NOTHING HEALS ME LIKE YOU DO

HARPER BLISS

nothing
HEALS
ME
like
YOU
DO

For my wife, who gave me the idea for this book

CHAPTER 1

Justine Blackburn shook her twenty-five-year-old self's hand. Alexis Dalton's grip was as light as the blue of her eyes. It wasn't exactly like staring into a mirror and seeing her much younger self reflected, but it was unsettling. It certainly was unlike anything Justine had experienced before—and she'd gone through a thing or two in her life.

She looked to Rochelle for emotional support during this odd moment, but her friend was going through the exact same thing. Rochelle was more laid-back about these things, however. She was already pulling the actor that would play the younger version of herself into a hug. Sienna Bright was older than Alexis, because Rochelle was eleven years older than Justine. What a fucking trip.

"You look just like I did back in the day," Rochelle said to Sienna.

Yeah right. In Rochelle's very distorted dreams maybe. But Justine refrained from rolling her eyes. Despite everything that had brought them here, this was a special moment.

"It's such an honor to meet you, Miss Blackburn." Sienna turned her attention to Justine while Alexis did the same with Rochelle. "I mean that from the bottom of my heart." Sienna

1

Bright's handshake was much firmer than her co-star's, and her unflinching stare into Justine's eyes was just as intense.

"Thank you." Justine made sure her grip was equally strong as she met Sienna's bold gaze.

"Casting really did an amazing job," Rochelle said. "I couldn't have done better myself." Rochelle had retired from her Hollywood casting director job only a few years ago. If it weren't for her, none of this would be happening. They wouldn't be shaking hands with these bright young things who were about to play them in a movie about what Justine and Rochelle had built together.

Justine had read various iterations of the screenplay and she felt there was too much emphasis on her love affair with Rochelle, which had ended decades ago. But she understood that a love story made a movie more interesting or, as Rochelle had called it, 'more watchable'. There were many parts of Justine's life that would be much harder to watch.

However, she had insisted with the director, Mimi St James, on a light tone, despite the heaviness of the subject matter. Agreeing to her relationship—or *romance*, as Mimi had called it —with Rochelle being included in the script was part of that. It was also true to life. All those years ago, Justine and Rochelle had fallen in love.

Now, Alexis Dalton and Sienna Bright were going to recreate it on the big screen. It was surreal to invite these two young actors into their lives for a little while so they could get to know them for this particular, extraordinary purpose.

Justine's motives for doing any of this had been crystal clear from the beginning. Rochelle had pitched her the idea in the only language she knew Justine would accept. Agreeing to this movie would bring in a ton of money for the shelter—and the shelter was what Justine lived for. If she had to sell the rights to her life for it—because that's what they called it in the 'industry'—then that's what she would do. She wasn't getting any younger and the shelter was always short of money. In that respect, it was a no-brainer. What was most baffling, really, was that someone wanted to make a movie about her life at all.

Rochelle ushered them into her living room and offered drinks. She busied herself in the kitchen, leaving Justine alone with Alexis and Sienna. She gestured for them to sit before settling into her favorite chair at Rochelle's house.

Whereas Alexis seemed to nearly disappear in the couch, Sienna took up all the metaphorical room in it. Justine's gaze was drawn to the actor playing her ex much more than to the actor who would be playing her. But maybe that made sense. Out of the two of them, Rochelle had always been the biggest attention-grabber. In that respect, the casting *was* pretty spot on.

"Here we are." Rochelle approached carrying a tray with four glasses and a pitcher of iced tea.

Sienna immediately offered to help, while Alexis seemed to fade deeper into the cushions.

"Let's not be coy about this," Rochelle said when everyone had been served a drink. "This situation is quite the mindfuck."

Justine could have done without this part of the process. She'd be quite happy to simply sign away her life rights and cash that check, thank you very much. But she recognized that actors playing real-life people wanted some modicum of access. To spend some time with Justine and Rochelle to see how they interacted and, perhaps, study the intricacies of their move-ments and the inflections in their voices. Now that they were all sitting here, deep down, it was quite thrilling. Although these were not the kind of youngsters Justine was used to dealing with—the privileged and the adored. Quite the opposite.

"It's so exciting to be here," Sienna said. Her voice didn't match her age. It was low and a little gravelly. "You must hear this all the time, but what you two have done and continue to do for the community is so inspiring."

This was beginning to sound like an awards acceptance speech already. Justine didn't care for awards, unless they came with a big fat check attached. Otherwise, they were a waste of time and energy. An award couldn't put a displaced kid up for the night. Justine shook off the thought—her brain perhaps spiraling because she was more nervous than she wanted to be —and focused on what Sienna had actually said.

"When you say community"—Justine fixed her gaze on Sienna's—"do you see yourself as a part of that?"

"Of course." Sienna met Justine's gaze and held it.

Justine had received extensive biographies of both actors, as well as a list of all the productions they'd been in. She knew full well Sienna identified as queer and Alexis didn't, but she was just testing the waters a little, ruffling some feathers because she couldn't help herself. Because it was her style.

Perhaps she was even doing Alexis a favor by showing her what kind of person she was—although the version of Justine that Alexis was asked to portray was very different from today's Justine who was, granted, being a bit difficult just because she could. Too much privilege on display could still get to her like that, but it was also what kept her fire burning, even after all these years.

"I'm not queer," Alexis said matter-of-factly. "I was told it wouldn't be an issue."

"It's not," Rochelle said, then shot Justine a look. "We've seen your work and it speaks for itself."

Rochelle often spoke for them both, usually making Justine look better, so she didn't mind that much. Justine didn't have a lot of spare time to watch movies—she barely had time for this encounter—and she'd seen no movies that either actor had appeared in.

She smiled at Alexis regardless. "I concur." Justine sipped from her iced tea and glanced at Alexis over the rim of her glass. The physical resemblance was there, although Alexis looked far glossier than Justine had ever done, especially at twenty-five.

Then, for the first time, Alexis widened her smile to full beam, and looked straight into Justine's eyes, as if to say, *why*

4

don't you just wait and see, and Justine caught a glimpse of that unrelenting fire that always—like a fever that never broke—burned within her.

————

Sienna was glad she'd be playing Rochelle rather than Justine—not that she could ever portray a blonde white woman with blue eyes. Where Rochelle was kind, inviting, and easy to talk to, Justine was a much tougher nut to crack. She wasn't cold per se, but Sienna figured, from the difference in their energies, that Rochelle was far more invested in this movie. Although, from a pure craft perspective, trying to get in the head, and under the skin, of someone like Justine could be a delicious challenge.

She focused on Rochelle instead, on her big hand gestures as she spoke—she clearly loved the sound of her own voice—and the warmth in her face when she smiled. Rochelle was instantly likable, one of those people who filled every room they walked into. But Justine was the heart of the movie—and despite her rather aloof demeanor, Sienna had nothing but respect for what Justine had accomplished. Although, from the script of *Gimme Shelter*, which Sienna had studied and already knew by heart, she knew Rochelle had been instrumental in getting their homeless shelter for LGBTQI+ kids off the ground. Sienna's part in the movie might be more of a supporting role—Alexis would be its undisputed star—but it was definitely significant.

"How do you feel about Nora Levine playing the part of your mother?" Sienna asked Justine when Rochelle stopped talking for longer than thirty seconds.

"I'm not sure I have any feelings about that," Justine replied, her face as expressionless as a blank sheet of paper.

An inadvertent chuckle escaped Sienna's throat. This woman was just too much.

"Sorry." Justine's shoulders loosened, and she sat up straighter. "I didn't mean to be flippant. This whole thing is just so weird. I mean, a movie about my life? Well, a very particular time in my life." She paused and, probably because it was the first time that afternoon that she'd spoken more than a few sentences at once, everyone let her. "I have nothing but respect for Nora Levine and her support of the LGBT Center. And I guess that any project that has her name attached to it will get extra buzz. If extra buzz equals extra cash, that's a double win in my book."

Rochelle cleared her throat. "What Justine is actually trying to say—"

Justine cut her off. "You don't have to speak for me, Roche. Besides, these girls are here to see what we're like. It would be awful to pretend being someone I'm not. That wouldn't serve them at all."

"I'm thirty-six," Sienna said, "I'm hardly still a girl."

"You *ladies*," Justine corrected herself, "need to know that unlike my good friend here, I'm not a Hollywood person. A fake smile and a bunch of hyped-up words mean nothing to me. To be completely honest, I never even go to the movies. I'll give you access to me and my life for a limited number of days, because of course I want this movie to work, but I'm *me*. I say it as it is. I don't sugarcoat things and I don't waste time with half-truths if I can help it."

"Would you mind if I made some notes?" Alexis asked. "This is pure gold for my performance."

When Alexis Dalton was first cast in the role of Justine Blackburn, Sienna had had her doubts, but she was beginning to see it was about more than pure physical likeness.

Alexis's question made Justine laugh out loud. "You know what?" she said. "I think I like you."

Alexis pulled her phone from her purse and furiously started to type.

"As you can imagine," Alexis said, while typing, "now that the ice is broken, I have a lot more questions."

"I'm sure you do." A small smile appeared on Justine's lips.

Sienna took it all in. Alexis was right. This access to the real people they were going to play was a gold mine for them as actors—although it added to the pressure to get it right. Sienna had only played fictional characters so far in her career and her father, who knew a thing or two about acting, had advised her against auditioning for the part because of his firsthand experience playing a real person and the havoc it could wreak on your career. Her father also had three Oscars on his vanity shelf.

Sienna sought acting advice only from her dad, because based on *her* firsthand experience, this was his only area of expertise. Yet she hadn't listened to him when it came to this movie. The Charlie Cross script had been too enticing and the prospect of telling an important story about actual lesbians too good to pass up. Being part of this movie meant something to Sienna on an elemental level that her father probably couldn't fathom.

"I'm here for all your questions too." Rochelle shot her one of her warm smiles.

"Do you remember when you first met Justine?" Sienna asked.

"How could I ever forget?" Rochelle's smile widened. "Although it was hardly love at first sight."

CHAPTER 2

Justine had told her story so many times, it didn't hurt her anymore. The pain had been plastered over with the good things she had built on its foundations. Pain, and anger most of all, was a powerful motivator. But sitting across from Alexis, across from the person who would portray her when she'd been in such a vulnerable, precarious stage of her life, was a little startling.

When Justine had met with Charlie Cross, the *Gimme Shelter* scriptwriter, she'd been matter-of-fact, listing the events of her youth as though dictating a shopping list.

When I was sixteen, in a fit of teenage rage, I told my parents I was a lesbian.

Just like that, they kicked me out of their house, because appearances were infinitely more important than how their only child felt.

I stayed at a friend's house for a while. Then another friend's, then another's. Until I ran out of friends.

Until I had nowhere else to go but the streets.

I made my way to Los Angeles.

I was homeless and hungry for too long.

The homeless shelters I turned to were not safe places for anyone, but certainly not for a lesbian teenager or for the fellow homeless queers I encountered.

I was young, furious, and helpless for a while, until I decided to change shit up.

Then I did.

In the end, I was one of the lucky ones.

"Look at me now," Justine had said to Charlie. "I couldn't care less about awards, but you have a couple on your mantel, and now you're writing my story. How about that? How lucky am I?"

"I'm mainly here for the bit where you changed shit up," Charlie had said. If that had not been the case, Justine would never have agreed to have this movie made. She wasn't interested in a sob story about how her parents kicked her out. Rochelle knew that and she'd made sure Charlie knew it too.

Alexis fixed her light-blue eyes on Justine. "Can I ask about your parents?"

"Sure." Justine shrugged. They were but a distant memory to her. Two people who might as well be dead. If they were, she didn't know and it made no difference to her in any significant way.

"There hasn't been a reunion?"

Justine shook her head.

"I'm really sorry that happened to you," Alexis said. "I just want you to know."

Justine waved off the remark. So many years had passed. Justine had lived so much life and helped so many kids along the way.

"The way I see it now, what happened to me did so because I was meant to do this." She gave a small smile. "Not this movie, obviously, but founding the Rainbow Shelter. I would never have done that if my parents hadn't put me out with the trash. I would never have found this strength inside me to turn my misery into something good and necessary. My parents aren't the only ones whose so-called love is entirely conditional on the fact that their child was exactly who they wanted them to be. I shouldn't be baffled by it anymore, but every time a kid tells me their story, it still surprises me that the people who are meant to love you the most can be so utterly cruel and selfish."

Alexis nodded and made a few more notes in her phone.

"What are your parents like?" Justine asked, not to be glib, but because she was genuinely interested.

"My parents?" Alexis seemed taken aback by the question. "They're, um, very nice and, like, completely regular."

"Are they?" Justine studied Alexis's face.

Eyebrows knotted together, she just nodded. "Is it important to you that I tell you about them?"

Clearly Alexis hadn't come here to talk about herself, a fact Justine respected.

"Yes. I'd like to hear more," she admitted. With all the horror stories she'd heard about abysmal parenting, sometimes she needed her faith restored that most mothers and fathers were responsible and willing to do their best for their children.

"Sure." A soft smile melted Alexis's face. "Mom's a dentist, and dad's an engineer. They live in New Hampshire. I'm their only child and we speak every day. They're very supportive of my career, even though it's so far removed from the professions they chose. They've always been supportive of everything I've done."

"Good." Justine replied with a smile of her own. "That's good." Alexis was twenty-five years old and a completely different generation to Justine. Her lovely-and-ordinary parents were probably the same age as Justine. "It's obvious they raised a confident daughter." Although Alexis was straight and Justine knew from decades of experience with queer kids that even parents who seemed very nice-and-ordinary could turn on their child when they came out. Apparently, there was a long and varied list of reasons to start hating your own flesh and blood simply because of who they loved.

Justine made a mental note to inquire about Sienna's

11

parents' reaction to her coming out, although they were Hollywood types and Justine knew from Rochelle that, behind the scenes, half of Tinsel Town was run by queers. That was another reason to agree to this movie. Representation and the chance to tell a queer story on a large scale.

Justine's phone rang. She didn't have to check the screen to know it was the shelter, because it always was.

"I'm going to have to take this," she said to Alexis.

"Of course." She focused back on her phone, perhaps to jot down more details about Justine. She wouldn't mind getting her hands on those notes later, just to know what a privileged young thing like Alexis made of the likes of her. Then she shrugged off the notion. If Justine cared one iota about what anyone else thought of her, she wouldn't be able to do this job— her fundraising skills were not based on flattery and smarminess, but on facts and utter necessity.

"Someone's come in asking for you specifically, Justine," Darrel, Justine's right-hand person at the shelter said. "I can set up a video call, if you want."

"No need." Justine looked at Alexis. "I'll be there in ten minutes and I won't be alone."

———

Half an hour ago, Justine had rushed onto the porch where Sienna was having a private and illuminating conversation with Rochelle, stating matter-of-factly that the four of them were going to the Rainbow Shelter for a research field trip. Rochelle didn't seem to mind and five minutes later, Sienna and Alexis were sitting in the back of a tatty old Subaru that Justine negotiated expertly through LA traffic. The shelter was only a ten-minute drive and as soon as they arrived both Justine and Rochelle were instantly accosted by people who worked there.

"How's it going with Justine?" Sienna asked Alexis, as she looked around. She didn't know what they were supposed to do with themselves. If anyone at the shelter had recognized them, they didn't let on. Or they were too busy to notice or care.

"Good, I think. She's more forthcoming than I had expected. Very frank and straightforward. You?"

"Rochelle's a sweetheart."

Someone walked up to them. "Hi there. My name's Darrel, they/them. Justine asked me to give you the grand tour."

They shook hands and exchanged pleasantries and pronouns—both she/her for Alexis and Sienna.

"Justine urged me not to make a big song and dance about it, but I'm your mother's biggest fan," Darrel said to Sienna.

"Color me surprised, as most people can't shut up about my dad," Sienna quipped. "But it's a lovely surprise." Being an actor, Sienna had huge respect for her father's career, but he was a good-looking white man. Her mother was the first Black female showrunner in all of TV's history. Sienna's admiration for her mother knew no bounds, because not only had she accomplished professional success against the odds, she'd also been Sienna and her sister's primary parent, and a damn good one at that. To hear a stranger gush about her mother for once made for a nice change.

"Of course, I'm also totally into you two," Darrel continued as they walked them to a door opposite the reception area. "This movie is like a dream for us working at the shelter and I love that you're both going to be starring in it." Darrel stopped in front of the closed door. They fixed their gaze on Alexis. "Good luck playing Justine." Darrel chuckled. "Lord knows I love that woman to absolute bits, but she's a piece of work." They followed up with a quick wink, then focused their attention on Sienna. "Rochelle's like the opposite. You can ask her anything. She's an open book. I'm not claiming you'll have an easier time of it because, well, what do I know about acting? But they're like ice and fire. Together, they create some sort of magic, though." They tapped their chest. "They both have a permanent place in here as far as I'm concerned. Justine has dedicated her life to making the lives of people like me infinitely better. She's completely selfless. She doesn't really want to do this movie. She doesn't want that kind of intrusion in her life and emphasis on her story, but this too, she's doing for us. For the kids who come knocking at our door with nothing but the clothes they're wearing and a few dollars in their pocket."

Obviously, like Rochelle, Darrel loved to talk. They had the same inviting warmth about them.

"I'd love to take you out for a drink," Alexis said. "You seem to know Justine well. How long have you been working here?"

"I arrived here when I was fifteen. The shelter helped me with literally everything." Darrel's voice cracked the tiniest of bits. "I got my degree in social work, just like Justine, and I've been working here ever since. I'll be thirty next month."

"Wow." Alexis's eyes went wide. "You must be a treasure trove of information on Justine." Sienna's co-star seemed to share Justine's kind of single-mindedness

"I'm so sorry you had to end up here," Sienna said, acknowledging Darrel's unimaginable-to-her ordeal.

"It is what it is, and I'm standing here with you two glitzy ladies now." They shot them an easy smile that probably hid a world of past hurt. "Have I said it's my honor?" They nodded at the door. "Shall we start the tour?"

Darrel showed Sienna and Alexis the dorm-style bedrooms, the gender-neutral communal bathrooms, and the dining area with large tables.

Sienna's parents were rich, and she had never had to come out. She'd never had to declare her sexuality to her parents—the way it should be. Even though she knew the *Gimme Shelter* script by heart, and could give an off-book performance there and then, actually being at the Rainbow Shelter, and seeing it with her own eyes, was a shock to her system. Despite its stark cleanliness, there was something inherently bleak about young people having to live like this.

"How are we getting on?" Rochelle had come out of nowhere.

"It's eye-opening to be here," Alexis said.

"Justine will probably be a while," Rochelle said. "I need to get home. My daughter called, and I've unexpectedly got my grandkids tonight. You can either hang out here and wait for Justine, or share an Uber with me back to my house."

"I can get a car home from here," Alexis said. "I have a thing tonight that I need to get ready for." She narrowed her eyes. "It's not possible to say goodbye to Justine?" There was genuine disappointment in her voice.

"If she's doing an intake, she's not going to interrupt that delicate process," Darrel said. "But I'll tell her you couldn't stay. Don't worry about it. She won't think you're rude."

"I'll be seeing her tomorrow, anyway," Alexis said in that direct manner she had. She dug her phone out of her pocket. "Can I ask for your number, Darrel? So we can grab that drink soon?"

While Alexis and Darrel exchanged numbers, Rochelle approached Sienna.

"Are you okay?" She tilted her head.

Sienna nodded.

"Despite the love we put into it, this place is not the Ritz."

This was not the time for Sienna to be fragile about her own privilege. "If it's okay with everyone, I'd like to hang around for a bit," she said, refusing to give in to the impulse to get out of there and retreat into the swanky penthouse her father had bought for her. Something compelled her to stay.

CHAPTER 3

Justine had never set out to be the face of the Rainbow Shelter. It had happened gradually and naturally, and it was a common occurrence for a kid to turn up and ask for her specifically, simply because they knew her name. She never denied the request because when someone had mustered up the courage to walk into the shelter—not something anyone did lightly—it was exactly the right moment to give them a tiny slice of her time. In Justine's book, it topped giving her attention to two Hollywood starlets doing research on her any day of the week. The kids always came first. Surely Alexis and Sienna would understand.

She hadn't expected either of them to still be there after she'd talked a young girl through her options and how the shelter could help her, but when she walked into the staff's break room, she found Sienna and Darrel huddled together, chatting like the best of friends. There was no sign of Alexis.

Sienna's brown eyes lit up when she spotted Justine. She managed a small smile in response. While Justine prided herself on her endless reserves of energy—how else to build a shelter out of nothing?—an intake conversation could be draining, especially if the girl reminded her so much of herself back in the day.

"I see Darrel has kept you entertained." Justine crashed into a chair. She just needed a few minutes and a strong cup of coffee and she'd be her fired up old self again. Although, admittedly, she was no spring chicken anymore, and every so often, she just needed some rest.

"Largest mug I can find?" Darrel said.

"Thanks so much, D. You're a saint." Justine was hardly in the habit of asking the shelter's staff to pour her a cup of coffee —they had far better things to do with their time—but Darrel couldn't help themself. If Justine remembered correctly, Darrel's shift had ended a while ago.

"Do you want some more coffee, Sienna?" Darrel asked.

Sienna shook her head. "No thanks."

She was probably used to complicated lattes that cost an arm and a leg, but Justine had long ago stopped holding other people's privilege against them. It served no purpose. And she needed people with money, like Sienna Bright, and their families to fund the shelter.

Darrel handed Justine an extra-large mug and Justine closed her eyes as she sipped. The shelter's coffee was bulk-bought run-of-the-mill fare, but it tasted exquisite right now. But why was she thinking about the quality of the coffee, anyway? Did Sienna Bright's presence really have that effect on her? Justine wouldn't have any of that.

"Did Darrel give you the tour?" she asked.

"Excuse me, ladies, but I have to run," Darrel said. "My evening class starts soon."

"Break a leg, D." Justine paid for Darrel's management course out of her own pocket because she wanted them to follow in her footsteps one day and run the shelter.

Darrel hugged Sienna goodbye as though they'd known each other much longer than the hour they'd just spent together.

"I hope you don't mind I'm still here," Sienna said. "I just… I don't know. Maybe it's because I'm queer that being here does something to me. It's, um…"

"Hard to fathom?" Justine pulled her lips into the warmest smile.

"Exactly," Sienna said. "I feel like I'm living the life of a princess when I'm here."

"Well." Justine chuckled. "You would be to any of the kids here. You were to Darrel. I could tell. They like you." Darrel was an excellent judge of character, Justine knew that much. They'd had to be to make it this far in life in their circumstances.

"They did say they admire my mom a lot." Sienna leaned back in her chair.

"Oh yes. Maxine Brewster, right? Darrel loves her stuff."

"Yeah."

From how that single word was spoken, Justine could tell that Sienna and her mother were thick as thieves, which reminded her of the mental note she'd made earlier.

"Can I ask how your parents reacted when you came out?"

"I didn't, not to my mom, at least. From when my sister and I were kids, she always referred to potential love interests as boys *and* girls. All options were our normal."

"And you're how old again?" While this was how it should be, it was not a tale Justine heard very often.

"Thirty-six and three months." Sienna grinned and she might as well have said twenty-six because the skin of her face was as smooth as anything.

"Please tell your mother from me that she's a rock star."

"That's high praise coming from the likes of you." Sienna slung one jeans-clad leg over the other, while flinging a braid over her shoulder.

"Yeah, and it really shouldn't be in this day and age, yet it is, and this shelter is still needed now more than ever."

A shadow crossed Sienna's face. Perhaps Justine had laid on the depressing side of the Rainbow Shelter a bit thick—she tended to do that. She was well-trained in tugging at the heart-strings of the rich and famous, but that's not why Sienna was here.

"All of that being said, I've seen so many kids blossom after passing through here. Take Darrel. They're thriving."

"They spoke very highly of you." A funny kind of smirk appeared on Sienna's face.

"Is that why you're grinning like that? Because of all the lovely things Darrel said about me?"

"They did also warn Alexis that you're a piece of work." Sienna obviously took great delight in sharing this information. The corners of her mouth tilted all the way up, making the windowless break room feel as though the sun was beaming inside nonetheless.

"That's a fairly accurate description of me." It was easy to respond to Sienna's smile in kind.

Sienna's full laugh was even more delightful. Justine could relax more around her because Sienna wasn't the actor playing her and she didn't make her feel as though she was trying to pick at all the scars on her soul. Additionally, Sienna was starting to remind her of Rochelle in more ways than one. She was easygoing, had a gorgeous smile, and a certain look in her eyes that was hard to not get sucked into.

"I'm starving," Justine said. "Do you want to grab some dinner?"

Sienna's thick eyebrows arched all the way up. Was that a hint of panic in her eyes?

"Not here," Justine reassured her. "Although there's nothing wrong with our food."

"I would love to," Sienna said, and freely gave away another one of her sunny smiles.

———

Justine walked them to a small Korean restaurant a few blocks away from the Rainbow Shelter. When they arrived there was a queue of hipsters waiting to get in, but Justine didn't seem to notice. She marched to the door as though it was her God-given right and the maitre d', a Korean woman of about the same age as Sienna, she guessed, hugged Justine as though she were a family member she hadn't seen in far too long.

Being Bobby Bright's daughter, Sienna had witnessed many times the kind of magic maitre d's can perform when it comes to conjuring up a table. The woman had the same trick up her sleeve. In no time, a small table was set up for the two of them, tucked away in a discreet corner of the restaurant, as though they were Hollywood royalty and their privacy was of the utmost importance.

"I'm impressed." Sienna leaned back in her seat and examined Justine's face.

"My job does come with certain perks, like lifelong gratitude from kids who have done extremely well for themselves against all the odds." She nodded in the direction of the maitre d'. "Min-ji came to us when she was seventeen. Together with the LGBT Center, we were able to get her a scholarship for the Culinary Institute, and now her restaurant is the toast of the town." Justine smiled the biggest smile Sienna had seen on her so far. "She always has a table for me."

"It's a bit like going to dinner with my dad," Sienna blurted out.

"The great Bobby Bright." Justine pursed her lips. "What was it like growing up in his shadow?"

Without having taken any orders, a server arrived at their table with water, bottles of beer, and a divine-smelling Korean pancake.

"Now I really do feel like a princess," Sienna said.

"You must be used to this." There was no sarcasm in Justine's tone, only curiosity.

"My parents divorced when I was five. I'm not close with

my father. My mom and stepdad raised my sister and me." Sienna picked up the bottle of beer and studied the label. "To put it bluntly, I could call my father up right now and ask for a hundred thousand dollars and it would be in my account immediately, as long as I don't ask him to talk about my feelings, let alone his."

Justine whistled through her teeth. "A hundred thousand bucks?" Her eyes went wide. "Please, do give him a call with my and the shelter's regards."

"Maybe I will." Sienna sipped from her beer. It was ice cold and wonderfully crisp.

"That was a joke, just to be clear, and one in pretty poor taste." For the first time since they'd met, Justine looked a touch uneasy. "How did Bobby react to you being queer?"

"As far as I know, he doesn't care who I fall in love with."

"As far as you know?"

Sienna shrugged. "As I said, we're not close. I see him maybe once a month. Less if he's abroad shooting or doing promo. I'm much closer to Eddy, my stepdad."

More food was brought to the table. Sienna hadn't even tried the pancake yet. She picked up a piece with her chopsticks and dipped it in the accompanying sauce. The piece of pancake slipped off and landed squarely in the middle of the dipping sauce.

"Oops." She grinned at Justine. "I'm usually more dexterous than this."

Quick as a flash, Justine fished the piece of pancake from the sauce with her chopsticks and held it in front of Sienna's mouth.

"There's nothing wrong with being a bit messy." She gazed into Sienna's eyes. "It's always the least of my worries, so here you go."

Sienna narrowed her eyes, then held up her plate so Justine could drop the piece of pancake on it. She wasn't going to eat it from Justine's chopsticks. Sienna considered herself way too cool for that.

"Thanks." As she successfully navigated the food to her mouth, she wondered what had just happened. The energy had somehow shifted. Then Sienna actually tasted the delicacy put in front of her. "Oh my," she exclaimed. "It's out of this world."

"I thought you'd like it." Justine pointed at another dish with the tip of her chopsticks. "Try the bulgogi. It's to die for."

Sienna focused on the delicious food while she adjusted to the sudden change in temperature. It was as though, after only a few sips of Korean beer, the weight that Justine seemed to carry around on her shoulders all day, had slipped off. It wasn't an entirely different woman sitting across from Sienna, but Justine looked a lot more relaxed. Sienna chalked it up to the hearty welcome they'd received at the restaurant and the amazing dishes they were treated to.

"There's a reason Rochelle invited you to *her* house. You should see my place," Justine confided in Sienna. "I don't spend a lot of time at home and after a while the messiness just becomes a part of the decor, you know?"

"And you couldn't be bothered to tidy up for two up-and-coming actors taking Hollywood by storm?" Sienna joked, because she felt as though she could now.

Justine tilted her head. "Alexis Dalton is definitely an up-and-comer, but you?" She sank her front teeth into her bottom lip. "I'd say you've very much arrived already."

Sienna looked into Justine's eerie blue eyes. "The praise just keeps on coming. And that from a woman who has no time for half-truths." If Sienna knew one thing, it was what flirting looked like—and she was staring it straight in the face.

"You're right." Justine painted on a small smile. "What do I know?" She tilted her head and kept her gaze on Sienna. She seemed to have lost interest in the delicious food in front of them.

"Have you seen anything I'm in?" Sienna braced herself for a hard no.

"No, but I can so easily imagine you as, um, let's see."

Justine narrowed her eyes. "Any type of smoldering leading lady, really. Surely you're aware of being drop-dead gorgeous?"

Although an expert at flirting, Sienna was thrown. She didn't know whether to laugh it off or go along with it. From the vibes she'd gotten from Justine throughout the day, she could only conclude she wasn't a woman who'd play games. Unless playing games was her preferred relaxation after another challenging day at the homeless shelter.

"A famous movie critic once wrote I won big-time in the genetic lottery, although he might have been referring to my status as a Hollywood nepo-baby rather than my looks." In the end, Sienna couldn't resist playing along. She never could. And most definitely not with a formidable woman like Justine Blackburn.

"Nah. I don't think so." Justine sipped her beer, all the while keeping her gaze trained on Sienna.

Sienna had focused most of her research on Rochelle's life, personal as well as professional. She'd need to do a deep dive into whatever there was to find about Justine's romantic history —or the lack thereof. Her best bet was probably to just ask Rochelle.

"Everything to your liking?" The maitre d' appeared at their table, carrying two more plates, and breaking the spell of what-ever game they were playing.

"It's all fantastic as usual, Min-ji." Justine beamed a wide smile at the woman. "I swear the food gets better every time."

Sienna took the pause in conversation to regroup. She inhaled deeply and piled some more of the mouthwatering food onto her plate.

"This one here…"—Min-ji pointed at Justine—"forgets to eat half the time, so I make sure there's plenty whenever she comes to my restaurant." She placed the dishes on the table. "I will not tolerate leftovers so, please, eat more." She suddenly sounded rather bossy. Min-ji glanced at Sienna and shot her a wink. "Sometimes, Justine needs a firm hand."

"Good to know." Sienna had a feeling she'd be coming to this restaurant again. "Thank you for this invaluable insider information."

"My pleasure." After another stern nod at the food, Min-ji walked away.

"She's right," Justine said. "I barely ate anything today. I got so sucked into things, I just forgot. And today's been a weird one, what with you and Alexis coming over." She averted her eyes and reached for more food. "That beer might have gone to my head a little and I'm a terrible flirt when tipsy." She looked at Sienna from under her lashes, a crooked grin on her lips. "Let me focus on this bibimbap first before I become even more impertinent."

"For the record, I don't think you were being impertinent at all." Sienna spooned a few bites of the divine-smelling bulgogi onto her plate. "And I'm a big fan of flirting, although I admit I wasn't expecting it tonight."

Justine shrugged. "I don't have many vices, but inappropriate flirting with beautiful women is definitely one of them." She didn't come across as extremely apologetic—it was stated like just another fact about herself.

"It's not inappropriate when reciprocated." Sienna could push the boat out as well.

In response, Justine widened her grin. "And you are very beautiful."

Between mouthfuls of food, Sienna asked, "Do you tend to flirt just for the sake of it or with a certain outcome in mind?"

Justine gave a hearty chuckle now. "Your directness is absolutely refreshing." She leaned over the table. "I don't usually hit on women who are so much younger than me so I'm not used to that, but I like it."

"Ten out of ten for not answering my question." Sienna was getting fired up—perhaps even getting a little carried away.

"Gorgeous and feisty. Fuck. I think I might be in big trouble."

"And still you persist with your non-answer."

"I'm nothing if not persistent." Justine took a sip of water instead of beer. "But fair enough." She tipped her head to the right. "While I do like a good flirt, that doesn't mean I'm very skilled at it and half the time, even if I have, um, a certain outcome in mind, my advances get rebuffed. Turns out that practice doesn't always make perfect."

"Persistent and brutally honest. Wow." Sienna was impressed with Justine's candor.

"That thing about not having time for half-truths also pertains to myself."

"It's good that you make time for flirting in your busy life, though."

"Thank you for being such a good sport about it." Justine caught a piece of kimchi between her chopsticks.

"Who says I'm just being a good sport about it?" Sienna pulled her lips into the kind of half-smile that had driven many a woman crazy—her own success rate with flirting and certain outcomes was much higher than fifty percent, especially since her first movie appearance. "Who says I'm not thoroughly enjoying it instead?" Should she or should she not? Why the hell not? "With a certain outcome in mind?"

CHAPTER 4

If Justine believed in anything, especially after a deliciously cold bottle of Korean beer, it was finishing what she started. In fact, she prided herself on it. No half-truths and certainly no half measures.

"In that case," Justine said. "I might just have to invite you to my messy house." That smile on Sienna's face was entirely impossible to resist and when it came to things like this, Justine was not one to overthink. Sienna Bright responding like this was not an opportunity she was going to ruin by imagining future regret—or possible reprimands.

"Shall we get the rest of the food to go?" Sienna finished her beer and put the bottle on the table with a slow, controlled gesture, all the while keeping her gaze trained on Justine.

Justine nodded and tried to find Min-ji. She was busy welcoming a sizable group of customers, but another server rushed to their table at the mere sight of her looking around, probably under strict instructions from Min-ji to swiftly cater to Justine's every wish. It was always like this when Justine came here—and why she kept on returning.

"Can you box this up to go, please?" Justine asked.

"Of course." The server made quick work of wrapping up

the food. Justine couldn't decide if the turmoil in her stomach was hunger or because of what was about to happen. Was she really taking Sienna Bright home with her?

"Leaving already?" Despite being rushed off her feet, Min-ji always kept track of everything happening at each table. She might be busy and, as she had repeated many a time, forever in Justine's debt, but that didn't stop her from giving Justine a puzzled look—or was that pure judgment in her glance? Justine brushed off the thought. Min-ji was certainly clever, but she was not clairvoyant. "I told you I wouldn't tolerate leftovers." She followed up with a knowing grin. "Make sure Justine eats all of it," she said to Sienna. Maybe she did have a touch of the clair-voyant about her then.

Also as usual, Min-ji refused payment, despite both Justine and Sienna's insistence to pay for their meal.

"Give the money to the Rainbow Shelter instead," Min-ji said. "A generous tip included."

"Deal." Sienna rose from her chair. "Thank you so much for all of this. Judging by the queue outside you don't need the extra promo, but I'll tell everyone I know about your amazing restaurant."

Min-ji hugged them both goodbye and a few minutes later Sienna and Justine were walking back to Justine's car. The shel-ter's parking lot wasn't far, but there was plenty of time to inquire further.

"Are you sure you want to see my untidy house?" Justine asked, the paper bag with food dangling from her hand.

"Truth be told, it's not your house that interests me, Justine." Sienna glanced at her sideways.

Now that they were out in the open and the fresh air cleared her head, Justine must be second-guessing herself, because she asked, "Is this part of your process somehow?"

"My process?" Sienna bumped her shoulder lightly against Justine's. "My acting process, you mean?" She slid her fingers under Justine's arm. "Of course not, although I've never played a real person before." She chuckled. "But I believe in seizing special moments that present themselves. I believe in the magic of spontaneity. In serendipity, if you will. I also quite like you." She gave Justine's arm a light squeeze.

"Quite, huh? That sounds pretty good."

Sienna stopped walking and turned her body to face Justine, dropping her hand. "Of course it's totally okay if you want to rescind your invitation. Just say the word and I'll get a car home."

"Are you crazy?" Justine reached for Sienna's hand. "I *quite* like you, too."

And so Justine found herself driving Sienna to her house, which was located between the shelter and Rochelle's house. The ride didn't take very long. As she unlocked the door, she tried to remember the state of her lounge—and her bedroom. Justine wasn't a very good housekeeper even though, for far too long, she hadn't had a house to live in. It was messy and, perhaps to someone like Sienna rather shabby as well, but this was *her* house. The furniture was all secondhand and the kitchen could surely do with a revamp, but it served its most important purpose without being glitzy or trendy. The house had Justine's name on the deed. It was her home, the first and only one she'd ever owned. And plenty of women had passed through without much complaint. Although as far as Justine could remember, Sienna was the first bona fide movie star to cross its threshold—and not one who had grown up in squalor until she'd made it, either.

Bobby Bright still fetched ludicrous amounts of money—multiple millions—for the movies he made and from Rochelle, Justine knew that Maxine Brewster had signed a multi-million streamer deal—whatever that was—a few years ago.

"It's cute," Sienna said and Justine opted to not look for condescendence in her tone. Sienna might as well mean it, although Justine would never think of her house as cute, more as functional.

Sienna's gaze was drawn to a picture on the sideboard . "Is that you with Raffo Shah?"

"It is." Justine pointed at a painting of an improbably feathered heart in deep rainbow colors above the non-used fireplace. "That's one of hers."

"No effing way." As if pulled by an invisible thread, Sienna strode toward the painting. "I have two Raffo Shahs at my place. She's so out of this world fantastic. That's one of my favorites of hers. I tried to buy it, in fact, but I was told it wasn't for sale."

"She made it for me."

Sienna turned away from the painting. "Did Raffo also stay at the shelter?"

Justine nodded.

"Fuck me." Sienna returned her gaze to the painting. "These colors. I don't know how she does it. Do you know her secret?"

"Goodness no." Justine knew the heartbreaking secrets of Raffo's past, however.

"It's one surprise after the other with you." Sienna spun on her heels and dug her fists into the pockets of her jeans.

Justine never took credit for anything the kids she'd welcomed at the shelter achieved later, because whether they went on to become a famous painter, an applauded chef, a school teacher or, like Darrel, a social worker—all equally successful in Justine's view—she was not responsible for that. Only they were, despite their crappy start in life. To go from almost nothing to something, that was the achievement. The option of something, no matter how big or small it was regarded by society, was what Justine tried to shine a light on with the kids that came to her.

Justine shrugged. "I'm going to put this in the fridge." She held up the bag. "Can I get you anything?"

"Hey? What just happened?" Sienna took a step closer. "Did I offend you?"

"You didn't. I just—" Justine let out a breath. "I wouldn't

want you to think that I took you to Min-ji's or have this Raffo painting on my wall to impress you. Or anyone else for that matter. These kids mean something to me that goes so much deeper than a work of art that sells for a couple of grand. That's not how I quantify what I do."

"That's the absolute last thing I would think of you." Sienna pulled her lips into that mad-driving smile again—the same one as at the restaurant earlier.

"I also don't want you to think of me as some kind of saint, because I'm anything but."

"Can't wait to find out about that." Sienna stepped closer still.

Justine was still holding the bag in her hand and no drinks had been poured. Her pulse picked up speed.

"I like you and I like sex." Sienna dipped her head. "Most of all, I like finding out what it's like to kiss someone new for the first time." She bridged the last distance between them, leaving only a whisper of space between their lips. "Would you like to find out what it's like to kiss *me*?"

The boundless, brazen audacity of privileged youth, Justine thought, before closing her eyes and leaning in. Sienna smelled like the height of summer. Like the promise of a hazy day in the sun with someone who utterly delights you.

Their lips brushed against each other, and Justine's shoulders relaxed. The first touch was soft and cautious. Explorative and promising. A tingle ran up Justine's spine. The bag of food dropped from her hand, to be forgotten on the floor.

Sienna's fingers glided across her cheek and wound their way into Justine's hair. They opened their lips to each other. The tip of Sienna's tongue dipped gently into Justine's mouth. Justine responded in kind, that tingle up her spine taking over the rest of her body.

She wasn't the type to question what another woman saw in her, but with Sienna, the thought did sneak up on her. Justine was almost twenty years older than the woman kissing her so tenderly, so deliciously. Objectively speaking, Sienna was the kind of woman who could be with anyone she wanted, yet here she stood, in Justine's cluttered living room, pulling her ever closer as their kiss deepened, their lips engaged in a delicate dance of sudden intimacy and promise of what was to come.

Sienna pulled back for a moment. "I haven't told you how beautiful you are," she whispered.

Before Justine could respond, Sienna continued their conversation without words, in the silent language of kissing. When their lips touched again, it was like the softest chord struck on a guitar, oh-so gentle yet deeply resonating.

The world seemed to pause and everything else in Justine's life became secondary to the electric tension crackling in the air between them. She gave in to the moment, this prelude to whatever would happen next, which was predictable but also not. Because just as Sienna liked finding out what it was like to kiss another woman for the first time, implying that it was different every time, so it was with taking someone new to bed.

They kissed and kissed, lingering in their embrace, in this newfound, exhilarating connection between them, their hands exploring more of each other's bodies, but remaining chastely above their clothes. Each kiss was a new discovery, each touch of their hands a declaration of intent.

"Do you want to go upstairs?" Justine breathed into Sienna's ear, after having kissed her way up there from her delicious, moreish lips.

"Fuck yes," Sienna said on a deep, heartfelt sigh.

"Come." Justine took Sienna's hand and led her up the stairs to her bedroom. And while the time for rational thought was long gone, Justine pondered how every time she invited a woman into her bed, as she was doing now, it was a small victory for her. It reminded her of what she had so gloriously managed to become—the very thing her parents had despised. It reminded her of who she was, of what defined her, of her core self and how that could make some people so profoundly uncomfortable, it made them turn on their own flesh and blood.

Sex could be uncomplicated, as Sienna had said earlier: *I like you and I like sex*—and that was that, apparently. That had been plenty of reason for her to kiss Justine and start things up between them. But for Justine, sex was tangled up with a whole host of emotions. Although she very much liked sex as well, and she'd had plenty of practice in her life, it was always complicated because, after all these years—decades, really—she still felt as though she had something to prove. That it meant something beyond the sheer pleasure it provided. Something beyond what happened in the privacy of her bedroom. Even though it took place behind closed doors, to Justine, it was still an act of outward rebellion. Because of who she was, where she came from, and what she had devoted her life to. She could scream from the rooftops how normal it was to be gay, but too many people on this planet still refused to believe her.

So she pulled Sienna onto the bed with her and kissed her with renewed abandon. She didn't just owe it to herself, she owed it to the world as well.

CHAPTER 5

Sienna gazed down into Justine's piercing blue eyes. She kissed the delicate slope of her cheekbone, the soft porcelain of her cheek, then trailed a path back to her divine lips.

They didn't know much about each other, but Sienna didn't need to know a whole lot about another woman to seduce her—because that's what she had done. She had seduced Justine. Justine had kicked things off, no doubt, but Sienna had hit the home run.

Sienna, quite simply, really did like sex. She had zero hang-ups about it like some of her friends did. She had no qualms saying that to another person—in fact, doing so quietly delighted her. She'd loved the look on Justine's face when she had told her. Justine, who had most certainly not been as welcoming as Rochelle had—and now look at her.

What Sienna could easily tell about Justine was that she had no idea how beautiful she was—and Sienna didn't mean the obvious kindness in her heart. Her presence was commanding. The tilt of her lips when she smiled irresistible. The blue of her eyes a pool to warmly linger in. Sienna hadn't set out to seduce Justine, but it turned out to just be one of those things that happened in life—a most pleasant surprise.

Sienna hadn't had a lot of bad luck in her life thus far, and most days, it felt like she was simply born to be happy—and she was. That's why going to the shelter had shaken her. Reading the script, and learning more details about Justine's life, was one thing, but actually being there had been a reality check. Sienna could just walk away from the place, never to return again, but she already knew she wouldn't, and not because she was in bed with one of the Rainbow Shelter's founders, planting kiss after kiss onto her delectable skin.

Their lips locked onto each other's while Sienna slowly unbuttoned Justine's shirt. In return, Justine slipped a warm hand under Sienna's top, finding the clasp of her bra. With a practiced move, she undid it, making Sienna break their kiss with an inadvertent smile.

She grinned down at Justine who had the most wicked smirk plastered across her face, as if to say, I'm not exactly new at this.

Neither was Sienna, who maneuvered around until she found enough balance to hoist her obsolete top over her head, taking her bra with it. That wiped the grin straight off Justine's face. Sienna was not movie star fit—far from it—but, thanks to her mother, she had never considered herself any less beautiful than her contemporaries with sculpted arms and impossible washboard abs.

Justine swallowed slowly while sliding her hand along Sienna's belly, up to her breast. She cupped it in her soft hand, gently rubbing her thumb across her rock-hard nipple. Justine swiftly pushed herself up toward Sienna and wasted no time taking her nipple into her mouth.

Sienna groaned low in her throat. She wasn't one to adhere to a script when jumping into bed with a stranger. She was a go-with-the-flow kind of girl, but experience had taught her that not every woman was like that. Some wanted to discuss before-hand—at length—what they enjoyed, while others were more into gentle guidance. Either way, these days, Sienna preferred to ask sooner rather than later.

With Justine's lips still wrapped around her nipple, she bent to her ear and whispered, "What do you like?"

At first, Justine only responded by drawing Sienna's nipple farther into her mouth, making Sienna all but forget about the question, until Justine pulled back, leaving Sienna's nipple moist and oh-so erect.

"I'm in my fifties," Justine said. "I need a lot of foreplay."

Sienna chuckled at Justine's delightful directness again. Justine was nothing if not true to herself, even in bed with a woman almost twenty years her junior. If this fazed her at all, she didn't let on—another definite turn-on.

"Right up my alley," Sienna said, and pushed Justine's blouse off her.

"There's a bottle of lube in the top drawer of the night-stand," Justine whispered into Sienna's ear as she drew her closer again. "Sometimes I need it, sometimes I don't. Either way, it's not a reflection on you." She smiled up at her. "You're fucking gorgeous," she said under her breath.

"Got it." Sienna kissed Justine again with no other intention but to make her feel good and wanted—because her own desire was quickly revving up. She slipped her hand underneath Justine's back and fumbled with her bra, unable to match Justine's earlier display of dexterity. Justine arched her back to give Sienna better access and soon enough, they were both naked from the waist up—excellent for a long bout of foreplay.

Sienna gazed down at Justine's ample milky-white breasts. She circled a fingertip around her nipple and it grew rigid under her touch. She lowered herself until she could take Justine's other nipple into her mouth and swirled her tongue around it. Justine's fingertips caressed her back lightly, as though skimming it with a feather. On their way down, though, her fingers dipped underneath the waistband of her jeans, digging into the swell of her behind.

Sienna ignored the throbbing between her legs, even though it was fairly ridiculous to still be wearing jeans—the fabric too thick for this kind of activity. Her clit pulsed against her panties as Justine's fingertips slowly made their way up again, getting lost in the tangle of her braids.

Sienna kissed her way from Justine's nipple to her neck, dotting soft pecks onto her alabaster skin. When she looked into Justine's eyes, the easy abandon in her gaze, the obviousness with which she wanted Sienna, quickened that pulse between her legs even more. But this was not a quicky. A one-night stand most likely, although there was really no way of knowing yet. All Sienna knew was that it was sex with a hot, intelligent, and intriguing woman—three qualities that in combination were irresistibly thrilling.

Sienna kissed Justine on the lips and the kiss swiftly deepened into an intimate, full-body embrace—making her jeans feel all the more annoying.

"I need to get these off," she said, and hurried out of her jeans, keeping her underwear on—for now.

"Can I?" she asked, pointing at the button of Justine's pants.

"Yeah." Justine's breath was ragged and uncontrolled.

Sienna slowly unzipped her, then peeled Justine's jeans off her legs, taking in their shapely contours.

She draped her almost-naked body over Justine's and kissed her again and again while her clit raged hot. Sienna didn't know what it was about Justine that drove her so crazy, but something inside her was about to explode.

Then it was Justine's turn to kiss a delicious path to Sienna's ear and say in a breathy voice, "Tell me what you like." With easy strength, she pushed Sienna off her and slid on top of her.

"No lube required," Sienna said through a snarky grin. "I'm so hot for you."

"So I gathered." Justine ran a fingertip between Sienna's breasts, all the way to the edge of her panties. "Let's see." Ever so slowly, she lowered her fingertip between Sienna's legs, all the while locking her eyes on Sienna's. "Oh, yeah," Justine whispered, obviously taking great delight in the effect she had on Sienna. She dragged her finger upward and the tip glistened with Sienna's wetness. The scene was so arousing, Sienna feared she might lose her mind altogether. Then Justine circled her wet fingertip around Sienna's nipple, bowed down, and softly licked Sienna's wetness off it.

"Oh, fuck," Sienna groaned, as though Justine had kissed her clit instead of her nipple.

"Do you want me to lick you?" she asked, looking up from Sienna's breast.

Sienna could only nod.

Justine hooked her fingertips under Sienna's panties and slowly pulled them down.

Sienna spread her legs for Justine, her clit, once exposed to the air, ready to melt.

Justine settled between Sienna's legs and nothing happened for a few long moments. Sienna looked down at her but could only see her tousled ash-blonde hair. Justine was taking her in— looking at her. Possibly deciding what to do next. It only made Sienna's heart beat faster.

Then fingertips skimmed along the inside of her thigh. Ever so lightly, they skated along her wet center. Justine caressed her so gently, yet Sienna felt it in every cell of her body. Justine's other hand rested on Sienna's belly and she clasped her own around it. Justine's fingers stopped mid-caress and gingerly pulled Sienna's lips apart, causing Sienna's breath to stall in her throat.

A moan escaped her, and in response, Justine squeezed Sienna's hand. Between her legs, Justine's fingers were replaced with the soft, hot tip of her tongue. As promised, she licked Sienna, but only along the edge of her sex—purposefully avoiding her clit. Justine sucked Sienna's lips into her mouth and her breath picked up speed now as her body surrendered to Justine's divine touch.

Justine teased her for a while longer, but then, finally, showed mercy. When the hot softness of her tongue landed on Sienna's clit, again, ever so gently, it started the first round of fireworks in Sienna's flesh.

Pure joy spread through her body as Justine, clearly very skilled at this, in a matter of minutes, licked her to an earth-shattering climax.

All the while, their hands had been entangled on Sienna's belly, and Sienna held onto Justine's for all she was worth.

CHAPTER 6

"What a day," Sienna said on what sounded like a deep breath of satisfaction.

"Fuck yeah." Justine pushed herself up and lay next to her, her body glued to Sienna's warm side.

"You're pretty good at that." Sienna planted a kiss on Justine's temple. "I have to hand it to you."

"It was exactly the foreplay I needed." A slow pulse throbbed between her legs.

Sienna's body shook as she chuckled. "Not in a million years would I have imagined this when I met you this afternoon." She examined Justine's face as if to ask, 'what about you?'

Justine just shook her head. Of course, she hadn't imagined this. At least she hadn't ended up in bed with the actor playing her—that would have been a too disturbing. Although, truth be told, being in bed with the actor playing Rochelle wasn't exactly straightforward either. Rochelle had been her lover—more than her lover. It might have been a long time ago, but Justine had loved her—had truly let herself love another woman without the shame and guilt her upbringing had instilled in her about that—and that meant a lot to her.

"Maybe I have a subconscious weakness for movie stars,"

Justine joked. "So it's a good thing I don't mix with your crowd very often."

"That's about to change though, isn't it?"

Sienna was right. This was only the beginning. *Gimme Shelter* would start shooting soon and it was beginning to dawn on Justine that she might have slightly underestimated what delving into her past would do to her. But she had a hot actor in her bed whose sweet, most intimate scent lingered on her lips, and whose cries of orgasm had just echoed through her bedroom.

"Yeah," Justine said, then prevented Sienna from saying any more by kissing her. God, she loved kissing her, this almost stranger she barely knew—she'd have to watch some of her movies now. She was curious.

Sienna's hand sneaked up Justine's neck, her fingertips curling into her hair. Their kiss grew more intense, as did the thrumming between Justine's legs.

"Would you like me to lick you too?" Sienna asked when they caught their breath.

"I wouldn't say no to that." Justine couldn't suppress the grin tugging at the corners of her mouth.

Sienna's brown eyes sparkled with delight or maybe it was desire. Justine didn't know, all she knew, all she could be sure of, was that Sienna was breathtakingly beautiful. The deep dark warmth of her eyes. That sculpted jawline. Her expressive gaze. The hot glow of her skin.

Maybe what tipped her over the edge the most, what had perhaps been the first unconscious step for them ending up here, was how Sienna had been visibly shaken by visiting the shelter. It told Justine, without words needing to be spoken, that she would have the right kind of sensitivity—as well as the pluck she'd shown all day—to play someone as amazing as Rochelle. And to co-star in the movie of Justine's life. Because no matter how much Justine liked to pretend that it wasn't a big deal, that she was only doing it for the money she could raise for the shelter, it was a big thing in her life. The evidence of that was in her bed right now. The kisses being strewn onto the delicate skin of her neck were a direct result of Justine saying yes to that movie. Life could be funny like that.

Sienna kissed her way down, lingering for long minutes at Justine's breasts, kissing and caressing with a tenderness that made more warmth blossom in Justine's chest. Maybe this night with Sienna Bright was some sort of a weird and unexpected full circle moment, because of who she was going to be in *Gimme Shelter*. Justine preferred not to waste her precious time thinking about things like that, but maybe she wouldn't have a choice.

Sienna kissed a path farther down, her braids fanned out on the pale skin of Justine's belly.

She might have meant it as a joke earlier, but fuck, it was a thrill to have Sienna go down on her. To feel her warm lips on her inner thighs. To have this hot young thing—as Rochelle had called her when the casting had been announced—lavish all of her attention upon her.

It was exhilarating to be in bed with Sienna, to have made her come, to flirt with her, and share this unforeseen pleasure with her. And yet, as soon as Sienna's tongue touched against Justine's clit, she knew it was a futile effort. She knew that a climax had, somehow, inexplicably, disappeared out of reach. This had started happening a few years ago. Not often enough for Justine to worry about at her age. But she had absolutely not expected it to happen tonight, in bed with Sienna Bright of all people. Perhaps the circumstances had a greater effect on her than Justine was able to admit to herself. Either way, right now, it was what it was.

"Hey," Justine whispered, while softly caressing the back of Sienna's head. "It's okay."

Sienna looked up at Justine from between her legs, her face a big question mark.

"It's, um—it's okay. Come here. I'll explain it to you."

"Explain what to me? I was just getting started."

"I know, but, um—" She looked into Sienna's eyes. "It's not about a climax for me tonight."

"Are you sure?" Sienna tilted her head as if to say, 'I'm up to any challenge if you'll let me.'

"I'm sure." Justine held out her arms.

Sienna crawled up toward her. "Are you okay?" she asked, her voice soft with concern.

"I'm fine, but I'm fifty-four. Sometimes… I just know it's not going to happen and that's absolutely fine. I love being here with you. It's more than enough for me."

"Maybe you have a toy we can use? A little something to grease the wheels, so to speak."

Justine chuckled. "Hey, this is not about you. You know that, right?" It certainly wasn't about how gorgeous and attractive Sienna was.

"My ego's not that fragile." Sienna shot her the sort of smile that couldn't be argued with. "But I'm here for you whenever you're ready."

"That's sweet, but I think I'll be just fine."

"Oh." Sienna knotted her thick eyebrows together. "This isn't your suddenly indirect way of asking me to leave, is it?"

Justine shook her head. "I would love for you to stay. Please, spend the night with me."

"So we can cuddle." A gentle smile spread on Sienna's lips.

"Why not?"

"There's nothing wrong with some good old cuddling." Sienna nestled herself in Justine's embrace.

Justine hadn't been lying when she'd said this was more than enough for her. She'd fucked up many a romantic relationship in her life, but she'd always have room for a warm body in her bed—and a beautiful woman in her arms.

CHAPTER 7

"Hey," a voice whispered in Sienna's ear. "Hey, gorgeous. Time to wake up."

Justine was standing next to the bed, fully dressed and her hair wet from the shower. She crouched so she was at eye level with Sienna.

"I'm sorry, but I have somewhere to be. I let you sleep as long as possible."

"What time is it?" Sienna groaned.

"Just after eight."

Sienna stretched her arms above her head and scrunched her eyes shut. When she opened them, Justine was unmistakably ogling her half-naked body.

"If you get up now, I'll make you breakfast. If you want to sleep more, you can. I'll leave you a key to lock up with. You can bring it to Rochelle's this afternoon."

"I'll have breakfast with you." Sienna was famished. "Just give me a minute."

"Sure. I'll see you downstairs." Justine brought her hand to Sienna's forehead and gently brushed the skin above her eyebrows. She looked quite perky for a woman her age having had only a short night of sleep—or was it ageist to think like that? Justine briefly looked into Sienna's eyes, then pushed herself up and disappeared from the room.

So much for waking up gently and, perhaps, giving Justine the orgasm Sienna hadn't been able to give her last night. Although Justine struck her as a woman who always had places to be and people to see with not a lot of time for idle lingering—and slow morning sex—in her life.

Sienna took a deep breath and threw the covers off.

———

Justine's coffee was nothing like the superior stuff the state-of-the-art machine at her apartment produced, but Sienna downed it nonetheless. Maybe Justine was one of those super women who thrived on only four hours of sleep per night, but Sienna needed at least seven hours, eight if she could.

Last night, they had bantered for a while longer, talking of nothing very significant, while Sienna lay in Justine's arms and then, somehow, Justine had ended up making Sienna come again—with her fingers this time—and when Sienna had checked her watch when they finally said goodnight, it had been almost three in the morning. She was exhausted and it probably showed on her face, but she tried to put on a smile for the short time she had with Justine. She would need to take a nap before Alexis's car service picked her up after lunch to spend more time with Rochelle—the person Sienna should be devoting most of her time to.

"Can we keep this between us for now?" Justine said. "I'm not sure I'll get the chance to tell Rochelle before this afternoon."

"So you're definitely telling Rochelle?"

"I tell Rochelle everything." Justine employed her businesslike, straightforward tone again—as if it was just a simple fact of life that she would tell her ex about sleeping with the actor who was going to play her in a movie.

"Everything?" Sienna gazed up from her coffee.

"Not all the details, obviously, but I will tell her we slept together. Do you mind?"

"I hadn't really thought about it, to be honest."

"That's okay." Justine shoveled some scrambled eggs onto her fork. Sienna didn't know if she was putting on a show for her—although she didn't strike her as the type—or if Justine took breakfast a lot more seriously than any other meal. There were eggs, toast, yoghurt, fruit, and lots of not-so-stellar-but-strong coffee.

"Do we, um, need to talk about what… it meant?" Sienna asked, not that she had a clue. But she was curious what Justine thought about their impromptu night together.

"We can if you want to."

Sienna huffed out a silly giggle. "Was it a one-time thing? Do you want to do it again? Do you want to go on a proper date?" She picked up her fork to attend to her rumbling stomach.

"I don't know. Why don't we just see where the day takes us? We're meeting again this afternoon with Rochelle and Alexis, anyway." Justine took a sip of coffee. "But, um, as far as dating is concerned, I think we have to be realistic about that. Last night was fun, but I hope you understand that we are not a good match in any respect."

"Okay. Gotcha." Sienna sounded more defensive than she wanted to. But Justine was right. Going on a proper date, like she had just suggested, was a bit out there.

"Let's just play it by ear." Justine pushed her chair back and walked over to her. "I absolutely mean no disrespect." She hunched over and found Sienna's ear. "I should only be so lucky to date someone like you."

———

Justine had skipped lunch, as she did most days, due to lack of time. Sienna and Alexis would arrive at Rochelle's in thirty minutes and she had decided to tell Rochelle about last night before they all met up again. Rochelle had some sort of sixth sense when it came to these things—when it came to Justine and who she slept with—and she didn't want to be scrutinized by Alexis the moment Rochelle's penny dropped.

"I'm early," she shouted after she knocked and walked in the back door.

"Hi, Justine." Rita, Rochelle's wife, was nursing a cup of tea in the kitchen "That's very unlike you."

Justine kissed her friend hello and smiled, even though she'd hoped to catch Rochelle alone. Although to tell Rochelle was to tell Rita—and vice versa.

"Rochelle's still putting on her face." Rita winked at Justine. "You'd think she's trying to impress these youngsters." She chuckled. "You might even suspect she has a thing for younger women." Rita was thirteen years younger than her wife and both she and Justine loved teasing Rochelle about that—even though, right now, that would make Justine a big hypocrite.

"Have you eaten?" Rita asked.

"I didn't have time." Justine sank into a chair. The short night was catching up with her.

"How about a sandwich? You know Mama Rita makes the best sandwiches," she said in the voice she now used with her grandkids.

"I could murder a sandwich." As if on cue, Justine's stomach rumbled.

"On it." Rita rose from her chair.

"Are you off work today?" Justine asked.

Rita nodded. "The students are on a field trip and, for once, my presence was not required." She took some stuff out of the fridge. "Which is excellent timing because it gives me a chance to meet Alexis Dalton and, even more interestingly, Sienna Bright, who will be playing my lovely wife." She went to work on fixing Justine a sandwich, an action Justine had long ago gotten used to—Rochelle and Rita loved to feed her. "Rochelle really liked her. What was your impression?"

"Um." Justine's cheeks flushed pink. Luckily, Rochelle waltzed into the room.

"You're early." Rochelle opened her arms wide and Justine got up to hug her friend.

"I think she wanted one of my sandwiches." Rita handed Justine a plate. "There you go. Tuna with tomato and a touch of pickled onion, just how you like it."

"Thank you so much. You spoil me." Justine sat again and tucked in.

"Someone has to," Rita said.

"How was last night? Did Sienna stay long at the shelter?" Rochelle asked.

"She and Darrel are already thick as thieves," Justine said in between bites, gathering her courage. She checked her watch. If they were punctual, Sienna and Alexis would be here soon. "I took her to Min-ji's after because we were both starving." She'd found the discarded bag of Korean food on her kitchen floor this morning—Min-ji would be furious if she found out its fate.

"Oh." Rochelle gave her a look. "And?"

"Things turned a little flirty and then, yeah, we went back to my place."

"Things turned a little flirty?" Rita's voice had shot up an octave.

"Did you sleep with her?" Rochelle cut in. "Did you sleep with Sienna Bright?"

"Yes," Justine admitted.

"Oh my god." Rita clasped her hands to her mouth as though Justine had just confessed she'd slept with her wife.

"I need to sit down for this." Rochelle pulled up a chair.

"Shall I get us something stronger than tea?" Rita's voice was still trembling.

"What happened?" Rochelle tilted her head and looked Justine in the eye. "I mean, *how*… did it happen?"

Instead of fetching booze, Rita sat next to them.

"We went to dinner. Had a few beers. You know what it's like with Min-ji. She always acts like I'm such a big deal. Conjured up a special table for us out of nowhere. The food was out of this world. And Sienna is just… really nice and forward about what she wants."

"Are you saying that she wanted you as a side with Min-ji's food?" Rochelle asked.

"We just spent the night together, as two consenting adults who knew exactly what they were doing. There's no need to make a big deal out of it. I just wanted you to know before she got here, because, well… you have that thing." Justine waved her hand about. "Where you just know stuff about me without me having to say and I didn't want the afternoon to be more awkward than it has to be."

"But, Justine," Rita said. "You slept with the actor who is playing your ex. Did that have something to do with it?"

"Of course not. Sienna's just… I just had the hots for her." And she for me, Justine thought, and wasn't that the strangest thing of all for a movie star?

"You put the moves on her?" Rochelle said.

Justine picked up the rest of her sandwich. "Come to think of it, I think she hit on me. I was just playing, you know? Just having some fun after a long-ass day. But she went for it. And I didn't say no."

"Are you honestly claiming that Sienna Bright seduced you?" Rochelle could sound a touch less incredulous. "*The* Sienna Bright? Bobby Bright's gorgeous, talented daughter who is, what? Twenty years younger than you?"

"Don't act so surprised." Although no longer that hungry, Justine took another bite of her sandwich.

"But I am surprised," Rochelle said. "I'm baffled, frankly."

Justine swallowed. "Because she's young and hot and…" She pulled up one shoulder. "I'm not?"

"That, too." Rochelle was nothing if not brutally honest, a

quality Justine greatly appreciated—and had been the basis of their long friendship after a difficult break-up. "But mostly that it happened. Just like that. You only just met her and… I don't know. I wasn't expecting this."

"Good for you." Rita seemed to have recovered from the shock. "Now I definitely can't wait to meet her."

The bell rang.

CHAPTER 8

Sienna was delighted to meet Rita and most of everyone's energy seemed to be focused on the introduction of Rochelle's wife, making Sienna's greeting of Justine feel furtive and a little weird—like they hadn't spent the previous night together. It was supposed to be a secret, of course, and Sienna had no problem with that.

In fact, over the course of the morning, she had decided that it would be for the best to move on as quickly as possible. Not to pretend it hadn't happened—there was no need for that. It had been good fun and unexpectedly thrilling and Justine was interesting to be around, but Sienna didn't want anything to jeopardize her performance in this movie. And the real work had yet to begin. Besides, she had to focus on Rochelle.

Like the day before, Rochelle took Sienna onto the porch so they could have a face-to-face conversation. Rita sat with them for the first half hour, but then gave them privacy.

"I'm sorry," Rochelle said as soon as Rita had left. "I hate to be indiscreet, but I have to say something." She pinned her dark gaze on Sienna. "Justine told me, about you and her. About last night. I know it's none of my business, but I can't ignore something like that. I'm just a little bemused by it, if I'm being honest."

Justine had already told Rochelle? These two really were the epitome of ex-lovers turned best of friends.

"Why?" Sienna asked, because the last thing she had to do was explain herself.

"You don't have to tell me what Justine is like. I've known her forever."

"What does that mean?" Sienna was intrigued. Was Rochelle judging her best friend? Or was she trying to tell Sienna something about her?

"The woman is a force of nature. She is unlike anyone I've ever met. She seems to have no off button when it comes to work—to her cause. But then she crashes and she has a beer and she forgets to eat again and… sometimes, she can get a little inappropriate."

"Inappropriate?" Sienna shook her head. "There was nothing inappropriate about it. Um, hello. I'm a grown woman and I was totally into her." Sienna scoffed—if anything was inappropriate, it was this conversation. "Why are you so upset about this?"

"I'm not upset, I'm just so excited about this movie. I think it's an important one and I'm sorry if that makes me sound self-important. I'm really not. At its core, it's not about me, even if it does focus on my relationship with Justine. It's not even about us. It's about systemic homophobia and the hurt it causes to so many people." Rochelle took a breath. "I'm sorry if I made you feel judged or uncomfortable. I've worked in the industry for my entire career and I know how hard it is to make a movie. I know what it costs in money, time, and energy. And talent, for that matter. You sleeping with Justine is just a bit weird. I guess it has thrown me. She told me minutes before you arrived. I'm still processing. But I do apologize for my too strong reaction."

"Are you always like this when it comes to Justine?" Sienna thought it a good idea to rise above this—for now—and take the chance to get to know Rochelle better. That was the reason she was here, after all. And this was telling her a lot.

"Justine is important to me. She's family and you know what family can be like. Relentlessly critical one moment, falling into each other's arms the next. In the end, I only want what's best for her, which is not something she always wants for herself."

"Can you delve a little deeper into that?" Sienna wondered if she had to share this conversation with Alexis—or with Justine. "If you don't mind." Sienna put on her most encouraging smile—a bit like the one she'd let loose on Justine last night.

"It has become second nature for me to look out for her and, sometimes, that includes the people she gets involved with."

"Why? What does she do to them?" Justine had been nothing but respectful of Sienna's boundaries.

Rochelle chuckled. "I feel like we're perhaps getting a little off topic."

"Not really. Your relationship with Justine is at the heart of this movie."

"My relationship with her thirty years ago, sure. But that was a long time ago. Neither one of us is still the same."

"Can I ask why you broke up?" The *Gimme Shelter* script may have a romantic happy ending, but clearly Justine and Rochelle's relationship hadn't lasted.

Rochelle slowly expelled the air from her lungs, as though Sienna had asked her to answer a hyper-complex question.

"Quite a few reasons, but I guess the biggest one was that I wanted kids and she absolutely didn't." She scrunched her lips together. "Justine was also a lot younger than me and at that time in our lives, that really did matter. My clock was ticking, you know? But it wasn't just that, believe me."

Sienna was aware of the privileged position she was in to gather all this information on the woman she'd slept with. It was hardly fair, but that didn't make it any less interesting.

"I know Justine loved me, but I wasn't the love of her life. Her work is. She is the perfect example of someone married to her job. She lives for the shelter. It consumes her. Maybe not as much as back in the day, when we started it, but still. Take yesterday. She got a call and off she went, even though we were meeting with you and Alexis. That's what she's always been like, but even more so in her twenties and thirties." Rochelle paused. "And then there's also… what happened to her, with her parents and after, but that's really not for me to divulge. She would hate it if she knew I told you about that. I'd tell you to ask her, but she won't talk about it so I'm actually advising you not to ask her about that specifically. But that's another reason why our relationship didn't work out in the end." Rochelle squared her shoulders and sat up a bit. "Do you want to see her again?"

"I don't know," Sienna said. "Has she said anything about that?" She was beginning to feel very unprofessional—so much for not letting her night with Justine affect her work.

"No, but…" Rochelle paused, took a breath, then stopped talking altogether.

"But what?" Sienna couldn't stop herself from pushing.

"Nothing." Rochelle grinned. "I know this movie is about Justine, but last time I checked, you're not the one playing Justine."

"Fair enough." Sienna nodded. Rochelle was right. "I'm taking advantage of the situation. I'm well aware." She followed up with an innocent chuckle. "Thank you for sharing."

"I know I'm far less interesting than Justine, and you and I haven't spent the night together, but is there anything else you'd like to know about me?" Rochelle's smirk said it all.

———

Justine tried to keep her focus on Alexis and her questions, but she was tired and her exhausted brain kept wondering what

Rochelle and Sienna were talking about on the porch. Knowing Rochelle, she'd probably already told Sienna that Justine had informed her about their night together—and she was probably grilling her. She'd need a thorough debrief with Rochelle after this.

"This must be hard for you to talk about, and I wouldn't ask if I didn't think it necessary for my performance, but, um, what was it like to live on the street?"

"Dehumanizing. Utterly undignified. Really hard and very fucking dangerous." Justine held up her hand. "I get that you wanted to ask the question, but I'm not going to tell you more about that time. For that, you'll have to use your imagination."

"Okay."

Justine appreciated that Alexis didn't break out into a flurry of useless apologies.

"I will say that it was so harrowing that I've dedicated my life to keeping as many kids as I can from the same fate." Justine regarded Alexis. "How did it make you feel to visit the shelter yesterday?"

"It was so interesting. Also to meet Darrel. I've already texted them. We're meeting up for drinks this weekend."

"So they can spill the beans on me?" Justine had no secrets when it came to running the shelter. "That's smart." Alexis had already left when Justine came out of her intake so she wasn't able to gauge her immediate reaction. She might ask Darrel about that later, to inquire whether she seemed shaken at all by the change in environment.

Justine was so tired, she had to do her best to suppress a yawn.

Alexis held her hand in front of her mouth as well. "I'm sorry. I swear you're not boring me, it's just seeing you yawn."

Justine chuckled. "You're not boring me either, but I didn't get enough sleep last night."

Alexis checked her watch. "It's about time to call it a day, either way."

"I hope this conversation was helpful."

"Every minute I spend with you is helpful." Alexis scrunched her lips together. "I don't suppose you've changed your mind about me shadowing you for a day? I find observation really key to nailing a character based on an actual person."

Justine huffed out some air. The prospect of having a movie star hot on her heels all day didn't exactly fill her with joy, on top of it being highly impractical in her job. She had many meetings of all kinds—although mostly about money—and the occasional intake conversation and none of those accommodated strangers listening in.

"I'll look at my calendar and I'll see when we can maybe spend an afternoon together at the shelter, but I can't make you any promises."

"I can volunteer if that helps," Alexis offered, surprising Justine.

"Let's see." Alexis and Sienna's presence at the shelter hadn't gone unnoticed. A few of the residents would give the little they had for a few hours with two movie stars—it was ridiculous, but it was simply how it was. "But yeah, I think you could make a few young people's day with that."

"Thank you." Alexis shot out of her chair, as though she suddenly had somewhere urgent to be—she probably had. Justine knew the feeling. Despite her fatigue, she wanted to go back to the shelter and check on the girl—Ashleigh—they had welcomed yesterday. When Justine had arrived at the shelter earlier today, Ashleigh had left, and Justine hoped she would return. She hoped to have another conversation with her.

"You're welcome, and have fun with Darrel." Justine rose as well. She should try for a quick nap before she went anywhere else, but she knew she wouldn't. She'd just try to go to bed early tonight.

"You'll let me know about volunteering?" Alexis asked.

"I will." Maybe she should drop Alexis Dalton's name if she

got to speak to Ashleigh again—maybe she could get through to her like that.

As if on cue, Rochelle and Sienna emerged from the porch.

"Do you want a ride?" Alexis asked Sienna.

"No. You go ahead. I'll make my own way home." Sienna looked at Justine. "I'd like to ask Justine some more questions before I go. Is that okay?"

Justine could hardly say no in front of everyone, even though she'd had enough of answering questions.

"Sure." Justine noticed how Rochelle's face strained.

Rita walked into the living room and hearty goodbyes were exchanged.

"Can I catch a ride with you?" Sienna asked Justine as they stood outside Rochelle's house.

"Depends where you're going." An inadvertent smile tugged at her lips. "I hope Rochelle didn't, um, I don't know, say something inappropriate to you. I told her about last night just before you arrived and she was freaking out."

"We had a very illuminating conversation." Sienna grinned.

"Meaning?"

"I could tell you all about it over dinner tonight."

"Over… dinner?"

"Or just a beer." Sienna's grin didn't disappear—on the contrary.

"I don't want to dismiss you, but I need to go back to the shelter. If you want to talk, I understand, but I'm not sure I'll have the energy for that tonight."

"How about tomorrow? It's Saturday. Maybe you'll be more rested." Weekends were always busy at the shelter and Justine rarely took a day off—only when she felt she really needed it, which was definitely not often enough according to Rochelle.

"Maybe you could come to my place? I'll show you my Raffo Shahs," Sienna insisted. "I'm also a pretty decent cook, even if I say so myself."

"Okay. Let's do that." Justine couldn't think of a good enough reason to decline this invitation from Sienna Bright.

CHAPTER 9

So much for moving on quickly, Sienna thought, as she added the tofu to the pan. But after that conversation with Rochelle, everything had changed. And Justine hadn't been very reluctant to agree to this dinner.

She took a sip of the Sancerre she had opened. The rice cooker was doing its job. The cucumber was marinating in the spicy dressing Sienna couldn't get enough of. As soon as the tofu was done frying in Sichuan peppercorn sauce, Sienna would be ready for Justine to arrive.

By the time Justine finally arrived—more than half an hour later than the time they'd agreed on—Sienna had finished more than her share of that bottle of wine.

"I'm sorry I'm late," Justine said, not sounding apologetic at all. "I also didn't have time to pick up something to thank you for your invitation. I know it's rude. I hope my awareness of that is enough." She looked around Sienna's apartment. "Well, fuck me. This place is humongous. Do you live here alone?"

"I do. My dad bought it for me, to be honest. It's his way of showing affection." The only way he knows how, Sienna thought.

"That's right. I need to give Bobby Bright a call one of these days. I'm sure I can get his number from you." Justine gave off a bizarre kind of passive-aggressive energy. Or maybe she was just nervously joking.

"Maybe later." Sienna tried to usher them toward the lounge area, but Justine was drawn to the walls of glass overlooking the city.

"I was surprised you lived downtown. I'd taken you more for a Bel Air or Beverly Hills type."

"Downtown is all the rage these days." Granted, Sienna's dad lived in Bel Air, while her mother lived in Beverly Hills. "What can I offer you to drink?" she asked. "And more importantly, do you need a snack first?"

"I had lunch so I should be okay." That was the first genuine smile Justine had sent Sienna's way since she'd arrived. "I'll have whatever you're having."

Sienna fetched her guest a glass and poured out the remainder of the bottle. She put some wasabi nuts in a bowl and brought everything to the lounge.

"Will you come sit with me?"

Justine strutted over. She was wearing jeans and a wrinkled shirt. Her shoulder-length hair was pushed back and looked unruly. She hadn't bothered to put on something special—or pull a comb through her hair—before coming here.

She huffed out a slow breath as she plopped down in one of the lounge chairs.

"Long day?" Sienna asked.

"There's this girl at the shelter. Her name's Ashleigh. She's hard to get through to. She's been through a lot and it's, um, yeah, it's hard, but I'll get there with her."

Obviously, Rochelle was right about Justine being married to her work. Sienna waited until Justine sipped from her wine and hoped the alcohol would relax her as it had done at the Korean restaurant.

Justine cut her gaze to Sienna. "I know exactly what you're

thinking. I'm a lot, I know that. I just need a minute to get my bearings."

Sienna chuckled and shook her head. "That wasn't what I was thinking, but it's true that you are a lot and I quite like it."

"Again with the *quite*." Justine sank a little deeper into her chair.

"It did the trick last time." So much for waiting until Justine had relaxed. But Sienna was not used to this. She hadn't met anyone like Justine in her thirty-six years.

"Oh, god. You're relentless." Justine smiled at her and it was the kind of smile that reached all the way up to her eyes. "Here I was thinking Rochelle told you a cautionary tale about me."

"Really? What did Rochelle tell you?"

"That you were very inquisitive about me and the reasons why she and I broke up."

"It's a fair question to ask in relation to the part I'm playing."

"Rochelle told me pretty much exactly what she told you about me." Justine left that hanging there, not giving any indication of how she felt about that.

"Do you think this is a date?" Sienna asked.

"A date?" Justine scoffed. "I thought we had agreed that us dating was a bad idea?"

"I'm not saying it is a date. I'm just curious what you think about tonight."

"I thought you wanted to talk about the other night," Justine said. "That's how I understood it. That's why I'm here."

"Okay. So we're on the same page."

"But you were flirting with me just now," Justine said.

"Hm. I guess I was."

"Let's talk, then." Justine ran a hand through her hair, making it look even more disheveled than before.

"Honestly," Sienna started, "if what Rochelle told me about you was supposed to be a cautionary tale, it had the opposite effect."

"Cautionary tales tend to do that." Justine took another sip of wine. "Although she might just have been replying to your nosy questions and I'm the one who concluded that she meant to warn you about me. About all my flaws and insecurities and the reasons why I royally suck at being in a relationship."

Sienna shook her head. "It wasn't like that. It's obvious Rochelle thinks the world of you."

"And I of her."

"Do you regret that things didn't work out between you?"

Justine huffed some air between her lips. "That was so long ago. But no, I don't regret it because I was not the right person for Rochelle. I could never give her what she wanted." Justine put her glass on the coffee table. "But enough of the twenty questions, please. Because of this movie, I already feel like my life and personality are being turned inside out. I'm not here for some more of that." Justine nodded at Sienna. "Tell me something about you. Why aren't you on a hot date on a Saturday night? It can't be down to a lack of suitors."

"Who says I'm not," Sienna quipped, because Justine had that effect on her. If she wanted someone to fawn over her, tell her how great an actor she was, how beautiful she was, she could have that in a heartbeat. But Sienna wanted the opposite —she always had. She wanted a challenge. A difficult woman with barbed wire for skin and a solid ice cube for a heart—at first.

"There you go again. It's truly impossible to get a straight answer out of you. It's hardly fair what with all the questions you've been asking Rochelle and me."

"You're right." Sienna was momentarily all out of quips.

"Just give me a glimpse. For instance, tell me about the last fling or relationship or whatever you want to call it you had." Justine reached for her wine glass and relaxed into her seat, as though settling in for a captivating tale.

"That was a couple of months ago. Her name was Dolly and she turned out to be a huge error of judgement."

Justine gave a small but encouraging nod.

"I was drawn to the fact she barely noticed me, or that she at least gave that impression. She played really hard to get and that's a game I can't resist. But, well, let's just say that the playing hard to get didn't stop when we got together. She was always canceling on me and blowing hot and cold over everything. I like a challenge, but I'm not into being treated like dirt."

"Thank you for sharing that with me."

Sienna swallowed a gulp of wine, then hid part of her face behind the glass, feeling as though she'd said too much.

"Are you hungry?" she asked, suddenly feeling too exposed —which was probably how Justine had been feeling when Alexis and Sienna visited her with the sole purpose of studying her movements and gaining insight into her personality.

"Starving." Justine shot her the kindest smile. Having a penchant for women who were hard to get was all well and good—and terribly exciting—but a warm smile from a woman who obviously had no clue of how gorgeous she was also went a long way.

CHAPTER 10

To say it all made sense now, that Justine understood Sienna's underlying reasons for hitting on her, was a bit much, but her confession about what kind of women she was into was still quite revealing.

"How old was Dolly?" Justine asked as she followed Sienna to the dining area.

"A not very mature thirty." Sienna headed into the spacious kitchen and turned her back on Justine, focusing on a pan on the stove.

Justine stopped at the large island separating the kitchen from the huge dining table. *Jesus. This place.* It must have cost a few million. The daily battles with insufficient funds in the shelter's accounts made Justine too aware of how other people spent their money. And of the ridiculous amounts of cash they were willing to spend on a house while so many people didn't have a roof over their head.

When she'd walked through the ornate lobby earlier, with its luxury furnishings and swanky chandeliers, her brain had already started doing inadvertent—and inappropriate—calculations. It was how Justine was wired after decades of fighting for money to shelter unhoused kids. She had to stop herself from doing the same as she looked around this place.

Then she spotted the Raffo Shah painting Sienna had told her about. It hung on a stark white wall next to the kitchen island that made its spectacular colors pop. Justine knew how much this painting was worth—just as she knew the value of the one Raffo had made especially for her. She hoped with every fiber of her being that she would never have to, but she also knew that if it meant she could create room for an extra kid who would otherwise have to sleep in the street, she'd sell it in a heartbeat—and Raffo would understand.

"It's amazing, isn't it?" Sienna put the pan on the table. "The other one's in my bedroom." She chuckled. "I'm just stating a fact, not insinuating anything."

Justine was drawn to the delicious smell coming from the pan.

"What's for dinner?" If she could help it, Justine never cooked. She considered it a colossal waste of time. Why spend an hour preparing a meal if you could pop a pre-made lasagna in the microwave and have an apple for dessert?

"Mapo tofu with jasmine rice and a spicy cucumber salad. I figured Asian food would be okay since you took me to a Korean restaurant."

"You really are full of surprises. That looks divine." Justine happily settled at the table. She didn't have any issues with a good-looking woman making her dinner.

"I like to cook. It relaxes me," Sienna said. "My stepdad was the chef in our house and I was always hanging out with him in the kitchen."

Oh, to have a father who buys you a multimillion dollar penthouse and a stepfather who teaches you how to cook.

Sienna put a plate worthy of a fancy restaurant in front of Justine.

"I'm really impressed with this."

"You haven't tasted it yet. Start with some cucumber. It's very refreshing."

"Yes, Ma'am." Maybe she could convince Sienna to volunteer in the shelter's kitchen—but again, she halted her train of thought. Justine was aware that her brain was constantly suffused with thoughts of the shelter. It was always at the forefront of her mind. It was hard to switch off from, even when having a delicious meal cooked for her by Sienna Bright. Justine speared a cube of cucumber onto her fork and popped it in her mouth. It tasted salty and acidic and spicy all at the same time. "I guess you can cook."

"It's really useful when eating good food is your favorite hobby," Sienna said. "The last few years, I've been cooking much more at home because it's getting harder for me to just rock up at the newest restaurant hot spot in town."

"Because you get recognized?" Justine tasted the tofu and that, too, was exactly the right combination of silky-smooth flavors and tanginess.

"And stared at and asked for selfies mid-meal. Things like that. You'd think I'd be used to it being Bobby Bright's daughter, but my dad didn't take us out that much. We didn't see him that often."

"But you're close to your stepdad?" Justine asked between savoring one tasty bite after another. "This is so good, by the way. If your acting career goes off the rails for some inexplicable reason, please become a chef."

Sienna smiled sheepishly, as though she'd heard that one a million times before.

"Eddy and I are very close. He's just a great dude, you know, and he gave me and my sister what my father couldn't: time and attention. He was there when we needed him, not for anything big in particular, just for all the mundane everyday stuff like homework or a scraped knee. And a lot of wonderful dinners at the kitchen table."

"And your mother?"

"Mom is not allowed near the kitchen. She's a terrible cook. She'd put lettuce in the microwave and stuff like that." Sienna chuckled. "But my mother is… I kinda hate how this sounds, but she's such an inspiration. Not just to me, but to so many girls and women of color. Not many women have accomplished what she has in the industry, let alone Black women."

"They both sound really great." Justine could only be happy for Sienna. She also couldn't help but needle her a little. "So why this fascination with women who enjoy stringing you along and pretending they're not interested?"

"It's not always pretense, I'll tell you that." Sienna shrugged. "But I guess it's more that I hate the opposite. You know that typical LA way of being hyper-friendly and calling someone you've just met amazing and wonderful. Ugh. It makes me break out in hives because being famous is absolutely not the same as being an amazing and wonderful person. On the contrary."

"Yet you decided to become an actor?"

"Because I love acting."

Or you're subconsciously angling for daddy's approval, Justine thought, but kept it to herself. This wasn't a therapy session. Come to think of it, she didn't really know what this was. Whether they called it that or not, it was beginning to feel a whole lot like a date.

"It's a strange profession, though." Justine filled her fork with more delicious tofu and rice. She couldn't get enough of this dish.

"Not for me. I grew up with it and so many of my first pictures are of me on set with my mom and dad, before they split up. Obviously, I don't remember any of that, but… it's all I've ever really wanted to do. To be part of telling a story like that. To disappear into a character. To understand them, to learn what makes them tick. It's so addictive. It's my art. It's how I create. I love it and I can't imagine doing anything else."

Maybe Justine should ask Sienna to give an acting workshop

at the LGBT Center, which the Rainbow Shelter worked with closely. *Argh*. There she went again. She shook off the thought.

"I'm happy for you that you get to do what you love."

"Don't you think I'm a spoiled brat who got everything handed to her on a silver platter?"

"Of course not. Why would I think that?" Of course, the thought had crossed Justine's mind, but that was before she'd actually met Sienna.

"The differences between us could literally not be bigger." Sienna pushed some rice around her plate. "I am aware of that, just as I'm hyper-aware of my privilege."

"I'm not one to hold anyone's luck against them. You simply can't choose the family and country and situation you're born into. It's like a cosmic lottery."

"I'm sorry that you didn't have that kind of luck," Sienna said.

Justine waved off the comment. Pity was the last thing she needed, although it did, at certain times, work wonders to make certain people open their wallets—but there was a time and a place for that, and it wasn't here tonight in Sienna's penthouse.

"I can't thank you enough for this delicious meal." Justine changed the subject—praise was always a good way to do that.

"I have dessert as well."

"God, you're spoiling me." Her belly more than full, Justine leaned back.

"Are you a dessert aficionado? Because you never know in this town."

"I am, although I guess it depends what's on offer." The food and wine had fully relaxed Justine and she looked straight into Sienna's eyes.

Sienna chuckled in response, seeming to catch Justine's drift. Contrary to Sienna, Justine appreciated someone easy to flirt with. Someone who didn't waste time playing games and being coy. Someone who was, very simply, up for a good time after a nice glass of wine and a delicious meal.

"It's just a dark chocolate mousse, nothing fancy," Sienna said. "Although maybe instead of coffee with it, we should have that conversation you came here to have."

"No coffee for me, anyway." Justine ogled her empty glass of wine. "I'll have some more of that, if you have it." Justine sat facing the kitchen and it was impossible not to notice the gigantic wine fridge in the corner. "And yes, let's talk. We were intimate and that at least deserves a conversation."

CHAPTER 11

Sienna refilled Justine's wine glass and presented her with a bowl of chocolate mousse. Then she sat down and waited for Justine to begin the conversation they'd been dancing around all night.

The entrée she'd prepared had gone down well, which pleased Sienna—cooking a meal for someone she liked was one of her greatest joys in life. And she liked Justine, that much had also become obvious over the course of the evening. She liked her no-nonsense attitude and her big heart, but also the delicate structure of her cheekbones, which gave her face a gorgeous, timeless quality that made you want to stare at it forever. Not to mention the captivating light-blue of her eyes.

"I enjoyed our night together." A sparkle lit up Justine's eyes. "Even more so because it made Rochelle and Rita act all out of whack."

"So I gathered." Sienna was still trying to work out the intricacies of Justine's relationship with her ex.

"But this is not about Rochelle, even though, let's be honest, it is very much a mindfuck that you're playing her."

"Do I remind you of her?" Sienna asked.

"In some ways, yes. But that might just be the power of

suggestion. The human brain is so susceptible to that. Maybe if I'd met you in circumstances that weren't you being cast to play my ex, you might not remind me of her at all, but I'll never know. Either way, you remind me of the best parts of Rochelle. Her gregariousness. Her warm smile. Her easy way, you know? I fell for her pretty hard back in the day. She was so kind and lovely—she still is, now." Justine paused. "But you are very much your own person, of course. And I know more than most that real beauty comes from within. That said, I find you very attractive. I'm not deluding myself about that. We didn't sleep together simply because I was drawn to the goodness of your heart. Although life has made me a pretty good judge of character and I sincerely believe you're one of the good ones." Justine's tone was slightly self-deprecating, as if she found her own words amusing but silly.

Sienna was melting under Justine's bright gaze. There was a lot to unpack in what Justine had just said, but the gist of it was, unmistakably, that Justine liked her as well. What Sienna was keen to find out, however, was where things were headed from here.

"I'd thank you," Sienna said, "but the particular shape of my face you're drawn to is merely due to genetics so I can't take credit for that."

"See, this is exactly why I'm attracted to you. You're incredibly down-to-earth for a nepo-baby movie star."

"How did you think I was going to be?"

"For starters, I would not have expected you to make that delicious meal." Justine briefly sank her front teeth into her bottom lip. "And, well, I also never would have expected you to respond to my inane flirting the other night at Min-ji's." She scrunched up her lips. "I guess I'm with Rochelle on that. It is quite perplexing if you look at it objectively."

"I don't think that it is. At all," Sienna said. "You're Justine Blackburn. You're a fucking legend and I rate you so much higher than the polished, media-trained movie stars this town has produced, even the ones that are gingerly starting to come out of the closet now. You make an actual difference in people's lives and you've been doing it for decades, since long before it was fashionable to be queer-friendly. I have so much respect for that."

"Thank you." Was that a hint of pink on Justine's cheeks? "That's very nice of you to say." She took a quick sip of wine. "But I did tell you the other night that I'm no saint. I can be a real selfish asshole, but it's easy enough to forgive myself because I know why I'm being selfish. It's harder for other people to understand. People I care about and who care about me."

"Rochelle did say something about that."

"I'm glad she told you those things. It saves me from having to tell you." There was straightforward Justine again.

"I'm acutely aware that I know much more about you than vice versa, but… can you give me an example? Could you, like, tell me about your last relationship-slash-fling?" Sienna turned on her best smile. "I know I'm too curious for my own good, but, please…" She turned up her smile to full-wattage.

"Oh, god." Justine glanced at Sienna from under her lashes. "I haven't been in anything serious for so long. I sound like a broken record, even to myself, but I simply don't have the time. I've always felt short on time, but at least I used to have more energy, you know? But now, I feel like I'm constantly out of time *and* energy and I just, um, I guess I don't put in the effort. That's what I've been told, anyway."

"What was her name?" Sienna pushed, because she was dying to find out a few salient details.

"Marcy," Justine said. "She was quite something, but I fucked it up. As usual."

"Where did you meet her?"

"At a Christmas party at the LGBT Center. I was letting my hair down after another long year and there she was. She caught my eye and I turned on my flirt. We hooked up, went on a few dates and then, yeah, it petered out. I let it because… Well, if my life has proven anything it's that I can't do both. I can't run the shelter and be the kind of attentive girlfriend most women want. Even with Marcy, whose expectations were actually pretty low. But still, she wanted more than I was able to give, and I don't hold that against her for a single second." A shadow crossed Justine's face. "Turns out you can't have it all."

Sienna would give a lot to meet this Marcy-with-the-low-expectations, to give her the third degree about what it was like to be with Justine, even if it was only for a short while.

"Are you saying that you want a relationship but your work doesn't allow you to have one?"

Justine shook her head. "My job is so much more than work. It's not just what I do, it's who I am. And it really is who I want to be. I'm willing to sacrifice other things for that, other things that most people would never compromise on, like a long-term relationship."

"Yet you are a relentless flirt," Sienna said.

"That I am," Justine admitted. "Always have been." Her face went from soft to stern in a split second. "But never with anyone from the shelter, though. That's a hard no."

Sienna nodded her understanding. "When was the last time you hooked up with someone?" she asked.

"A couple of nights ago with this really hot chick who's playing my ex in a movie about my life." Justine snickered.

Sienna responded with a chuckle of her own. "Before *that* particular hot chick, I mean."

Justine didn't immediately reply but, instead, gazed into Sienna's eyes.

"A few months ago, I think. I don't remember the timing exactly, but I remember the woman." The grin that appeared on Justine's face ignited a pang of jealousy in Sienna.

"What happened afterward? You just went your separate ways?"

Justine nodded. "She wasn't interested in anything more."

"And you?"

"I'm not one to push. Yes, I flirt, but then I'm very happy to leave the initiative with the other party. I don't want to give anyone the wrong idea of who I am and what I'm after."

"What about, um, this... What about tonight?"

"I don't know." Justine stared into her bowl of chocolate mousse. Neither one of them had touched dessert. "I don't know what to make of you, but I'm glad we're having this conversation. I like talking to you." She arched up her eyebrows. "But it's high time to turn the tables again. Tell me what it is you want? You're how old? Mid-thirties? You must be asking yourself some big questions about wanting a family and all that?"

"I don't want kids," Sienna said. "I don't have the mother gene, if that's a thing. I figure that if I wanted a child, I would have taken steps to make that happen by now, but I don't have that need inside me. Not like my sister has, for instance. She has two kids and, fuck, being a mom is hard, right? It's easy enough to see when I look at Taissa, but she always had that unyielding desire to be someone's mother. And I don't." Sienna'd had enough conversations with her sister about this to understand the fundamental difference between her and her sibling.

"Your honesty is refreshing. I love it," Justine said. "That kind of clarity is so rare, believe me. I have a shelter full of kids whose parents should have thought twice before having them, because they couldn't give them the one thing they needed the most, the one single thing they should have in abundance— love."

Conversation with Justine always, naturally, seemed to flow back to what was at the center of her life: the Rainbow Shelter.

"Good for you that you're so clear about that and are able to be completely honest about it. It's still not a given for a woman, even now. I truly applaud you for it." And then she could come out with the kind of heartfelt compliment that made Sienna's stomach flutter. "What about relationships? What's your view on those?"

"My view?" Sienna toyed with her spoon. "I'm not sure I have one, I just… seem to have a tendency to be attracted to women who are not always very good for me." Sienna couldn't help but wonder if Justine thought about herself that way right about now.

"The emotionally unavailable type, you mean?"

"I wouldn't put it that way, but maybe. I have been in two long-term relationships, but they didn't work out." Sienna resolutely picked up her spoon. "But I don't really want to get into that right now."

All Sienna wanted to find out was whether Justine wanted to take things further—and whether that was a good idea. From what Justine had confessed about herself, probably not. But her words stood in stark contrast to the warm vibe of the evening and the easy but profound conversation between them. "How about some chocolate mousse instead?" she asked.

CHAPTER 12

Justine didn't know what to do. If she'd had this kind of conversation with Sienna at Min-ji's—if she'd allowed herself to take the time for it—she might not have invited Sienna to her place. She might not have slept with her because she liked her too much. In fact, there was very little not to like about the woman sitting across from her, licking her dessert spoon. The more the evening went on, and the more wine she drank, the more Justine wanted to have sex with Sienna again. But she shouldn't. There was actually something at stake here and Justine knew what she was like. Although she had just been very honest about that as well. So, she figured she'd do what she always did: leave it up to the other person. To Sienna.

"Once again, utterly delicious." Justine looked into Sienna's eyes—because it was one thing to leave the initiative to her, it was another to not convey interest.

"Thanks." Sienna returned her gaze. "And for the record, I don't really know what to make of you either, nor of... this." She waved her spoon about.

"That's a dessert spoon. Probably a very expensive one, but that's really all it is."

Sienna chuckled softly as she shook her head. "You must

79

have broken quite a few hearts," she said. "You're very easy to like and, well, I didn't just sleep with you because you're a legend either."

Here we go, Justine thought. "Maybe I'm easy to like, but I'm much harder to love. Trust me."

Sienna shrugged. "I'm not looking for love tonight." She licked her spoon as she returned Justine's gaze again.

"Just so you know," Justine said. "If you come on to me, I'm not going to resist you."

"Because you can't or you don't want to?"

"Maybe a little of both." No matter how delicious, Justine was no longer in the mood for dessert. "I've been meaning to ask: is Bright your father's real name? Because it does such a good job of describing you."

"You're such a delicious flirt. I really *quite* like it."

"I figured as much." Justine waited. "And ditto."

"Would you like to see my other Raffo Shah painting?" Sienna asked, putting her spoon down.

"Raffo would never forgive me if I didn't enjoy her work when given the opportunity."

"Come on, then." Sienna pushed her chair back. "I'll show you."

Justine followed Sienna up the glass-and-steel staircase to the top floor of her gigantic duplex loft, into her master bedroom, its color scheme seemingly picked to complement Raffo's painting.

Justine made a spectacle of examining the work, exaggerating her reaction, probably because she was a touch nervous about this.

"Raffo's so talented." She marveled at the vibrant hues of the painting. Justine had never seen it before, yet it felt keenly familiar.

"Do you ever stop to think that you gave Raffo the opportunity to develop her talent?" Sienna stood behind Justine and, without further ado, slipped her arms around her waist.

"Nope," Justine said resolutely. "Because that's not why I do what I do."

Sienna chuckled and her breath was warm on the back of Justine's neck. Sienna's hot whisper of breath was soon followed by the soft touch of her lips on Justine's sensitive skin there.

"You don't seem to care much that making art can be the most important thing about a person," Sienna said softly in between gentle kisses.

Even though potentially interesting, this was not a conversation Justine wanted to have right now. She pivoted in Sienna's embrace and faced her.

"Is it the most important thing about you?" she asked, not because she was desperate for Sienna's answer, but simply because she wanted to prolong the moment.

Slowly, Sienna shook her head, then tilted her head forward and brought her lips a mere fraction of an inch away from Justine's.

Justine inhaled her divine scent and brought her hands to Sienna's cheeks.

"Actually," she said, her lips almost touching Sienna's as she spoke. "I don't think I *can* resist you."

———

Sienna lay naked on top of Justine, her knee between Justine's legs as she kissed and kissed her. How divine was it to kiss Sienna Bright? How utterly wonderful and butterfly-inducing and like-you-never-wanted-it-to-end. Then the kiss did end, but only because Sienna nuzzled a soft path to Justine's ear.

"This time, I am going to make you come," Sienna breathed into Justine's ear, then followed up with more kisses, making it impossible for Justine to respond that, sure, a climax was always great, but it wasn't the be-all and end-all of sex for her. And Sienna might have boldly claimed the other night her ego was not that fragile, but that might very well just have been posturing.

Because of all the kissing, Justine's clit was throbbing furiously against Sienna's smooth leg. And Sienna didn't stop. Her tongue danced inside Justine's mouth, her teeth softly pulled at her lower lip, while her hands roamed everywhere they could go. Until she slipped off Justine and gazed down into her eyes.

"Do you have lube?" Justine asked.

"Which sexually active woman doesn't?" Sienna simply said and leaned over toward the nightstand.

You'd be surprised, Justine thought, but maybe it was different with the next generation, for whom sex was much more openly discussed—especially pleasurable sex for women.

Justine adored Sienna's complete lack of complicated feelings toward this—toward being in bed with an older woman. In fact, it might be more complicated for Justine. She wasn't in the habit of picking up younger women. She enjoyed flirting in her own age range and above. Later, she'd take a moment to consider if it meant something, apart from the fact that Sienna was—of course—playing her ex-girlfriend when she'd been much younger. But they'd both been a lot younger then.

Right now, the sight of Sienna squirting lube onto her fingers was far too arousing. Justine swallowed hard. Her breath hitched in her throat. She felt as though she might be wet like a river, but the truth was that she didn't know. Either way, it wasn't an issue. Sienna surely was proactive about that. Moreover, this whole scene was so breathtakingly hot, it made Justine's clit pulse even harder with unquestionable desire.

"Hey." Sienna sidled up to her and glued her warm body to Justine's side. This time, she didn't kiss Justine, just looked into her eyes as she brought her wet fingers between Justine's legs. She slowly skated them along Justine's lips, then upward to her clit, where she ever-so-gently drew a circle.

"Oh, fuck." Instantly, Justine knew Sienna would be able to

make good on the promise she'd made earlier—and effortlessly so.

Sienna's finger swirled around Justine's clit with increasing intensity and while it made Justine feel like endless slews of butterflies were flapping their tiny wings like crazy in her stomach, what made her ready to tip over the edge most of all was how Sienna peered into her eyes, the smallest hint of a smile tugging at her lips—not a smug smile, but one brimming with warmth and kindness. That and her easy sexiness. The supreme hotness that made the camera love her, the charm that made Sienna Bright pop on the big screen. She was so fucking gorgeous and her wet-hot finger was stroking Justine's clit with just the right amount of pressure and, oh, Sienna sure knew what she was doing—those butterflies in Justine's stomach were about to take flight—and her eyes were so incredibly friendly and expressive and Justine was reading so much—too much, probably—into them, but she didn't care.

Heat traveled through her flesh at lightning speed. Her muscles contracted. The butterflies had spread all over her skin, making it tingle, until whatever it was she'd been holding onto exploded in her core, and she let Sienna give her that climax she'd so craved—she hadn't been the only one.

Justine was about to catch her breath, when Sienna's fingers slipped inside her. Breathing properly would have to wait as all the air was expelled from her lungs with the deep moan coming from her throat.

"I've been wanting to fuck you for days," Sienna said, taking things to a whole new level of hotness.

Sienna's fingers moved slowly but with purpose inside Justine, with a deftness that betrayed a lot of experience. All these women who had the audacity of playing hard to get with Sienna. How Justine wanted to tell them what fools they were, although that was easy enough to think when Sienna was doing this. When she was stroking deep inside of her with a look on her face that only confirmed what she'd just said. She'd been wanting to fuck Justine for days. Really? It was probably just something she said.

"Oh, god, Si—" Justine moaned, no longer capable of pronouncing Sienna's full name.

Maybe, subconsciously, Justine had been wanting this for days as well. She must have by the way her body was reacting to Sienna, who was still looking into her eyes, gauging her face, making this much more intimate than Justine was used to. Sienna's soft gaze on her created a cocoon of closeness between them. It made Justine feel as though they were the only two people on the planet. It made her feel as though Sienna only ever wanted to do this with her, until the end of times. As though she might do more than *quite* like her. It made Justine feel special—not something she often felt, no matter how many times someone told her she was a 'legend' or something else to that effect.

Sienna wiggled her fingers in the most delightful manner and leaned closer toward Justine. She could feel Sienna's hot breath on her lips, mixing with her own desperate groans of pleasure. When Sienna's soft lips touched against Justine's, she surrendered to Sienna once again. To this warmth between them. The flirting they couldn't seem to help. The dexterity of her fingers and how a kiss from Sienna felt like a kiss from the best and brightest goddess from the heavens up above—something Justine didn't even believe in. Still, that was how it felt.

Sienna broke their divine kiss and slid her fingers out of Justine.

"That's some lube," Sienna joked, yet her face looked earnest.

"Everything in this apartment is clearly super-deluxe." Justine chuckled at her own silly words. To make up for it, she pulled Sienna close and whispered, "That was really something."

CHAPTER 13

"When was the last time you slept with the same woman twice in less than a week?" Sienna asked as she presented Justine with a cup of coffee from her fancy machine.

"You ask a lot of questions early in the morning." Justine sniffed her mug, as though she didn't quite trust what Sienna's coffeemaker had produced.

"It's ten a.m." Sienna held out her hand. "Come. Let's drink our coffee outside."

Justine took her hand, and they went onto one of the patios that wrapped around Sienna's apartment.

"Jesus. I didn't even notice this last night." Justine shook her head. "It's obscene how some people live."

Sienna chuckled in response. Admittedly, she got a small kick out of doing this, not because she enjoyed showing off her home, but because of Justine's blunt reaction to it. In a city of fake smiles and all too blatant phoniness, Justine was refreshingly real.

"Because you only had eyes for me?" Sienna sat in one of the lounge chairs by the glass railing.

"It quickly became obvious you invited me here for one

purpose only." Justine sat opposite her and smiled at Sienna. "Despite your preposterous claim of only wanting to talk."

"We did talk." They'd talked so much, in fact, that Sienna had only grown to like Justine more. Not just the slope of her cheekbones and how, when she looked into your eyes, she made you feel as though everyone else in the world ceased to exist, but the delicious contradiction of how she could be so self-deprecatingly honest about herself, yet at the same time could play coy like the best of them. Despite her direct manner, Justine didn't strike Sienna as an easy woman to get to know— there was a thick shield around the most vulnerable parts of her —and, despite painful past experiences, Sienna found that wholly irresistible.

"Do we now have to talk about our talk?" Justine sipped from her coffee, then moaned low in her throat like she'd done a few times in bed last night. "Yum."

Sienna shook her head. "We don't have to talk, although it would be nice if you could answer my question from before."

"What question?" Justine was not very good at playing dumb.

Sienna just tilted her head and waited.

"That hasn't happened in a while." Justine wrapped her hands around her mug. "Probably when I was with Marcy."

"Were you together long?" Sienna couldn't help herself. She might as well probe a little now that Justine was still here. It was Sunday and surely even someone as committed as Justine took a Sunday off once in a while.

"I wouldn't say we were together per se." Justine was surprisingly forthcoming, but Sienna guessed that last night's intimacy had something to do with that. Making Justine come had been special—wonderful, even. "We went on a few dates and slept together a couple of times. That's it. The whole thing didn't last much longer than… I don't know. Two months or so, not even that."

"Did it hurt you when it didn't work out?"

"Didn't we cover this last night?" Justine's foot found Sienna's and she tapped against it. "I hope you remember what happened after your last interrogation."

"How could I ever forget?" Sienna caught Justine's rogue foot between her feet. She meant it. She wasn't about to forget their exceptional night together.

"Are you trying to make it happen again?"

"Of course not. I wouldn't expect that from a woman your age." Sienna tried to keep a straight face.

Justine rolled her eyes in an exaggerated fashion. "I won't even dignify that with a reply."

"Would you like it to happen again?" Sienna surely would.

Justine exhaled slowly. "Sitting across from you, looking at your beautiful face, and the memory of last night still thrillingly fresh, I can hardly say no. But that doesn't mean it's necessarily a good idea."

"Because of the movie?" Sienna was aware that her behavior as a cast member wasn't very professional—and she vividly remembered Rochelle's speech from the other day. She'd also heard plenty of outrageous tales from her father about how on-set affairs gone awry could derail production schedules, but times were different now. It might not be professional to sleep with the subject of the movie they were making, but Sienna considered herself professional enough to separate the two. No one on set even needed to know. She certainly wasn't planning on telling Alexis, let alone the director, Mimi St James.

Justine nodded.

"I get it. I really do." Sienna smiled. "It can be our secret." The prospect of that was also rather exciting—perhaps a bit too much. In the end, they were making a movie, not performing high risk surgery on someone whose life depended on it. It wasn't even a big-budget movie—movies like this never were.

"Also." Justine tipped her body toward Sienna. "Sleeping with someone twice in less than a week doesn't change who I am or my priorities in life."

Ouch. That was Sienna told. But maybe it was what she needed to hear. At the same time, it made Justine even harder to resist, because of course Sienna relished the challenge of being the one woman Justine did want to be with. The one woman she would change her stubborn ways for. Although Sienna was hardly that naive. She might be a lot younger than Justine, but that didn't make her a lot more stupid.

"Let's play it by ear then, like last time," Sienna said.

"Sounds like a plan." Justine finished her coffee, then regarded Sienna over the rim of her cup.

"What?" Sienna slid off her sandal and ran her toes over Justine's shin. Pity she was wearing jeans.

"Nothing."

"Tell me." Sienna painted on her best smile again—the one Justine had not been able to resist twice now. "Please."

"I'm just glad you're not inviting me to do something today, which I then would have to decline. You know, that whole song and dance."

Ouch again. It wasn't as though Sienna hadn't considered it. She wouldn't mind spending some more time with Justine, getting to know her a little better—at least the parts of her she freely offered up to others.

"I'm seeing my family today," Sienna said, although she'd only be going over to her mother and Eddy's house for dinner much later.

"Good." As though Sienna had just asked her to leave, Justine rose from her chair. "I want to go by the shelter on my way home to check on Ashleigh." She hadn't mentioned the shelter in the hour or so since they woke. "She's in a bad way." Just like that, the vibe changed. Justine's thoughts had drifted back to the one thing that mattered to her most.

"Okay." Perhaps Sienna's sigh was a bit too obnoxious. "Don't let me keep you then."

"Hey." Justine reached for her hand and tugged at it. "As I

said before, you're really something, Sienna Bright. Really, really something."

"I guess I'll see you on set when we start shooting." They had a week of rehearsals first. Sienna intertwined her fingers with Justine's despite the shift in mood.

"Alexis might volunteer at the shelter next week to prepare for the role. Is that something you'd be interested in?" Justine asked.

"To do what exactly?" Sienna looked into Justine's bright-blue gaze, already knowing she'd say yes, regardless of what she'd have to do.

"Basically to just hang out with the residents for a bit. I think it would make a lot of people's day. So you wouldn't have to do all that much. Just be there, really."

"Will you be there?" Sienna grinned.

"I'm pretty much always there."

"Then I'll see you at the Rainbow Shelter." Sienna kissed Justine goodbye—for now.

———

"Cover your ears, sweetie." Sienna put her hands over her niece's ears. "I have to tell your mom something."

The girl shook herself free. "Why can't I hear what you have to say to Mom?"

Granted, Sienna hadn't been very smart about this.

"Do you hear that, pumpkin?" Taissa pointed a finger at her ear. "That's Grandpa calling you. He needs your help in the kitchen."

"Okay." Zara was only six and Sienna didn't know if that meant she believed the fiction her mother had just invented, but it did mean she sped off to supposedly help Eddy, who loved nothing more than having his grandkids in the kitchen with him—just as he'd enjoyed Sienna and Taissa's company when they were kids.

"What's up?" Sienna's sister asked, a smile already playing on her lips.

"You know that movie I'm about to start shooting?" They were sitting in the backyard of their mother and stepdad's house, the pool shimmering in front of them.

"*Gimme Shelter*, about Justine Blackburn, directed by Nora Levine's girlfriend Mimi St James."

Of course, Taissa knew—there wasn't much she didn't know about her sister's life.

"I might have, um, slept with the movie's subject." Sienna scratched an imaginary itch on her nose.

"No way." Taissa narrowed her eyes. "You? *You* slept with Justine Blackburn?" She made it sound as though Sienna had just told her she'd slept with some mediocre cishet man.

"Twice. One of those times last night, in fact." Sienna drank from the wine her mother poured generously whenever the family was together.

"Isn't she, like, in her sixties or something?" That was what Taissa was focusing on? Although Sienna could hardly hold it against her sister.

"She's fifty-four, Tai."

"Oh, well, excuse me, then."

"The first time was okay. I mean, it was hot and unexpected and great, but last night was… it was different. It was still hella hot, but it was more than that. For me, at least." Sienna knew it was best not to kid herself about last night meaning something more than just sex to Justine. "It had a tenderness to it that surprised me. It was intimacy more than sex, I guess."

"You felt something?" Taissa asked.

"Yeah," Sienna admitted, also to herself.

"Are you seeing her again? Not just for the movie, but as a thing between you?" Taissa tapped a finger against her chin, as though pondering the ramifications.

"I'm volunteering at the shelter next week, but she made it pretty clear that I shouldn't get any romantic ideas in my head."

"Oh. And is that what you're doing?"

"No." Sienna shook her head. "But I would like to see her again. I invited her to dinner last night and we really clicked. We had a real connection, you know?"

"You like her." Taissa grinned. "You like a white lady in her fifties." She pulled her lips into a judgmental pout and slowly nodded her head.

"Which white lady in her fifties?" Their mother had snuck up on them.

"We're having a private conversation, Mom," Taissa said.

"You should have gone somewhere more private than my backyard, then." Maxine Brewster was not one to be brushed off by her own children. She pulled up a chair, refilled her glass of wine, and looked at Sienna. "Tell me."

"No, Mom. We've talked about this. There are things a mother should not know about her children. You agreed. Remember?"

Her mom shook her head. "I don't remember that at all."

"Yeah right. You're just curious."

"Of course, I'm curious. You're my daughter. I will never not be curious about you." Her mother rested her gaze on Sienna. It made her think of the kids the Rainbow Shelter took in—kids whose parents lost so much more than their curiosity about them. "Either way, you can't back out now. I heard about the white lady in her fifties. Who is she and what are you doing with her?"

Their mother had always had a bossy streak and she'd been overseeing hundreds of employees at her production company for decades, which had only made her bossier. Maxine Brewster had always refused to take no for an answer—even rock-hard 'nos' that caused friction, awkwardness and disappointment. It was one of the things Sienna admired about her mother the most—although perhaps not so much in this moment.

"Before I tell you anything, you need to promise you won't

freak out," Sienna said, even though she could perfectly predict how that would go down with her mother.

"I will do no such thing." She locked her gaze on Sienna's. "You've made me even more curious, though."

"I slept with Justine Blackburn," Sienna blurted out. So much for it being her and Justine's secret. But this was her family and they didn't have many secrets between them—not on this side of her family, anyway.

"You did not." Her mother burst out laughing. "You're just riling up your too-nosy-for-her-own-good mother now." She held up her hands. "Fine. I deserve it. Well-played, girls." She gave them a thumbs-up.

"I warned you, Mom." Sienna was a lot like her mother when it came to certain things, being tenacious was one of them. "There are things a mother shouldn't know. Maybe that will teach you to no longer eavesdrop on us."

"Are you saying that you're telling the truth?" She gulped down some wine. "That you actually slept with Justine Blackburn?"

"And that she likes her," Taissa butted in.

"God knows I have a lot of respect for that woman and what she does, but… I'm not seeing it. You're Sienna Bright, for heaven's sake. I know you have a thing for difficult, unattainable women." Her mother rolled her eyes. "But Justine Blackburn?" She knitted her sculpted eyebrows together. "I can't see it. As your sister said, what are you doing with a white lady in her fifties?"

"First of all, can we leave the fact that she's white out of it? Dad's white, for crying out loud."

Her mother acquiesced with a terse nod of the head. "What is it about her then? Is it this movie? You haven't even started shooting yet. I know a movie set can be like a pressure cooker of emotions—false and real alike—but…" Her eyes went wide. "Was she inappropriate with you?"

Sienna huffed out a desperate breath. "Mom. Stop. Just stop."

"She's right, Mom," Taissa finally backed Sienna up. "You're freaking out."

"I didn't promise that I wouldn't." Her daughters ganging up on her had never once intimidated their mom—nothing much did. Except, perhaps, her youngest daughter hooking up with a woman in her fifties.

"So." Her mom regrouped. "You actually like her?"

"Kind of, but... I'm not sure it's mutual."

"Of course it's mutual." Her mom couldn't help herself. "What's not to like about you?"

"This is not helpful, Mom," Taissa said.

"Look, it doesn't matter," Sienna said on a sigh. "It's not going to be a thing, so don't worry about it. In fact, let's forget about it. Let's pretend I never said anything and it never happened." *Yeah right.*

"I'm visiting that set in a few weeks," Sienna's mom said. "And I won't have forgotten by then."

"Promise me." Sienna made sure to look her mother square in the eye. "That you won't go all embarrassingly mother hen on me. If you don't promise, I'll make sure you won't be granted access to the set."

"I'm Maxine Brewster. Who's going to stop me?" Her mom grinned. This was her way of saying she agreed, and that she wouldn't confront Justine about this if and when she met her.

"Thank fuck," Sienna said. "Sometimes, I think you forget I'm thirty-six years old."

"Language, please." Her mother winked at Sienna. "But if you do want to talk about it, I'm always here. You know that."

CHAPTER 14

"She's gorgeous, isn't she?" Darrel said. Justine hadn't noticed them coming up to her. "I told you this movie would be a blessing for the shelter." They were both looking at Sienna, who was surrounded by six people who all wanted a piece of her.

Justine ignored what Darrel had just said about Sienna, although she wholeheartedly agreed.

"It's astounding what meeting someone who has been in a few movies can do to people. Look at Ashleigh. She's a different person around Sienna."

"They're all starstruck. It's so cute."

"Sounds like you're a little starstruck as well, D." Justine glanced at her co-worker from the corner of her eye. They were positively beaming.

"It never hurts to glam this place up a bit. And that's what Sienna does. It's hard to explain."

"I think for these kids she's like a canvas on which they can project their biggest dreams," Justine mused. "Despite Sienna's obvious privilege."

"It probably means something different to everyone." They bumped their arm against Justine's. "Good job getting her here."

"Where's your other new best friend, Alexis Dalton?" Justine asked.

"She texted that rehearsals are running late. She has a big part to play, after all, and she has to properly prepare." Darrel delighted in this a bit too much to Justine's liking, although she fully understood. The shelter was not a glam place—as they'd put it—and to have Sienna, and later Alexis, spend a few hours here hanging out with some of the kids momentarily changed the vibe from bleak to sparkling. It was as though Sienna added a vivid splash of color to its beige walls just by being here—a bit like a Raffo Shah painting. Thinking of Raffo made Justine's mind wander to last weekend—to when Sienna wanted to show Justine her other Raffo painting. And show her she had. An inadvertent smile spread on her lips.

"You like her, don't you?" Darrel said. "I can tell. Your body language's different, so don't even bother denying it."

Justine thought a change of subject was the best course of action. "Didn't you have a hot date with Alexis Dalton over the weekend to gossip about me?"

"Gossip? Moi?" Darrel clutched their hand to their chest. "Besides, I only have good things to say about you."

"Like when you told Sienna and Alexis that I'm a real piece of work." Justine arched up her eyebrows and looked Darrel straight in the face.

"In a good way, obviously, boss." They winked at her. The thing with these shelter kids who'd managed to change their lives, kids like Darrel had been, was that once they'd made it to the other side of all the rejection and pain, they were stronger and more resilient than most—and there wasn't much left that could unnerve them. Least of all a half-hearted scolding from Justine.

"Why am I such a piece of work, according to you?" Justine was actually curious.

"Where to even begin?" Darrel returned her gaze. "You built this place from scratch. You fight for kids whose parents have given up on them. You take zero shit from anyone. You're tough, because you've had to be. But as one of the shelter's most valued employees and someone who has worked with you for years, I know you have a heart of the purest gold underneath all your posturing and fronting."

"Jesus, D. I wasn't asking for a psychological assessment of my personality." Warmth blossomed in Justine's chest nonetheless. But Darrel was a success story and even though other kids had gone on to do extraordinary things after knocking on the shelter's door—like Raffo and Min-ji—they were the exception. For every kid the shelter could help, there were several who couldn't cope, because every single person handles being kicked out by their family differently. Compared to life on the street, staying at the shelter might be a definite improvement, but it was never how a teenager's life and development was supposed to go. No matter how hard she tried, Justine couldn't save them all. That was what frustrated her the most, what kept her up at night, and what kept her going most of all. And what kept her screwing up most of her personal relationships—not that she cared a great deal about that. That was probably what Darrel really meant when they'd claimed she was 'a piece of work'.

Her gaze was drawn to Sienna again. Justine had work to do, some of it urgent enough that she should have finished it days ago, but she found it hard to tear herself away from this room that Sienna brightened up so spectacularly. So she stood, side-by-side with Darrel, looking at Sienna a little while longer.

———

"Knock, knock." Sienna appeared in the doorway of Justine's makeshift office, which was more like a broom closet with just enough room for a tiny table on which she could rest her frantically-whirring old laptop.

Again, a smile spread on Justine's face. If Sienna had that

effect on the kids, Justine could hardly blame herself for not being immune to Sienna's abundant charms.

"Hey. They loved you. I can't thank you enough for doing that."

Sienna scrunched up her lips. "I can think of a way." She held up her hands. "Not that I need to be thanked. Seriously, these kids are great. They're already asking when I'm coming back."

"Are you?"

"Sure. Why not?" Sienna took a step inside but there wasn't much space to maneuver. "My part in *Gimme Shelter* is not as big as Alexis's. I'm sure I can spare the time to spend a few hours here." Without any qualms whatsoever, she looked Justine deep in the eye. "As long as you're here."

Justine wasn't sure she should flirt back, but she also didn't know how to stop herself. "If that's the incentive you need, I'll be here."

"Hey, um, I talked to my dad." Sienna leaned her shapely hip against the table. "He's making a nice donation to the shelter."

Justine eyes grew wide. "He is?" Her stomach tightened with excitement.

Sienna nodded. "There is one condition, though."

"What's that?" There wasn't much Justine wouldn't do to secure a 'nice donation'.

"He insisted you come to dinner again at my place." Sienna all but licked her lips.

"That really is a strange thing for your dad to insist on."

"People are strange. I'm sure you know that." Sienna chuckled. "My fridge is stocked and I'm free tonight."

"You're serious about this?"

Sienna shook her head. "Nah. He already made the transfer. The money will be in the shelter's account soon." She leaned over the table. "But I'd really, really, *really* like you to come over again." She ran the tip of her tongue over her lips. "I have some other works of art I haven't shown you yet."

"Seriously though, Sienna. Thank you so much. I so appreciate it." Justine wanted to check the shelter's account now to see if the money had arrived yet. "All jokes and flirting aside. It means a lot."

"I'll be adding my fee for this movie as well. It's outrageous that I get paid to play Rochelle, the co-founder of this place, while the shelter needs the money so much more than I ever could."

Darrel had been right earlier. This movie was a blessing for the shelter—and so was Sienna.

"I'm truly lost for words," Justine admitted. "And I would love to have dinner with you again." It was a no-brainer now. Not because of the money Sienna had pledged, although, truth be told, money for the shelter was a good way to buy Justine's affection any day of the week, but because of how Sienna, just like that, had made good on her word—on something Justine had believed to be a joke. And even more so because of what it said about who she was as a person—someone whose privilege didn't stand in the way of her generosity. In her decades of fundraising for the shelter, Justine had met too many ultra-rich people who believed that the ever-growing amount of money in their bank account was far more important than helping unhoused queer kids. "Although I should be the one taking you to dinner."

"It doesn't matter to me." Sienna beamed her a warm smile. "In case you missed it, I'm mostly interested in spending more time with you."

Why? Justine wanted to ask, but this was not the time for that question. Instead, she said, "You'd best take me home then."

———

Justine would rather sit in rush hour traffic for an hour than spend money on an Uber, but Sienna had talked her out of driving into downtown LA. They sat in the backseat of a car, that was just as stuck in traffic as Justine's own car would have been, her phone burning a hole in her pocket—she was dying to find out how much Bobby Bright had donated to the shelter.

"I just need to check something," she said, cursing herself for losing her cool as her cheeks flushed instantly.

"Sure." Sienna shot her a knowing smile.

Justine fished her phone out of her bag and, hands trembling, consulted the shelter's bank account. Sure enough. There it was. Bobby Bright's name next to a much higher amount than Justine had been expecting.

"Oh my god." She no longer saw the point in trying to hide from Sienna what she was doing. "Your father donated two hundred and fifty thousand dollars." There were only two things in life that made Justine Blackburn well up. When a kid left the shelter and she knew, in her bones, that she and her team had put them on the right path. That they wouldn't succumb to self-destructive behavior or turn to drugs or, sadly also too common, just give up on life altogether. When she knew that she'd made a difference. That, and a spontaneous huge donation to the shelter that would make the residents, the staff, the many volunteers they relied on, and her life so much easier for a little while. Enough money to give them a little space to breathe. She tried to swallow the emotion out of her throat, but her eyes didn't cooperate and got all ridiculously watery.

"He's nothing if not generous with his money," Sienna said matter-of-factly. She probably didn't have a clue of what that kind of money did for the shelter.

"I will send Bobby Bright a heartfelt thank-you letter and I should also give him a call."

"I'll give you his details, although I can take care of all that for you. I'm not saying he's not interested in the shelter, but he did it because I asked him to. That's just how he is with me and my sister, although he was a touch more generous than I thought he was going to be." She shrugged. "Although what's two hundred and fifty grand when you get paid millions for one single movie?"

"It's a lot of fucking money." It would be easy for Justine to be cynical about how this donation was a perfect illustration of the inequality in their country—and the world, for that matter—but for her own sanity, she refused to go down that route. "And I'm going to call him tomorrow to thank him for it."

"Okay. He'll like that, but, um…" Sienna painted on a devilish grin. "It would be wise not to tell him about tonight."

"What do you mean?"

"He's my dad. Best he doesn't know what I have in store for you." Sienna's confidence was reaching greater heights by the minute.

"That must be a very special dinner you have planned," Justine said, her stomach flip-flopping with delight, and not just because she'd finally, among many other things, be able to replace her dying laptop, have the drab beige walls repainted, and perhaps even get that secondhand minibus she'd been dreaming of forever to take the kids out with.

"You have no idea." Sienna put her hand on Justine's knee and gave it a squeeze that was not to be misunderstood.

CHAPTER 15

"I hope you don't think I'm in your bed because of money," Justine said.

"I hope you don't think I flashed my dad's money around to get you into bed," Sienna replied. She lay in the crook of Justine's arm, her skin still glowing from a trembling climax.

"Maybe we're both a little guilty, but it doesn't bother me in the least."

Sienna let out a soft laugh. Only Justine would have the balls to say something like that—and as post-orgasmic pillow talk no less.

"My intentions were pure," Sienna said.

"Sure they were." Justine gently stroked Sienna's cheek. "But I respect that you fully go for what you want. I also presume that you wouldn't have made me return the money if I had not accepted your invitation."

"It's not my money," Sienna said.

"I do have a question I've been trying to ignore since we were in the car." Justine's fingers drifted to Sienna's back.

"Shoot."

"When I was here last weekend, I made it pretty clear that, well, I am who I am and, um..." Justine struggled to find the right words. "You came on pretty strong earlier. Surprisingly strong, actually."

"I like spending time with you." Sienna skated her fingertips over Justine's belly. "I like having sex with you."

"That's it?" Sienna's touch made Justine's breath come out a little ragged.

"We agreed to play it by ear and that's what we did."

Justine's fingers meandered up to Sienna's ear. "Your ears must have some kind of special powers then." She stroked the edge of Sienna's ear.

"Why? Don't you like me?" Sienna wanted to turn on her side so she could look Justine in the eye, but she resisted the temptation.

"Oh, I like you a lot."

"Well, then. It doesn't have to be more complicated than that." Of course it was a lot more complicated than Sienna made it out to be. Since last Saturday, she hadn't been able to stop thinking about Justine. Rehearsals for the movie hadn't helped. Her life right now pretty much revolved around Justine. On set, she was going to play falling in love with a young Justine, played by an actor, but still.

Most powerful of all, though, was the real Justine. The woman she had become. All tenacious drive and delicious stubbornness. Sienna wanted nothing more than to scratch a little at the sturdy surface of the armor she carried around with her, and then, if she could be so lucky, plumb the depths of her soul. Justine was one of the most interesting, complex, and intriguing people Sienna had ever met. And they'd ended up in bed three times since that first meeting. Sienna was not going to walk away from that just because of Justine's abysmal track record in relationships—on the contrary, it was exactly the kind of person she ran toward, arms spread wide.

"As long as we're on the same page about that." Justine pinched Sienna's earlobe.

"Aw," she play-acted. "I'm going to get you for that."

"Oh, I can't wait." Justine's belly shook as she laughed. "I think it's time I tried that present you got me."

———

There was nothing complicated about how Justine slipped the toy inside Sienna. She did it with the kind of verve that drove Sienna wild from the very first second. Because it was one thing to give another woman a strap-on as a present, but it certainly wasn't a given that the other woman would appreciate it—a lesson Sienna had learned years ago, but still, she hadn't been able to resist with Justine. Now, it was paying off big time.

Justine moved the toy inside her slowly, but quickly amped up the rhythm. Sienna spread wide for her, her legs as open as her heart felt in that moment. She tried to return Justine's gaze but the ecstatic sensation traveling through her flesh made her eyes fall shut. Sienna moaned breathily, her body surrendering to Justine, to her enthusiasm, but also to the speed with which she'd come home with her, to the banter she was so good at, to how she was—Sienna truly believed—leaving the doorway into her soul ajar for Sienna to glimpse at.

It only delighted Sienna more, made her feel more, made her dig her fingertips into the soft flesh of Justine's back deeper as she moved inside her—as she cut off Sienna's breath with pleasure.

Justine looked so fucking gorgeous while she did this, so sunk into this special moment, so completely in tune with Sienna—as though, for the time being, she could finally forget that she ran a homeless shelter for LGBTQI+ youths. And sure, it was a little immoral for Sienna to use her father's money like that, a little sleazy even. But the outcome was a win-win for everyone involved. Especially for Sienna, right now, as Justine took her to ever new heights of delight.

"Fuck," Sienna said, and not just because of how much she enjoyed what Justine was doing but also because she felt more than she let on, than she could admit to Justine without having her run for the hills. She'd have to be careful and strategic, and while it might become a dangerous game for her heart to play, for her mind—and her flesh that always wanted more—it was a pure delight. To have Justine fuck her like this felt, if not like a victory—that, too, sounded a little sleazy—then at least like gaining some ground on the difficult terrain of Justine's whole being.

There was no denying that Justine wanted her. She could say whatever she wanted about how she was—she could claim to be as emotionally unavailable as a rock—it was not how she acted. And it was that very paradox that drove Sienna maddest of all, that she couldn't get enough of. It was her weakness. She had the scars on her heart to prove it. Yet, she only wanted more. And how she wanted Justine Blackburn.

"Oh fuck, fuck, fuck," Sienna groaned between heavy breaths. Justine's body was hot on hers, her lips kissed her neck while her mouth produced the most divine little grunting sounds in Sienna's ears.

Sienna's body tensed all the way up, the prelude to surrender—to the biggest pleasure she knew. Her skin glistened with sweat. Her hips bucked wildly upward. Her muscles contracted, then released, as the fire in her belly spread its flames throughout all her cells. Sienna came hard and long and, fuck, all she could think of, even in the throes of that profoundly satisfying climax, was how soon she could get Justine to do that for her again. It was part of Sienna's most persistent character flaw not only to chase after a woman who was wired to play hard to get, but to do it over and over again.

———

"Was that worth two-fifty grand?" Justine had the most delicious smug smirk on her face.

"Wow." Sienna was still catching her breath and the sight of

106

Justine with the toy strapped to her hips didn't make that any easier. "That's the first thing you ask me?" Sienna shook her head. "You're so bad."

"It's beginning to dawn on me that you quite like that." Justine pressed her lips to Sienna's cheek and the kiss soon morphed into something hot and lingering again, only confirming to Sienna that Justine couldn't get enough of her.

"I like *you*," Sienna said after they broke from their kiss.

"Ditto," was all Justine said.

Sienna could most definitely work with that.

CHAPTER 16

Justine had lived in Los Angeles since she was seventeen, yet she'd never been to a movie set before. Not even on one of the studio tours that tourists went on—she wasn't a tourist, after all, and it wasn't as though she had any family visiting her.

Equally, she'd known Rochelle, who'd worked in Hollywood all her career, and had been a casting director for most of it, for the better part of her life. But Rochelle knew that visiting a sound stage where actors pretended to be fictional people would just be a waste of time for a woman on a singular mission like Justine.

But to see, with her own eyes, the earliest version of the Rainbow Shelter rebuilt on set, was even more of a trip than meeting Alexis Dalton for the first time. What was even more complicated for her to grasp was to see Alexis, dressed in the kind of clothes Justine wore back then, her hair styled to look as messy and uncared for as Justine's did, interacting with Sienna, who somehow suddenly resembled thirty-six-year-old Rochelle as though she was her twin.

Obviously, Justine knew how movies were made, yet she couldn't believe how this was possible.

Everyone she'd spoken to had warned her that it might be odd, definitely weird, perhaps even a little off-putting, but no one had predicted it would be this emotional. Justine had to bite back unexpected—and very silly—tears as she watched the scene Alexis and Sienna were playing. Just like that, it transported her back to when she was a naive, angry-but-hopeful-nonetheless twenty-five-year-old. And of course, Justine knew what acting was, still her brain could not comprehend how Alexis, whom she'd spent a little but really not all that much time with, could portray her so accurately. With the kind of intense and raw vulnerability Justine stomped through life with back then.

"Cut," Mimi, the director, said. "You ladies are blowing my mind." She beamed at Alexis and Sienna. They'd started shooting a few days ago and Rochelle had implored Justine to come to the set for this scene specifically—the moment when Justine and Rochelle had met. "Let's do another take just to be sure," Mimi said. "Have a breather while we reset."

"Are you okay?" Like no other, Rochelle could sense a change of mood in Justine. "It's quite something to watch."

Justine nodded. "Yeah." Inadvertently, her glance skittered to Sienna. They'd hooked up again last weekend—Sienna was insistent, and she had a way about her that Justine still found impossible to resist—but, apart from a couple of texts back and forth, they hadn't really spoken since the shoot had started. Sienna had said the beginning of a shoot was emotionally very engrossing and time-consuming.

Alexis was the first to walk up to Justine and Rochelle.

"No hugs or kisses." She came across as a lot more relaxed than before. Maybe she was most in her element in this particular environment. "Makeup will kill me."

"Consider our minds fully blown as well," Rochelle said. "Look at you."

"The power of make-believe," Alexis said. "What did you think?" She looked at Justine.

Justine exhaled dramatically. "I don't know. Obviously, it's amazing what you can evoke, but it's hard for me to wrap my brain around. To see you as me. It's, um, quite astounding."

"That's to be expected." Alexis smiled. "I guess it also means I'm doing a good job. I'd have to ask myself some serious questions if you weren't somehow a little shaken by it."

Suddenly, the vibe on the soundstage changed, as though a current of electricity crackled through the air.

Nora Levine, followed by a man and a woman—Juan and Imani, Justine knew from Marcy—walked onto the set.

Justine's muscles tensed. Not because she disliked Nora Levine—on the contrary, there was a lot she absolutely loved about Nora, mainly her involvement with, and generous checks to the Los Angeles LGBT Center—but because she knew who Nora was playing in this movie. Her mother.

"She's probably just here to see her girlfriend," Rochelle said.

"Nora and her entourage have been here every day. She's extremely supportive of Mimi," Alexis said. "It's kinda cute. I hadn't really imagined Nora like that." Alexis brought her hand to Justine's arm. "Nora's scenes are only scheduled for next week."

Justine was certainly not planning to visit the set on the day those particular scenes were being shot. She knew they were part of the movie, and she had given her approval, but she had no desire to relive the drama of her parents kicking her out of the house. She had no intention of opening up that old wound, even though she was pretty sure the layers of scar tissue that had grown over the years would not open very easily—possibly never, not if she could help it.

She scanned the set for Sienna again. She wouldn't mind looking into her pretty face right about now, just for a touch of comfort, to be pulled out of all of these emotions swirling within her.

Nora must have spotted them and walked over. They

exchanged polite hellos. Justine was grateful that Nora's personal trainer—her ex, Marcy—wasn't part of her entourage, because that would surely have tipped her over some sort of edge right now. Where was Sienna, damn it? Perhaps she was keeping a respectful distance in order to avoid anyone finding out about their affair—if you could even call it that. They hadn't agreed on a code of conduct. It hadn't seemed important when they'd said goodbye last Sunday at Sienna's penthouse.

"Places in five," someone said over the speakers.

Alexis said her goodbyes and Nora wasn't really one to linger—Justine knew that about her.

Then, finally, Justine caught Sienna's gaze.

———

Sienna didn't know what to do. She couldn't predict how she'd behave if she stood too close to Justine. Besides, she was working. She had to focus. It was hard enough with Justine and Rochelle watching. Alexis seemed to thrive under their gaze, but Sienna, for the first time, was starting to think that maybe sleeping with Justine before this shoot had even begun was not such a good idea.

But she was also curious about how coming to the set, and watching Alexis play her and Sienna play Rochelle, affected Justine. Because it was certainly getting to Sienna playing opposite Alexis-as-Justine.

She caught Justine looking at her. Their gazes locked. But the assistant director was about to call time. She had to get back in place, and fully in character, for the next take. Hopefully it would be the last one Mimi needed for this scene and they could take a long break while the next scene was blocked.

Sienna averted her gaze and tried to find her focus. She owed it to this movie—and to Justine and Rochelle—to be the best actor she could be in this movie. It was important to her for so many reasons.

———

Sienna had barely looked at Justine for a few seconds. She hadn't even managed a smile. But Justine understood better than anyone how annoying it was to be disturbed while trying to do your job—although she considered her own job a lot more important than making this movie.

Rochelle gave her a look. Justine hadn't talked more with her about Sienna, but of course she knew they were still sleeping together. Rochelle always knew. The strength of their friendship was that, more often than not, they didn't need words to understand each other. Although Justine was pretty sure Rochelle didn't understand *this*—and that she very much disapproved.

Justine watched Alexis and Sienna's different ways to prepare for a take. Alexis went fully still and seemed to turn deeply inward in order to unearth Justine's character from the depths of her own soul, while Sienna clenched her fists and took a few long, loud breaths. Then someone yelled 'Action' and Justine was watching a version of herself she was proud of in some ways, but had also chosen to forget vital parts of.

Delicate negotiating and subtle strategizing had never been Justine's forte, especially not back then. She was a doer. She got shit done. It was the only way to get the shelter off the ground.

Justine was neither a politician, nor a naive dreamer. She was someone with firsthand knowledge of what it was like to sleep outside—and not in a romantic, under-the-stars kind of way. She knew what it was like to never, not even for one split second, let your guard down. To sleep on a flimsy piece of cardboard with one eye open. To protect yourself from constant threat. To be so hungry you'd eat anything and so unwashed that your clothes felt hard instead of soft.

She knew how important it was to limit that damaging experience for anyone to as short a time as possible, but especially for vulnerable teenagers whose brains were still developing. If she had to shout at someone to make that happen, then so be it. If she had to step on some toes and make a bunch of city council suits feel uncomfortable, that was an easy price to pay compared to what she—and many others like her—had been through.

But time and age had softened Justine's sharpest edges, and she was no longer that version of her that Alexis was playing, eyes blazing naked anger and muscles perpetually strained with the utter unfairness of it all. But oh, to see herself like that again. To look into this time machine mirror and have those emotions wash over her again. To watch Alexis-as-herself meet Sienna-as-Rochelle for the first time. To witness the subtle mellowing of her features that Alexis portrayed so well in response to Sienna's radiant smile, was stronger than Justine's will to not let any of this get to her. Because it did get to her. Because meeting Rochelle had changed her life, and only ever for the better.

Silently, she reached for Rochelle's hand and held it in hers throughout the rest of the scene.

"Fuck," she said on a sigh as soon as the director said 'Cut'.

"It's quite something." Even Rochelle's always loud voice had dimmed. "Are you okay?"

There was no way she could stop the tears streaming down her face, so Justine didn't even try.

"Hell no," she said. "I don't think I'll become a regular visitor to this set."

"Maybe we underestimated what this would do to us." Rochelle still held Justine's hand and gave it a light squeeze. "Especially to you."

"This movie's been on my mind for so long." Justine inhaled sharply. "It was one thing to agree to it and to read the script. Even to meet Alexis and, um, Sienna. But to witness this…" She shook her head, tears dangling from her lashes. "That's a lot to process."

Justine couldn't put into words what it was doing to her—not yet. And maybe she shouldn't even try. Maybe she should just let it be what it was, and not return to this movie studio again. There would be a big brouhaha about the premiere eventually, but that was a long time from now. She didn't need to worry about that yet.

"I know." Rochelle rubbed Justine's arm. "I'm glad you came, though. I think it's important."

Justine shook her head. "I prefer to look to the future instead of delving into my past like that." She pursed her lips. "That's really not my thing."

"I know, but still." Rochelle looked Justine in the eye. "Sometimes it's good to look back."

"Hey."

Justine had been so wrapped up in her emotions that she hadn't noticed Sienna approach.

"We're having some feelings," Rochelle said.

Damn it. Now Justine was crying in front of Sienna. Justine never went out of her way to look sexy for someone she was casually dating—she didn't have the time—but to stand in front of Sienna with her cheeks all wet and her eyes puffy was not exactly her intention either. Moreover, what she wanted to do more than anything was pull Sienna close to her. To feel the warmth of her skin against hers. To just, very simply, hold her in her arms for a few seconds, or minutes, or longer if possible. But this, too, was not how Justine was wired. Her life simply didn't accommodate too much sentiment. She had bigger fish to fry and she was always on a tight timeline—this included her emotions as well.

"Are you okay?" Sienna put her hand in the small of Justine's back and it took everything she had to not burst into tears again, to add some more moisture to her already soaked cheeks. What the hell was happening to her? "Do you want to go to my trailer? I have a break."

"Yeah." Justine wiped her face and squared her shoulders. It's what she did. Still, she gladly followed Sienna, who looked so much like Rochelle it really did feel like time had just collapsed in on itself.

CHAPTER 17

They'd slept together a few times and, according to Sienna at least, each time, more tenderness had crept into the act. Still, Sienna's dreams of scratching deeper at the surface of Justine's armor had not yet come true. Until now, apparently.

"I'm sorry about being such a blubbering mess." Justine sounded nervous and unlike her usual self. "This fucking movie."

"Here." Sienna handed her a bottle of water and let her fingers linger on Justine's. Obviously, she was shaken by the scene she'd just witnessed, which, in Sienna's view, was perfectly normal—and also a little flattering. "It might be difficult and strange, but I'm glad you're here."

"Are you?" There was the first half-smile of the day. "Is it not weird for you to have Rochelle and me watching you?"

"It's not weird." Sienna took a step closer. "It's special."

"Special, huh?" Justine's face softened. With her eyes red and her face covered in streaks from crying, she looked more vulnerable than Sienna had ever seen her.

"*Very* special." Sienna took another step closer so that Justine was backed against the door of the trailer. She hadn't told anyone on set about her dalliance with Justine—it was nobody's business. "Just as it is a real privilege to see the great Justine Blackburn like this."

"Like what? A blubbering mess?" Justine huffed out some air. "Best not get used to it, because it won't happen again."

It drove Sienna crazy when Justine spoke in absolutes like that, when she went all brazen and arrogant and was very likely to overplay her hand. Because surely Justine hadn't expected to burst into tears when planning her visit to the set today, yet here she was. Sienna couldn't get enough of it. She loved the soft Justine that she so expertly, so stubbornly, hid beneath her tough as nails exterior.

"Sure." Careful not to mess up her hair too much, Sienna kissed the side of Justine's neck. "Do you want to come over tonight?"

"I thought you didn't have the emotional bandwidth for that at the beginning of a shoot."

Justine was melting under Sienna's touch already.

"Just the first couple of days and besides, now I'm thinking it might be helpful to spend time with you." Sienna kissed her way up, until her lips reached Justine's.

"Well then, if I can be of help." Justine didn't even pretend to be busy. "I don't really want to be alone tonight."

"I'm looking forward to it already." Sienna was about to press her lips to Justine's, when her phone rang. She checked the screen. "It's my dad," she said, wondering what he wanted. He'd probably forgotten she was shooting.

"Please, don't keep the best donor the Rainbow Shelter has had in a long time waiting," Justine said, sounding deadly serious.

Sienna took the call.

"Hey, Doll. Surprise. I'm here. At the studio. Which sound-stage are you on?"

"What do you mean you're here?"

"Surprise set visit from your old man. I figured you wouldn't let me if I told you in advance." Typical Bobby. "Also,

I've been looking into the Rainbow Shelter after I talked to Justine Blackburn, and I find myself fascinated." Wow. Bobby Bright fascinated by something else other than his own navel. Still, to hear her father say that about Justine made Sienna's stomach flutter. "Is it okay if I visit? I'm here now, so I might as well."

In theory, Sienna could say no, yet she didn't—for many reasons. She told her dad where he could find her and hung up.

"Surprise. Daddy's here."

"Really?" Justine's face lit up. "I'd love to meet Bobby. He and I had a wonderful conversation when I called to thank him for his generous donation."

"I bet you did." Her father was nothing if not extremely charming—and Justine was clearly under the influence of the money he'd given to the shelter. "He doesn't know about…" Sienna waved her hand about aimlessly. "This. About us."

"Of course." Justine pulled Sienna back toward her. "I will most certainly not be the one to tell Bobby Bright about that," she said before exiting Sienna's trailer without having properly kissed her.

———

Sienna had long ago accepted that her father was not cut out for parenting. While her mother excelled at presence, patience, and unconditional love, her father had tried to be the fun dad. Both Sienna and Taissa had seen through that act soon enough and they'd learned that, for Bobby Bright, no other person—not even his kids—could ever be more important than himself.

Whenever Sienna was with her dad, he was generous with his attention—as generous as with his money—but the thing about affection was that, if it wasn't backed up by time willingly spent together, by shared memories that came naturally when someone raised you, it felt a little off. And with Bobby, also quite performative at times.

So Sienna accepted his hug and she had no problem smiling through the unnecessary introductions she made—everyone knew who Bobby Bright was—and the inevitable fawning from people in the presence of her dad, as if being a movie star automatically made you the best person in the world.

Even Mimi, who had never struck Sienna as someone easily impressed by the phony allure of fame, seemed pulled in by her father's magnetism.

Both Rochelle and Justine were all over him, tripping over themselves to thank him for his generous donation to the shelter. Sienna's father had a way with ladies of all persuasions and he had Rochelle and Justine snickering at his lame dad jokes in no time.

Sienna had become used to sharing her father with everyone everywhere they went. He was the kind of man with such a giant hole in his soul, he could never get enough attention. He was the life and soul of the party. The center of gravity in every room he walked into. And that afternoon on the *Gimme Shelter* set, he was the person everything suddenly revolved around.

"You can take away all his money," Sienna's mother had once said about her father, "but don't ever take away his fame. He's addicted to it. He feeds off it. He's nothing without it."

Sienna could understand how constantly being treated better than anyone else was easy to get used to, but she didn't want to become like her dad. To her, fame was the least appealing side-effect of being an actor, although it hadn't stopped her from becoming one.

"I had to come see my girl," Bobby exclaimed to the group of people in a circle around him as though he was some sort of guru. Everyone on this set worked in movies, and you'd think they'd be immune to an old movie star's impromptu visit, but it was the star power of Bobby Bright that clearly no one was. Not even Justine.

"Come here, Doll." Her dad beckoned her toward him.

Sienna dutifully obliged, out of habit and also because she

knew he wouldn't stay very long, and there was no use making a scene, either way.

Bobby threw his arm around Sienna's shoulders. "I'm so proud of you for doing this movie." He pointed at Rochelle. "You have big shoes to fill." Then he turned to Justine. "I'm in awe of both of you. You're such powerhouses."

On surface level, it all sounded wonderful. After her dad left, everyone would be talking about how friendly and accessible and 'normal' he was. About what an utterly good guy Bobby Bright was. It wasn't even a facade, because this was what her dad was genuinely like. Warm-for-now but his attention always fleeting. He'd keep you simmering in the flame of his awareness just long enough to make you feel good, and then withdraw. Or just disappear for a few months. It was all Sienna had ever known. As though, throughout her life, she'd only ever caught glimpses of him. And sure, she could call him and ask him to donate money to a queer homeless shelter and he would do it without thinking about it—and to some, that must be a lot—but that was, in reality, about the extent of their father-daughter relationship.

Bobby turning up like this on set out of the blue wasn't for Sienna's benefit—to be honest, to her it was just a distraction—but for his own. For his ego. For the power he felt when he walked into any movie studio. For the gazes he drew, the whispers, and the endless admiration. Bobby Bright lapped it up like a puppy whose thirst could never be quenched—and it couldn't.

Sienna went through the motions, indulging her dad as everyone else did—she'd long given up on calling him out on his behavior. As her therapist had said back when she was trying to come to terms with the kind of person her father was, "Use your precious energy on other people. On people who make you genuinely happy." That's exactly what Sienna did.

After the whirlwind of Bobby Bright stopping by had passed, Sienna took a moment to herself in her trailer. Her next call time was fifteen minutes away. She closed her eyes and took a few deep breaths. She'd call her sister later to vent. Taissa always understood.

There was a knock at the door. Instantly, Sienna hoped it would be Justine, because Justine made her feel better about everything. She might as well admit to herself that she had a crush on Justine Blackburn, despite Justine's ridiculous fawning over her dad.

"Come in," Sienna said.

"Hey." Rochelle appeared in the doorframe. "Just checking in with you and, well, letting you know that Justine left."

Sienna's eyes widened. "She left?"

"Something with Ashleigh at the shelter." Rochelle smiled apologetically. "Can I come in?"

"Of course." Sienna had met Ashleigh last week and she'd seemed to be doing quite well at the time, but of course, just like when they met her dad, people put up a front when they met Sienna—she knew that much. Nevertheless, Justine could have taken the time to say goodbye to her. Sienna motioned for Rochelle to sit.

"Between us," Rochelle said, "it's not easy for Justine to be here. To be confronted with her past in such a vivid manner. It's doing a bit of a number on her."

"She still could have said goodbye before leaving," Sienna said.

"Absolutely, but…"

"That's Justine," Sienna said, even though she was starting to get sick of that phrase already—that catch-all non-excuse for Justine's occasional rude behavior.

"I know that, um, you and she are still hooking up," Rochelle said. "Justine doesn't talk about it, but it's written all over her face."

"Yeah." Sienna studied Rochelle. "I find it quite hard to stay away from her." Her lips tilted into a silly grin.

"You do you, but… don't let her walk all over you. That's all I'm saying."

"It's not like that." Sienna didn't get the impression that Justine was walking all over her. On the contrary.

"Good." Rochelle looked Sienna in the eye. "Call her out on her bullshit, then. She needs it sometimes and she can take it." She held up her hands. "That's all I'm going to say about it."

Rochelle was not someone whose advice Sienna should ignore. Rochelle knew Justine better than anyone.

Just as the call came for the next scene, Sienna received a text from Justine:

Sorry I had to leave. I hope we're still on for tonight. Can't wait. xo

CHAPTER 18

"Your dad was a hoot," Justine said after sinking into Sienna's plush couch.

"I get why you would say that, but that's not how I see him." Sienna looked a little tired—a day of playing Rochelle would do that to a person—but still resplendent and, frankly, good enough to eat. Justine couldn't help but smile when she looked at her.

"He showed up. Doesn't that mean he cares?" Bobby Bright had paid plenty to be in Justine's good books for the foreseeable future. But Justine was also well aware that money could temporarily blind her to a person's otherwise obvious flaws. "I'd really like to know."

"Why do you want to know?" Sienna slung one leg over the other and leaned back, away from Justine. "You couldn't get enough of him this afternoon."

"I want to know because I care about you." Justine had cracked much tougher nuts than Sienna Bright. She threw in her warmest smile.

"More than about Bobby's money?"

"Oh yes." It didn't feel like a lie to Justine.

"I'd ask you to prove it, but I'm not that insecure." Sienna smiled back.

"You can talk to me, you know. I'm a really good listener. It's a big part of my job."

"I'm not going to complain about my dad to you. That would just be inappropriate, really."

"I don't think so. We all have our own crosses to bear and there's no point in comparing your pain to others." That was a bit of a white lie. Compared to someone like Ashleigh, Sienna didn't have much to complain about. But Justine had just claimed that comparison was futile, and it was in certain ways, but hearing stories like Ashleigh's over and over—unbearably sad stories of abuse and harm and human cruelty—had made Justine immune to lesser, loftier issues, like the ones Sienna obviously had with her father.

"I don't want to talk about my dad, anyway," Sienna said, and glanced at Justine from underneath her long lashes.

"What do you want to talk about, then?"

"You," Sienna said. "And how you felt when you were on set."

"I don't really feel like talking about that."

"Yes, well, Rochelle told me, verbatim, I may add"—Sienna lifted a finger—"to call you out on your bullshit, so." Sienna sat there grinning like someone who'd bet big on the winning horse.

Oh Christ. It was just like Rochelle to stick her nose where it didn't belong. But Justine knew she had been wrong about something.

"I do apologize for leaving so abruptly. I should have come to see you before, but Ashleigh… she's, well, I can't tell you what she's been through, but it's a lot. An unimaginable lot and she's really taken to me and—"

"Babe, please." Sienna calling Justine 'babe' easily stopped her mid-sentence—or should that be mid-excuse? "This isn't about Ashleigh. It's about you."

"What about me?"

"Come on." Sienna narrowed her eyes. "You were visibly shaken today. Your cheeks were wet with tears. This movie is about you, about your past, about all the shit you went through. Yet when I ask you about it, you don't want to talk about it."

"It's hard for me to talk about." Justine averted her gaze. "It was hard for me to be on that set today. To see Alexis play me. It was like a punch to the gut, to be honest." Like someone sharpened a knife and drove it right through the decades' worth of scar tissue around Justine's heart. "Like getting the wind knocked straight out of me."

Sienna sidled up to her, but didn't say anything, just put her hand, chastely, on Justine's knee.

"As I said in your trailer. *This fucking movie.*" Justine let her head fall back onto the couch. "I thought I only agreed to it for the money, but now that I'm actually seeing it being made, I'm suspecting some subconscious, ulterior motive, and I really hate that. The last thing I want to do is dredge up my past and all the nastiness with my parents and what happened to me after. I'm so done with that stuff. And I knew that about myself. But if I really did, why did I say yes?" All Justine could see—wanted to see—when the producers approached her was a big, fat check for the shelter. Because when it came to funding, tunnel vision worked wonders. Just not this time. Because this was about her life—the really wretched part of it before she and Rochelle had founded the shelter.

"Maybe it's just like you say it is. Maybe you haven't fully reckoned with your past and this is a good opportunity to finally do so."

"Please don't take offense if you don't see me on that set anymore." Justine turned to look Sienna in the face—always a comforting sight. "It's not you; it's me."

Sienna smiled sphinxlike.

"What's with that smile?" Justine asked.

"I think you'll be back." Sienna tilted her head. "And not

127

just for me." She shot Justine a wicked grin before she, finally, kissed her. And oh, if only Sienna's divine kisses weren't such a potent balm for just about anything. For forgetting about the day. For, just for the time being, putting Ashleigh's troubles aside. For banning all the emotions being on set had stirred up inside Justine, even though Sienna was, of course, inextricably linked to that damned movie.

When Sienna kissed Justine, none of it mattered. Justine could disappear in the sensations created by the soft touch of Sienna lips on her own, in the levity it brought, in the downright silly belief that, when they kissed, everything would simply be all right.

So Justine happily surrendered to Sienna touch, to the tug of her hands as she pulled her on top of her. She gladly obeyed Sienna's wordless instructions because she couldn't get enough of her. Of the delicate features of her face, of that naughty twinkle in her eyes, of the addictive smoothness of her skin and, perhaps most of all, of how she spoke to Justine. With such confident directness—a trait she also possessed when doing this. Because Sienna's fingers had already dipped inside Justine's jeans, all the way into her panties.

Justine looked into Sienna's face. That grin was enough to make her clit throb even harder, to make her want Sienna even more. Justine wanted Sienna inside her so badly. She wanted to feel all of her.

"Fuck me," she sighed, her own words turning her on even more. "I want your fingers."

Sienna didn't immediately oblige—she was a tease like that. Instead, she gazed up at Justine, her teeth sank into her bottom lip, and slowly she withdrew her hand. Her eyes locked on Justine's, and she brought two fingers to Justine's lips. Instinctively, Justine opened her mouth and moistened Sienna's fingers. She twirled her tongue around them and made sure they were plenty wet.

As she lowered her hand, the look on Sienna's face changed

to more solemn than smug, although there was definitely still a hint of arrogance in her gaze. And Sienna might have looked like a young Rochelle on set earlier, and she might have, impressively so, acted like Justine's former lover in that scene, but in this, they couldn't be more different. Being with Sienna wasn't some sort of deluded nostalgic trip for Justine. It wasn't some twisted way to make up for what she lacked when she'd been with Rochelle—what did she know back then, anyway? She was only twenty-five when they met. Even though she'd had to grow up hard and fast, in many ways, Justine had still been a child—an unloved teenager looking for love everywhere she could find it.

Justine was no longer looking for that kind of love. Yet, she was finding something with Sienna, something she couldn't quite put a name to.

Ever so slowly, Sienna slipped her wet fingers inside Justine. The angle was difficult because of their position and the clothes they were wearing, but it didn't matter. All that mattered was that Sienna's fingers slid inside her, and simultaneously made her feel, as well as forget, everything.

———

Later, in bed, both of them finally fully naked, Justine turned to Sienna and peered deep into her gorgeous eyes.

"I don't know what it is about you that drives me so crazy, but there's certainly something," she said.

"Maybe you just like me." Sienna smiled that unbearably seductive smile of hers. "I've been told I'm very likable."

"If there's such a thing as too likable, you're definitely it." Justine gently caressed Sienna's cheek with the back of her fingers. "Too hot as well."

"Is that why you left the set without saying goodbye this afternoon? Because I'm too likable and too hot?" Sienna was the only woman who could ask Justine a question like that without annoying the hell out of her. When Sienna asked, her eyes sparkling and her voice deliciously throaty, Justine didn't mind at all. She even wanted to come up with a more elaborate excuse than the one she'd given earlier.

"I'm sorry about that," she said again. "I get like that when I receive a call from the shelter. I go into a kind of panic mode and forget everything else."

"Even me?" Sienna cupped Justine's breast. "After all the sweet love we've made?" She grinned broadly, making her choice of words sound ironic.

"I've lost too many kids," Justine said, unable to make light of what they were talking about. "By not being there."

"I'm sorry." Sienna's face turned serious and she removed her hand. "Please never think that I take what you do lightly. To be honest, most of the time, I have no idea."

"It's good that you have no idea, because it means you didn't have to go through the misery most of the shelter kids have gone through. That's always a good thing."

"And what you went through." Sienna's voice was soft, her tone understanding—even though she could never fully understand. "To think I wanted to complain about my dad."

"I'm sure even the great Bobby Bright has his faults. We all do." Justine swiped her thumb over Sienna's cheek. "I meant what I said earlier." Justine really did this time. "It's not because my parents were awful that you can't tell me about yours. That's not how these things work."

"What things?" Sienna's lips drew into a smirk. "Relationships, you mean?"

"We do have a relationship." Even Justine, with her obvious and many flaws when it came to them, could not deny that they were in some sort of deepening type of relationship. "You and I."

"After the first time we slept together, and the little speeches both you and Rochelle gave me, I really hadn't expected you to be so forthcoming with your subsequent affections."

"To be fair, neither had I," Justine admitted. "I blame this fucking movie and, for the record, that's what I'm calling *Gimme Shelter* from now on." Justine didn't need to know a lot about closeness to know, in her bones, that this was what it felt like. This lying naked in bed together, touching each other with a lot more than body parts. This gentle sharing, this slow unearthing of what was important to the other person and what wasn't.

"You should be really careful," Sienna said, her voice all melted butter.

"Of what?" Something sparkled deep inside Justine's core—something that had been dormant for long decades.

"I might just fall in love with you," Sienna said, and followed up with a kiss so obliterating, Justine could only conclude that, despite herself, that feeling might be entirely mutual.

CHAPTER 19

"I'm a middle-aged woman who's fucked up every meaningful relationship I've ever had in my life," Justine said. "So yes, you should be very careful."

"That's exactly why I can't resist you," Sienna said.

"We're definitely putting the 'fun' in dysfunctional," Justine replied.

Sienna snickered because it was funny and true—and what else was she going to do? But she stubbornly refused to believe that she was setting herself up for a fall with Justine. For all the verbal warnings Justine had given about her personality and her track record of failed relationships, she hadn't acted like that with Sienna at all—and actions spoke so much louder than words.

Justine kept turning up, kept returning her calls, kept initiating hookups herself. They were in the early stages of a relationship and it was quite obvious that it was exactly where they both wanted to be.

"Maybe I should introduce you to my dad as my lover one of these days, now that he's in town and apparently very eager to spend time with me. He even told me that he was fascinated by you."

"Fascinated? What does that mean?"

"You must have impressed him when you talked to him on the phone after his donation." Sienna could easily see why. So much about Justine was impressive and, unlike so many people in this city, she wasn't all talk. She literally changed young people's lives.

Justine just shrugged. She seemed completely immune to any kind of compliment—unlike to cold hard cash in the shelter's bank account.

"By the way," Sienna said. "My mom and sister already know about you."

"What?" Justine did a double take. "Seriously?"

"We're very close on that side of the family." Sienna grinned. "So I told them I was hooking up with a middle-aged white lady."

"What did your mom say?" Worry crossed Justine's face.

"Relax." Sienna wasn't sure if she should share with Justine what she'd told her mom and Taissa—that it wasn't serious. "My mom's chill. And I'm thirty-six so more than old enough to make my own choices." She'd make sure they didn't visit the set on a day that Justine was there, which shouldn't be too hard since Justine had claimed she wouldn't visit anymore—although Sienna didn't believe a word of that.

"But still," was all Justine added.

"Don't worry about it." Sienna considered that, when she saw her family next, she might have to retract some of the things she'd said about Justine, because it was already so much more than what she'd made them believe. It was getting serious. "Hey, um…" Sienna pushed herself against Justine's warm, comforting body. "Alexis and I are doing an intimate scene tomorrow." Sienna looked Justine in the eye. "I'm literally getting it on with you tomorrow."

"Oh, god." Justine shook her head.

"I think I need to get in some more practice."

"This fucking movie," Justine said on a sigh, although her

tone of voice was anything but annoyed. "I was led to believe the intimate scene was fade to black. Did the script change?"

"Scripts change all the time." The script hadn't changed that much regarding this particular scene, but it was too delightful to rile Justine up like this. "Although I can assure you that the movie version will never be as sexy as being in bed with the real Justine Blackburn."

"Ah, so you think I'm sexy, huh? Does that mean you're into fifty-something white ladies?"

"Not usually," Sienna blurted out. "But I'm so into you. You have no idea."

"I have a pretty good idea." Justine pushed one of Sienna's braids away from her face. "So much so, in fact, that I'd like to invite you to something this weekend."

"As your date?" Sienna's blood suddenly seemed to tingle in her veins.

"It's not really a date kind of situation." Justine smiled apologetically. "We're hosting a drag benefit for the shelter on Saturday. I'd love it if you could come. If you don't have any other plans, of course. I know it's short notice."

"I'll happily rearrange whatever I've got going on. What's your role? Are you dressing up?"

"Me?" Justine chuckled. "No, but a few of the kids are. We've been doing some drag workshops. It's not all doom and gloom at the shelter." The smile that broke on Justine's face could only come from a place of deep joy. "If you want to make a surprise drag king appearance, you're very welcome, of course."

"How about I just show up?" Sienna studied Justine's face. "Should I bring some friends or is it too soon for that?"

"Too soon for what?" Justine grinned. Playing innocent was not her forte.

"If I bring my friends, I'll want to introduce you."

"We're pretty much sold out." Justine was still grinning,

though. "But we always have a few spare tickets for VIPs. You can bring a friend or two."

"Maybe Alexis and my sister?"

"You want to tell Alexis about us?" Justine's eyebrows arched up.

"Maybe. Yeah." Sienna hadn't given it a lot of thought. She was just going with the flow, but now that they'd started shooting, and she and Justine were still hooking up, and even kind of dating, telling Alexis, the actor playing Justine, was the only right thing to do—mostly because keeping it from her felt wrong. "I think I should."

"I don't know how things work on a movie set," Justine said, "or what it's like to do what you do. To act like you're someone else opposite another person."

"Even though it's called acting, truth is at the heart of it. For that reason alone, I think I should tell her." Sienna found Justine's hand under the covers. "I wasn't really sure before, but now I'm starting to believe there's actually something to tell."

"In that case, I should probably have another conversation with Rochelle." Justine squeezed Sienna's hand. "For some insane reason, I don't even mind." She gazed into Sienna's eyes —Sienna gazed back, ready to drown in Justine's bright-blue eyes. A wave of happiness rolled over her. It had all started so casually, yet here they lay, only a few weeks later, completely besotted with each other.

"Now, about practicing for my scene tomorrow." Sienna inched her face closer to Justine's. "It's mainly a lot of kissing."

"You don't need any practice in that department," Justine said, bridging the last of the distance between them. "You're already the best."

———

Justine hadn't come to the set anymore that week, yet she and Sienna had spent a lot of time together. Even tonight, the Friday before the shelter's drag benefit, Justine had magically found time to come to Sienna's place—she really seemed to like it there.

"I always thought actors hated watching movies they were in," Justine said while she waited on the popcorn in the microwave.

"I sat through so many of my dad's movies when I was younger, with him right next to me," Sienna said. "It's not an affliction actors in the Bright family suffer from." Earlier that week, Justine had admitted she hadn't seen a single movie Sienna was in. Hence, their movie date night.

"I like that about you." Justine stood there grinning, looking sexy again in her cheap clothes and disheveled hair. For Sienna, the fact that she didn't give a damn about what she looked like, or what anyone thought about her for that matter, contributed greatly to how hot she actually was. "That you love watching yourself."

"You don't think it's vain?" Sienna walked over to Justine, as if drawn to her by an invisible string.

"It's what you do. It's your job as well as your art. It's such an important part of you, so no. In my opinion, vanity has very little to do with it."

"I value your opinion greatly." Acting wasn't just Sienna's job—it was her calling.

She might not be close to her father, but he had given her a passion for this strange profession from a young age—and thus he had given her one of the most important things in her life. He had led by example and Bobby Bright might have been a pretty absent—and not very good—parent, but he was one hell of an actor.

"My dad taught me how much I can learn from watching myself. I have to see my performance for myself. I can't trust anyone else to tell me how I did." Her father was the only person she did trust 100% when it came to critiquing her work. She knew that, at the very least, he was always honest about that.

The microwave pinged. Justine grabbed the bag as though it wasn't hot and painful to the touch. Her tolerance for pain was far greater than Sienna's. She tore open the bag and poured the popcorn into a bowl Sienna was holding—the two of them the perfect and most unlikely picture of domestic bliss.

Sienna had picked the first movie she was really proud of for them to watch together. It was the fifth production she'd been in and the first time she'd felt really confident on set, like she knew what she was doing. Like she belonged there. Like she was contributing to a wonderful movie, instead of feeling like a liability or—worst of all—the one actor the critics couldn't help but review badly. It was the kind of movie where everything had come together, despite all the uncontrollable stuff that always goes on behind the scenes, and had worked out the best way it could.

Better Days was a modest indie feature about a young woman, played by Sienna, grappling with the sudden loss of her sister. Sienna's character embarks on a road trip with her sister's journal as her guide. Along the way, she forms an unexpected bond with a series of women from different walks of life, each teaching her lessons about love, loss, and laughter—a lot of laughter. For a movie about grief and death, it had so many jokes.

Sienna and Justine sank into the couch together, shoulder to shoulder, the bowl of popcorn wedged between them. Justine watched the movie as though she was studying a work of art, her gaze focused, her facial expressions intense. She didn't utter a single word for the next hour and a half—and seemed too entranced even to eat any popcorn. She only spoke when the credits rolled.

"Wow," she said. "That was really moving."

Sienna reveled in Justine's perfect reaction. A smile beamed on her face.

"I should watch movies more often," Justine said.

"Stick with me and you will."

"Gladly." Justine narrowed her eyes. "I might be biased, but you were amazing. I'm no movie buff, but I feel that in here." She brought a hand to her belly. "You have a gift for transporting the viewer."

Throughout her career, Sienna had gotten her fair share of good and bad reviews, but these words about her acting from Justine meant more to her than the best write-up in the most reputable industry outlet. Because Justine was always honest and forthright—another unmistakable draw for Sienna.

"Thank you." Sienna grinned from ear to ear.

"I was completely mesmerized." Justine grabbed Sienna's hand. "It's rare that I get so absorbed by something." Justine averted her gaze and seemed suddenly very focused on Sienna's hand. "I might have fallen for you even more," she murmured.

Sienna understood loud and clear. She brought their entwined hands to her lips and kissed the inside of Justine's wrist.

"Maybe you'll even watch *Gimme Shelter* with me," she joked.

"We'll have to see about that." Justine didn't smile. "I will watch all of your other movies, though."

"You know you're going to be my date for the premiere?" Sienna blurted out. *Oops.* That event was many months away. Who knew what might happen before then?

"What?" Justine did paint on a grin now. "Me next to you on the red carpet?" She shook her head. "I don't know about that."

"Why not?" Sienna could easily picture it, although she understood that a lot of other people—Justine included—might not be able to.

"I truly don't know. I haven't thought about it at all. It's weird enough that you're now shooting this movie about my life, that you're playing my ex, and that we're also seeing each other. Honestly, for my own sanity, it's best that I don't have a lot of spare time to think all of this through."

"For the record, I can totally envision us on the red carpet together," Sienna said. "And it would be an honor to walk it with you." It would be the greatest honor of Sienna's life to turn up to the *Gimme Shelter* premiere not only as its co-star but as Justine's date—or partner, even.

"I'd only be obliterated by your dazzling beauty and star quality," Justine said.

"Not a chance in hell," Sienna said. "I know you don't care about clothes and makeup and red carpets, and movies for that matter, but when the time comes, you will be the one to dazzle on that red carpet. There's not a single doubt in my mind about that."

"Really?" Justine's features softened; her voice was as light as a summer breeze.

"Definitely," Sienna said, meaning it from the bottom of her heart. Because she saw Justine's pure, authentic beauty, and not just her magnificent cheekbones, which had probably never been accentuated with the right kind of makeup, or her face that always radiated the hard-won wisdom she carried inside herself, but the beauty of her soul—and the infinite kindness in her heart, despite the life she'd lived. A life that could just as easily have turned her bitter and cold, but Justine was the exact opposite of these things. She was also clueless about certain things, which was endearing, really, and very stubborn about others, which was also a quality to greatly admire. There wasn't much about Justine that Sienna didn't admire and the more time they spent together, the deeper her affection grew.

CHAPTER 20

"So." Sienna was sitting between her sister and Alexis in the back of the car. "Before we arrive, I need to tell you something." She turned to Alexis, because her sister already knew— although Taissa surely didn't know how fond Sienna had grown of Justine these past couple of weeks.

"Shoot." Alexis was all glammed up in that quietly luxurious way that was all the rage these days. She would turn a lot of heads tonight.

"Um, well, I've been spending a lot of time with Justine lately."

"Did you do more volunteering at the shelter?" Alexis didn't have a clue—and why would she.

"No." Sienna should have, but she'd been too busy, in between shooting the movie, whiling away the hours in bed with Justine. "It's different. We've been, um…"

"They've been hooking up," Taissa blurted out.

"What the hell?" Sienna shot daggers at her sister with her eyes.

"I'm just trying to help," Taissa said matter-of-factly. "We're almost there."

"Wait. What?" Alexis said. "You've been hooking up with Justine? Since when?"

"Since the day we met," Sienna said, a warm glow spreading through her.

"No way." Alexis angled her body fully toward Sienna. "All this time?"

"Yeah." Sienna threw in her best smile. She didn't know how she would feel if things were the other way around—it was impossible to think of without a violent pang of jealousy coursing through her. "It was very casual at first, but now, it's, like, a thing."

"They're in *luuurrve*," Taissa said.

"Are you?" Alexis knotted her eyebrows together as though that was the strangest news she'd heard in a long time.

"We, um, like each other a lot," Sienna stammered. "I thought you should know, going forward with the shoot, and also because we're going to this show together tonight. It's not something I want to lie to you about."

"Are you actually in love with her?" Taissa asked.

Yes, Sienna wanted to scream, but the back seat of this car was not the place for that. She and Justine had broached the subject and neither of them seemed very reluctant to admit to their growing feelings, yet it was still so early and delicate.

"It's early days, but we're kind of officially dating now, so," Sienna said, wholly unable to wipe that stupid grin off her face.

"I didn't know you were into older women," Alexis said in that laconic way she had.

"She's not," Taissa said. "She's into difficult, hard-to-get women."

So much for having her sister by her side for moral support, although this was perfectly predictable Taissa behavior.

"Oh, yes. Then I totally see it." Alexis smiled. "Although, honestly, having done all this research on her, I think underneath whatever it is Justine's trying to present to the outside world, she's a real sweetheart."

"She so is," Sienna said, because she couldn't help herself. "She's rough around the edges, but she's such a presence."

"Fuck," Taissa said. "You *are* in love." She patted Sienna's knee. "I so can't wait to meet this wonder woman now." She left her hand on Sienna's knee for a moment. "She'd better not break your heart or she'll have me to deal with." That, too, was very much Taissa.

"I appreciate you telling me." Alexis smiled sweetly at Sienna.

The car came to a stop and a few moments later, the doors were opened.

———

Justine didn't look like Justine at all—not the Justine Sienna knew. She was dressed in what could only be a bespoke two-piece suit, its fabric embellished with sequins in a multitude of colors, creating an amazing glittering effect. Her blonde hair was swept back stylishly—and was that a hint of lipstick on her lips?

Sienna had to stop herself from doing a double take at the sight of her.

"I'm so happy you could come." Justine opened her arms wide to Alexis. Earlier, on the phone, Justine and Sienna had agreed on no public displays of affection to avoid the inevitable fuss that would be made of it.

"That's Justine Blackburn?" Taissa whispered in Sienna's ear. "I think I might have just become gay for your girlfriend. She's a stunner."

"She is," Sienna sighed. She wanted to throw the no-PDA rule out of the window there and then and kiss Justine on her gorgeous lips.

"You must be Taissa." It wasn't just Justine's looks that were different. It was as though wearing that suit had injected her with a shot of the warmest gregariousness. She hugged Taissa, a stranger she had never met, as well. "Really lovely to meet you."

"And you." Taissa had suddenly grown demure—which was the opposite of who she was.

Justine wrapped her arm around Sienna's waist discreetly and found her ear with her lips. "It means a lot that you're here," she said, and Sienna nearly melted into the floor. Oh yes, she was very much in love with Justine Blackburn.

"Who the hell are you and what have you done with Justine?" Sienna's lips couldn't stop stretching into the widest smile.

"Sometimes, dressing up comes with the job. I could hardly put on my worn jeans for drag night." Justine's hand drifted up to Sienna's neck and gave her a light squeeze—just a little token of affection, that made Sienna glow hot inside.

"Give a girl a word of warning next time," Sienna said. "Even my straight sister has the hots for you now."

"Hello strangers." Rochelle and Rita walked up to them. They didn't need Sienna to introduce her sister. They took Taissa in their arms as if they'd known her for years.

Justine pulled Sienna away from the little group that had formed.

"I'm going to be busy talking to just about everyone, but I'll see you later, okay?"

"You'll be doing a lot more than just seeing me. Let there be no doubt about that." Sienna wished the show was over already so she could take this other version of Justine home with her.

"You look amazing, like always," Justine said, her features as soft as her voice. Then her gaze drifted away from Sienna. "Mimi and Nora are here," she said. "Have fun tonight. We'll talk later." She shot Sienna a quick wink while she briefly touched her arm, before being swallowed up by the crowd and all the people that wanted a piece of her.

―――――

It was the kind of night Justine thoroughly enjoyed, and not just because it was good for the shelter's bank account. A lot of the work she did was hard and spiked with grief and sadness, but tonight was all about joy—the indisputable, incomparable joy of being queer.

There was no better way to celebrate queerness than by having a bunch of queens and kings on stage. The smiles on the teenagers she had such difficult conversations with every day only confirmed that. And then there was Sienna in the audience. Justine had brought dates—possible love interests even—to events like this before, but she'd never felt this way about them. And Sienna was already so much more than a mere love interest.

Darrel sidled up to her at the side of the stage.

"You're a rock star, you know that," Justine told them. Darrel was in charge of organizing the event and, as usual, they had done an outstanding job.

"And you look like one," they said. "Are you ready?"

"Yes." Justine gave a confident nod. Her only job at this event was to be there, be nice, and give a speech to wrap things up.

After thanking everyone who had performed and donated money, she said, "In a world where LGBTQI+ youth still face significant challenges, the Rainbow Shelter stands as more than just a safe haven. It is a place that affirms the inherent worth and potential of every young person who walks through its doors. Our mission extends beyond offering a warm bed and a meal; we are committed to breaking down the barriers of prejudice and discrimination that have impacted the queer community for far too long.

"To be queer is simply to be human—with all the beauty, complexity and dignity that entails. Every day, we strive to create an environment where LGBTQI+ youth can show up as their authentic selves and know that they are valued, supported and celebrated. While much work remains to be done to build a world of true equality and inclusion, the Rainbow Shelter will continue to be a light in the darkness for those who need it most. Together, we can keep making progress toward a future where every young person, regardless of their identity, feels safe, loved and empowered to reach their full potential."

Justine smiled at the crowd. She fixed her gaze on the row where Sienna was sitting with her sister and Alexis.

"Each cheer tonight wasn't just for the queens and kings who owned the stage. It was a cheer for every young person who has had to navigate the stormy waters of identity in a world that can be so unkind. It was a cheer for the joy of being gay—for the love that refuses to be hidden, for the colors of pride that paint our streets every June, and for the everyday acts of courage that go unseen."

Justine wasn't one to hold back in speeches like this. She, in fact, believed that moments like this were meant for the dramatically joyful words she spoke.

"As we move forward, let our efforts and your support echo the message of tonight's show—that every act of love and acceptance tilts the world toward a brighter, more inclusive future.

"Thank you for standing with us, for celebrating with us, and for contributing to a future where every young person can embrace who they are, love who they love, and just be their true, authentic selves without any fear. Thank you."

Justine basked in the applause. As the face of the Rainbow Shelter, she delighted in giving rousing speeches, seeing them as an important part of her role. She called Darrel on the stage with her, so they could enjoy the standing ovation together.

She witnessed Sienna cupping her hands around her mouth and cheering wildly. Then she looked at Ashleigh who, to Justine, had become the very symbol of why she did what she did—why this was her calling. Ashleigh was smiling from ear to ear and her smile reminded Justine that every sacrifice she had ever made, including the ones that she'd been forced to make, had been worth it just for that.

———

"I'm exhausted," Justine said. "I'm not young like you." She laughed despite herself, because Sienna was kissing her neck, and with every kiss, Justine felt a few years younger.

Sienna stopped kissing her. "I don't want you to take off this suit, anyway."

"You want me to sleep in it?" Justine really was bone-tired. A night on her feet, talking to what felt like every single person in the room, would do that to her.

"No, this suit is not made for sleeping in. It's made for showing off." Sienna took Justine's hand in hers. "Where did you get it?"

"Someone made it for me."

"No kidding." Sienna ran a finger over the sequined fabric. "This must have taken so much time." Sienna fixed her gaze on Justine. "It looks like it cost a fortune."

"It was a gift from a very sweet guy called Francis Delgado."

Sienna's mouth fell open. "This is a Francis Delgado?"

Justine nodded. "One of the sweetest people you'll ever meet."

"Oh my god, don't tell me. He spent time at the shelter?"

"Not as a teenager himself," Justine explained. "He and his husband are foster parents and they've taken care of quite a few of the shelter's kids."

"And he made this for you?"

"He did." Justine tugged at Sienna's hand. "You like it?"

"I love it." Sienna's voice dropped an octave. "Seriously, babe, I feel like I've reached a whole new level of being crazy about you after tonight."

"Just because of this glittery suit?"

Sienna slowly shook her head. "Because of who you are and

what you said and what you mean to people. You're so special. So absolutely, utterly extraordinary."

"Let's not get carried away." Justine also felt the residual effects of the euphoria the night had provided, but she would never think of herself as special, let alone extraordinary.

"The fact that you don't think of yourself in that way at all, that it almost sounds like an abomination to you, makes you a thousand times more special to me."

But Justine was too tired to argue against her own extraordinariness. Besides, when Sienna said it, it almost felt like she could believe it, because Justine was very fond of Sienna Bright —and maybe the fact that she was now dating a movie star was what made her special most of all. Because, in Justine's eyes, Sienna was the special and extraordinary one—the butterflies in her stomach told her so, and she trusted them not to lie.

CHAPTER 21

"It's so easy with her, Roche," Justine said. "I don't get it." They were sitting on Rochelle and Rita's porch and Justine had come over specifically to talk about this, because she truly didn't get it.

"You're smitten," Rochelle said. "That's why it feels so easy."

"I've been smitten before." Justine drank from her tea. "I was quite smitten with Marcy. Don't you remember?"

Rochelle shook her head. "I don't."

"Really?" Justine studied her friend's face to make sure she wasn't pulling her leg.

"Yes, really. You're not exactly an open book about who you date and, on top of that, you barely have time for your girl-friends, let alone have them spend time with me."

Justine shrugged, because Rochelle was right—she usually was about these things. "That's what so baffling, though." She took a beat. "For Sienna, I suddenly have all the time in the world."

"Because you want to." Rochelle grinned at her. "You make the time."

"Maybe." It must be a subconscious process because it felt

like a normal part of her day to drive to Sienna's penthouse after work or to sit through movies with her or, most of all, to sleep with her. "But what I definitely don't get is why, out of all the women in Los Angeles, this hot, talented, clever, super-fun thirty-six-year-old actor wants to be with me."

"You never understand why someone wants to be with you. You didn't get what I saw in you, and you still don't, even after all this time."

That much was definitely true. Justine was not an easy woman. She had accomplished some things in her life, like founding a shelter, which seemed a huge achievement to many, while for her, it had been a necessity. People loved to confuse Justine's relentless drive and endless zeal for sacrifice and hard work, but it never felt like that for Justine. It was simply what she did.

"It's pretty obvious Sienna looks up to me." Justine ignored Rochelle's remark. "She says all this stuff about me being special and blah-blah-blah. I'm not special. Like millions of other people on this planet, I just get things done."

"You run a homeless shelter for queer kids. You're very visible, and they're making a movie about your life," Rochelle stated. "That's hardly like millions of other people."

Justine needed some levity so she batted her lashes. "Don't tell me you think I'm special, too."

"That's your biggest problem right there." Rochelle squared her shoulders. "And I get it. I've always understood, from the moment I met you, I got it. Where it came from. This need to make things into a joke, to run away from your feelings and bury yourself in work and purpose and being important in the lives of kids just like yourself. It's why I warned Sienna about you after that first time you slept together." Rochelle wasn't mincing her words. "You spend so much time trying to convince the kids at the shelter that they're worthy of love, that being rejected by their own parents doesn't automatically make them unlovable, and you're damn good at it, except with yourself. At fifty-four, deep down, you still believe you can't be loved."

"Not that old chestnut again." Justine and Rochelle had had a version of this conversation countless times over the years, usually after one of Justine's ill-advised affairs had crashed apart again.

"I may repeat myself, but that doesn't make it any less true." On some level, Rochelle was right, but not as much as she liked to believe.

"Clearly," Justine said, because that's why she'd come here —not to rehash her so-called biggest problem but to show Rochelle she'd moved past it. "I'm letting myself be loved now."

"Are you?" Rochelle pinned her dark gaze on Justine. "You just literally said you don't get why Sienna has feelings for you."

"I may not get it, but I'm letting it happen." *And every minute of it is utterly glorious.* "When we first started hooking up, Sienna said she finds women who play hard to get irresistible, but I've never done that. Quite the opposite, actually."

"Sometimes, it's as simple as two people liking each other and having the hots for each other, which is obviously the case here. The question is… what happens next?"

"We just go on liking each other and having the hots for each other," Justine said, perhaps not quite believing it could be that simple.

"You have no idea how much I want that for you." Rochelle smiled at her. "I know I give you a hard time, but I'm doing it for a reason."

"Because you still love me." Justine wasn't quipping now.

"I do—and you know it."

"I love you too, Roche." Justine huffed out some air. "But this movie." She shook her head. "I think this movie might also have something to do with me spending so much time with Sienna."

"Because she's playing me?" It was Rochelle's turn to bat her lashes.

"Yes." Justine was adamant. "It's all connected. That time when you and I met, Roche. I was so damaged and angry and hurt. It's a challenge to go back there." Justine hadn't returned to the set. Not only because she had far better things to do with her precious time, but also because she didn't want to see Alexis play that young, vulnerable version of herself that Justine had left behind a long time ago. "That was not a good time."

"I know, but look what you made it into."

Justine shook her head. "Not you as well."

Rochelle rolled her eyes. "This movie is being shot as we speak. It's happening. I know firsthand how difficult it is to get a production off the ground in Hollywood, but this one is really happening. Your story's being told." She paused to give Justine a poignant look. "I know your reasons for agreeing to it are very different than mine, and the last thing you want is some sort of glory off the back of it, or to revisit a challenging time in your past. But it's all happening, because life can be fucking funny that way. Have you thought about that? When I was watching that scene being shot of us meeting thirty years ago, my mind was blown, because not only was I watching our first meeting being turned into a movie scene, but I was also thinking of how crazy it is that this movie is actually being made. When you think about all the pieces that needed to fall into place for that, and the lives we've lived since. It's hard to wrap my head around sometimes."

"It's such a trip." Before she'd been approached for this movie, Justine hadn't thought about that time in her life for decades. Even though she had to dig into her own emotions and experiences when relating to the shelter residents, she had found ways to do that so that her personal experience felt like a strength instead of a weakness. This movie messed with that big time. No wonder she kept turning up at Sienna's door, because Sienna was extremely skilled at taking Justine's mind off things.

"I think you should visit the set again," Rochelle said. "I know you don't want to and that every cell in your body is screaming no-no-no, but sometimes you have to do the thing you feel like doing the least in order to heal. I genuinely think it will help you mend some of the wounds from your past."

Justine shook her head. "I think me simply finding the courage to watch the finished product once, alone in the privacy of my own home, is more than enough."

"That, too." Rochelle shot her a warm smile. "We'll watch it together, okay? But..." She pursed her lips. "Being on that set is special. Seeing that movie being made is such a privilege. To feel that energy and see all these people working together toward the goal of telling your story. To be around Alexis and Sienna. It's magical and most certainly a once-in-a-lifetime experience."

"You don't think there'll be a sequel? Sienna told me sequels are all the rage these days."

"How about I pick you up tomorrow?" Rochelle said, ignoring Justine's banter. "We'll go together."

"Which scenes are they shooting tomorrow?" After what Rochelle had just said, Justine might consider it—if only to surprise Sienna.

"I have no idea," Rochelle said. "Let's just take a chance."

"Okay," Justine acquiesced easily, because she trusted Rochelle and, perhaps, some of the things she'd said held more than an ounce of truth.

CHAPTER 22

"So," Mimi said. "You and Justine, huh?"

More than a week had passed since Sienna had told Alexis—and word had spread. Now it had obviously reached the director of *Gimme Shelter* as well. "To be honest, I did not see that coming." Mimi arched up her perfectly sculpted eyebrows.

"I hope you don't think it has affected my performance," Sienna said, even though she'd been sleeping with Justine since before the shoot had started—but she'd only really acknowledged her feelings for Justine very recently.

"Of course not." Mimi smiled and shook her head. "I would like to invite you and Alexis to dinner at my house this weekend," she said. "You can bring a plus-one, of course."

"You mean Justine?" Sienna grinned.

"I'd love to see you just… be together."

"Is Alexis bringing anyone?"

Mimi shook her head. "No, but don't let that stop you from bringing Justine."

"Is Nora going to be there?" Sienna asked.

"Yes, and she'd love it if Justine came along." Mimi winked at her. "Also, if you're keen to see a long-term age gap relationship in action, dinner with Nora and me will be an excellent opportunity." She followed up with a chuckle.

"Nora is very supportive of you." That was easy enough to see. Nora Levine turned up to the set all the time, although never for very long, and always making sure—somehow—that she wasn't the center of attention, unlike when Sienna's dad had visited.

"If it weren't for Nora, this movie would not be happening. You should ask her all about it over dinner on Saturday evening."

"I'm in." During a shoot, Sienna liked to keep her social calendar as empty as possible, in order to keep focus but also to facilitate impromptu get-togethers with the cast and crew of the movie she was working on. "I'll let you know about Justine soon."

"Let you know what about Justine?" Was that Justine's voice or Alexis in character—she had a real knack for mimicking Justine's voice.

"Speak of the devil." Mimi turned to Justine. "What a lovely surprise."

"You say that now." Justine kissed Mimi on the cheek while Sienna's stomach turned silly somersaults in her belly.

"Hey, you." She locked her gaze on Sienna's and shot her a warm smile, which didn't help with the flip-flops in Sienna's belly.

"I was just inviting Sienna to dinner at my house on Saturday. Nora and I would love it if you could join," Mimi said. "Alexis is coming as well."

"Oh." Justine narrowed her eyes. "I need to check my calendar, but I'll let you know."

The first assistant director walked toward them, calling for Mimi.

"Do you want to go on a date with me at Mimi and Nora's?" Sienna asked. "Also." She took a step closer to Justine. "It is such a wonderful treat that you're here. To say I wasn't expecting you would be an understatement."

"I couldn't stay away from you." Justine tugged at Sienna's hand. "And Rochelle gave me one of her emo speeches, so." She shot Sienna a grin before kissing her on the lips.

"What did Rochelle say to you?" Sienna asked when they broke from the kiss.

"You don't want to know the things Rochelle has the audacity to say to me, babe." She pulled her lips into a lopsided grin.

"I might not have been to makeup yet, but, er, I'm playing Rochelle, remember? I think it would even be fair to say that I *need* to know everything she says to you."

As if someone on the production team had overheard, a call came over the intercom, asking Sienna to go to the makeup trailer.

"We'll talk later. Go." Justine tapped Sienna lightly on the ass.

"Will you go with me on Saturday?" Sienna brought her lips close to Justine's again.

"I just might." Justine's face was all lovey-dovey softness, accurately echoing how Sienna felt. "I can't seem to stay away from you. In all the time I've lived in LA, this has never happened to me with a celebrity before."

It was hard for Sienna to tear herself away from Justine as well, but she couldn't be happier that she had shown up. She blew Justine a quick kiss before hurrying to makeup.

––––––––

While seeing Sienna was wonderful, all the reasons Justine had for not coming to the *Gimme Shelter* set quickly became clear to her again. Being here, witnessing her past come to life, tore her right open. Justine prided herself on the defenses she had built around her heart, around her weakest spots, but on this set, they crumbled to nothing in the space of a heartbeat.

Because there was a replica of the first shabby sign they'd put up at the Rainbow Shelter—just a sheet of paper with the words scribbled on, slipped into a plastic folder. There was the soundstage where they'd rebuilt the interior of the very first iteration of the shelter, which was just two adjoining rooms, one with secondhand army cots and scratchy blankets, and one with the barest minimum of what could constitute a bathroom. It looked like nothing, but it was so much more than nothing— and it was definitely better than a makeshift tent on the street.

The current budget of the Rainbow Shelter was humongous compared to what they'd had to start with. Justine had always strongly believed that, as time went by and the years grew into decades, they would need less funding simply because times changed and attitudes shifted—and being queer would be as normal as having blue eyes or brown hair. That had never happened—on the contrary. Most nights, the shelter, despite adding beds every year, was at full capacity. Wasn't that the most heartbreaking of all in a time when so many young people —one out of three, according to the latest study Justine had read —identified as queer or, at the very least, not straight?

That was another reason for agreeing to this movie—for signing away her 'life rights'. Because representation and awareness were still of vital importance. The battle Justine had fought all her life had not yet come to an end, and it surely wouldn't in her lifetime. But at least, because of this movie, she could leave a little piece of herself in the memory of everyone who watched it.

Most emotional of all, was seeing Alexis as her younger self. She emerged onto the soundstage wearing what had passed for Justine's business attire in the nineties—a suit Rochelle had lent her and a T-shirt that had once been white. In the scene, Justine and Rochelle had a meeting with a city councilor—one of the many men they'd had to beg for either funds or permission along the way. While Charlie Cross, the screenwriter, had done a great job of bringing some much-needed lightness to the script, and Justine knew this scene had plenty of dry wit and sharp dialogue, the general tone of the movie didn't matter while she was standing there, reliving her past.

Because when she'd been twenty-five, Justine had barely processed what had happened to her, and her heart was still full of the pain of rejection. She had dealt with it the only way she knew: by doing something. By building something. By using what she knew from experience and turning it into something tangible, something that would make an actual difference. But standing there, looking at the determined but still-so-lost version of herself that Alexis captured so well, she also realized that ever since she'd started the shelter, she hadn't stopped. Justine didn't take vacations. She hardly took the weekend off. Justine's 'off' mode only kicked in when she had exhausted all her energy, when she was too tired to do anything else but crash into bed.

But now, there she stood, all the emotions she had so expertly kept at bay for decades, catching up with her in the time it took to act out one single scene.

Justine tried to focus on Sienna, who was captivating and gorgeous and also made her feel all sorts of things, but Justine's attention kept being pulled back to Alexis—to herself. To the person she was and all the despair and sadness she had pushed to the outer edges of her conscious mind, so she didn't have to feel it anymore, and could focus on what was most important: founding the shelter.

When she looked at Alexis in the reconstructed Rainbow Shelter, on the set of this fucking movie, Justine could see, clearly for the first time ever in her life, how the shelter was built on her own personal pain. Its very foundations were made up of her bottomless anger, its walls were bricks made of her frustration, and those rickety beds were all the love she went without.

Tears streamed down her cheeks again. A tissue appeared in front of her. Justine took it and accepted Rochelle's arm around her shoulders. No words were required. Justine was convinced that Rochelle knew exactly what was happening to her—it was why she'd talked her into coming back in the first place. No wonder Justine had resisted so much.

Because healing was so damn painful.

———

It was also obvious why being with Sienna was so easy, so utterly delightful, and fun. Just as Rochelle had done when Justine was twenty-five, Sienna brought a lightness to her life Justine desperately needed. Without Sienna, and all she stood for in Justine's life—entertaining company, amazing sex, and big celebrity perks like her father's donation—coming to the set would be completely unbearable. No matter how much healing it might inspire.

"Come here." Sienna opened her arms to Justine.

"You'll ruin your hair and makeup," Justine said.

"It's not that hard to make me look like Rochelle." Sienna's voice was gentle, almost a whisper. "Come," she insisted.

Justine stepped into her embrace, and it felt so right and so comforting.

Sienna's hand slipped into her hair and she held her tight. Justine tried not to cry, but she couldn't stop herself. The floodgates were well and truly open.

"Oh, fuck," she breathed into Sienna's ear.

"No one here can truly imagine what this is like for you," Sienna whispered. "But every single person on this set respects the hell out of you, so just let it out."

"This movie isn't supposed to be my personal therapy," Justine muttered.

"So what if it is?"

Justine had sat through plenty of hours of counseling in her life. She was a trained social worker and she acknowledged the importance of talking and working through your feelings, but mainly for other people.

Witnessing this movie being made was next-level therapy. It was more than Justine could handle, if she was being completely honest, hence Sienna's tear-soaked blouse.

Instead of burying her face in Sienna's hair for much longer, Justine thought it better to look at her gorgeous face. To feast her gaze on Sienna's pronounced cheekbones. Her dark, soulful eyes. Her full lips and that tiny, crazy-driving dimple just next to the corner of her mouth. The confident serenity she carried herself with, as though, like Rochelle, she was more than a decade older than Justine, and instinctively knew how to comfort her.

Justine took a breath. "Thank you," she said. "You're not just extremely hot, but very kind as well."

Sienna chuckled in response. "I'm always available whenever you need some kindness *or* hotness."

Justine hadn't considered herself unfortunate since the Rainbow Shelter had opened its doors almost thirty years ago, but to have Sienna Bright, of all people, say those words to her, she must now be the luckiest person on the planet.

CHAPTER 23

Sienna was a little starstruck—something that didn't happen very often. But to be this close to Nora Levine felt special. In their teens, especially during weekends at their dad's, she and Taissa had binged all seasons of *High Life* several times. And just like most other viewers, Emily Brooks had been their favorite character.

Mimi had introduced Nora the first time she'd visited the set, and they'd had a brief, polite conversation, but afterward, whenever Nora came to the set—and she came often—she seemed to have this bubble around her that made her difficult to approach. She was always flanked by two of her friends, like she has a human shield around her.

But tonight, Sienna was sitting opposite Nora Levine at the table—and, as Mimi had promised, she was watching an age gap relationship in action. When Sienna had told Justine this, she had given her a skeptical look, as though it was the first time she had contemplated their own difference in age.

Justine and Nora had a lot in common and neither Sienna nor Alexis could get a word in edgewise while Mimi—clearly the cook in this particular age gap relationship—was busy in the kitchen.

"In liberal circles," Justine was saying, "it's almost frowned upon to be straight these days. It's astounding, if you think about the attitudes toward gay people only thirty to forty years ago. Twenty even. The hideous things people said about gays. It's easy enough to forget, but I will always remember." Justine's face always lit up so brightly when she smiled, as she did now. "My point being that I really can't applaud you enough for coming out of the closet, Nora."

A while ago, when promoting a movie about lesbian spies she was in with Elisa Fox, Nora had done a one-off big interview with *Vanity Fair* in which, after years of tabloid speculation, she had come out as bisexual and in a relationship with a woman.

"I was only surfing the wave that Ida Burton and Faye Fleming started," Nora said.

Justine shook her head. "Every single coming out is hugely important. It's so easy to think it no longer matters when someone in the public eye comes out, but it so does. It has the kind of impact we tend to underestimate, but so many of the kids I talk to found the courage to come out because someone famous inspired them." A shadow crossed Justine's face. Sienna knew why. Because those kids had still ended up at the Rainbow Shelter—no matter how many celebrities busted out of the closet.

"Well, thanks." Clearly, Nora Levine wasn't one to bask in the glory of something as trivial to her as telling the world she was in a relationship with a woman. "But, really, Justine, you're the one who needs to get all the applause at this table. Coming out when I did was low stakes for me."

As Sienna predicted, Justine waved off Nora's comment. You really couldn't embarrass Justine Blackburn more than by giving her a heartfelt compliment. She simply couldn't accept it.

"Did you ever consider coming out in your *High Life* days?" Alexis asked, skillfully working her way into what had pretty much been a dialogue between Justine and Nora since they'd sat down.

Nora shook her head. "Not even for a second, although, in hindsight, I should have."

"Times had to change first," Justine stated matter-of-factly.

"And she didn't have me back then." Mimi approached the table, carrying a stack of plates.

"I was single and it's quite possible no one would have even believed me then," Nora said. "Bi-erasure was and is still very much a thing."

"Let me give you a hand with those." Sienna rose and followed Mimi back to the kitchen.

"Nora's very comfortable with Justine." Mimi glanced at the dinner table. "I can tell by the way she's talking to her that she's the kind of person Nora truly appreciates."

Now that she was alone with Mimi, Sienna took the opportunity to assuage her curiosity about something. "Does Nora live here with you? I see all these pictures of your kids and grandkids, but nothing Nora-related as far as I can tell."

Mimi smiled. "Nora and I don't live together. It's not her thing and that's absolutely fine with me. She needs her own space and lots of privacy and I have four kids who are in and out all the time, so not living together works really well for us."

Sienna nodded. "Sure. Why not?" If things with her and Justine progressed to thoughts of living together, Sienna couldn't picture herself moving in with Justine—but she really shouldn't be thinking about something like that yet.

"Can you take these, please?" Mimi handed her a handful of cutlery. "Just put them on the table. I'm very casual when it comes to dinner parties." Sienna liked Mimi a lot, mainly because of her levelheadedness. She was a modest director without delusions of only directing Oscar-worthy movies. More than anything, on set, Mimi radiated the pure joy of being there, of having the coveted job of director and getting to do what she loved the most—something Sienna totally understood.

Just as she deposited the cutlery on the table, Sienna's phone rang. She fished it out of the back pocket of her jeans. Her mother's name appeared on the screen. Sienna excused herself and headed into the lounge to take the call, wondering why her mother would call her on a Saturday night.

"Sienna, darling. Where are you?" Her mother's voice was all choked up. "Are you alone?"

"No, I'm at Mimi's with Alexis and, um, Justine. Why?"

"It's your dad. He's had an accident." Her mother's voice tightened even more. "On his motorcycle. He—" The silence on the other end of the line was interspersed with sobs. "He didn't make it, darling. I'm so sorry."

"What?" Sienna sank into the nearest couch. "What are you talking about?"

"He's dead, baby. Bobby's dead." Her mother exhaled deeply. "Give me the address of where you are. I'll send a car. Come to the house. Your sister's on her way."

"Mom." As the news slowly registered in her brain, Sienna's eyes filled with tears. "I don't get it. Dad's… dead?" *What the fuck?*

"I'm so sorry, baby. Come be with me. You need to be with your family now."

Justine had walked into the lounge and crouched next to Sienna.

"What's going on?" she asked.

Sienna's hand dropped to her lap, her phone tumbling to the ground.

Justine picked it up and talked to Sienna's mother for a few moments.

Sienna just sat there, trying to absorb the news. Surely, it couldn't be true. She'd need to get her phone from Justine as soon as she hung up so she could call her dad. She would speak to him and he would tell her none of this was true. It was all utter nonsense. It was just the worst nightmare Sienna had ever had.

"I'll bring her over right now," Justine said and ended the call. "Hey." She swallowed hard. "I'm so sorry, babe. I'm so very sorry." She tried to fold her arms around Sienna, but Sienna shrugged out of her embrace, her muscles rigid.

"No, no, no," Sienna muttered, fumbling for her phone. She retrieved it from Justine's hand and immediately dialed her father's number. It went straight to voicemail.

"Dad, call me back as soon as you get this. Please. It's urgent." She hung up and called again, her fingers trembling. Voicemail. Again.

Sienna's mind raced with possibilities. He was on set, caught up in a scene. He was out with friends, his phone on silent. He was asleep, his phone charging in another room. There had to be a reason he wasn't answering. Any reason except the one her mother had given her.

She called a third time, desperation rising in her chest with each unanswered ring. When his familiar voice came on, asking her to leave a message, a sob escaped her throat. "Daddy, please," she whispered, the phone clutched to her ear. "Please, pick up. Tell me this isn't true."

Justine gently took the phone from Sienna's hand and set it aside. She wrapped her arms around Sienna once more, and this time, Sienna didn't resist. She collapsed into Justine's embrace, her body shaking with the force of her grief. Tears streamed down her face as the reality of her father's death began to sink in.

"I've got you," Justine murmured, holding Sienna tightly. "I'm here. You're not alone."

"Everything okay?" Suddenly, Mimi was standing next to them.

Justine whispered to Mimi for a while. Was she really saying to Mimi that Sienna's father, *the* Bobby Bright, was dead? Was Bobby really gone? How could that even be? A fist of the hardest, coldest steel wrapped itself around Sienna's heart.

———

Sienna huddled against the car door, her forehead pressed against the cool glass of the window. Tears streamed down her face in a silent, endless cascade as Justine drove through the busy streets of LA. The city's nightlife carried on around them, people laughing and enjoying themselves, blissfully unaware that Sienna's world had just shattered into a million pieces.

How could they be doing this? How could life continue as normal when her father was gone? It seemed impossible, a cruel joke the universe was playing on her.

As they stopped at a red light, a motorcycle pulled up beside them. Sienna jerked forward in her seat, her heart leaping into her throat. For one brief, desperate moment, she thought it was him. It had to be him. This was all a mistake, a terrible misunderstanding. Bobby would pull off his helmet, flash her that Bright grin, and tell her everything was okay.

But it wasn't him. The biker was just a stranger.

Sienna doubled over in her seat, her arms wrapped tightly around her middle as if she could physically hold herself together.

Justine reached over and placed a hand on Sienna's back, rubbing soothing circles between her shoulder blades.

"Breathe," she murmured, her voice thick with emotion. "Just try to breathe."

But breathing seemed impossible. Everything seemed impossible.

As they drove on through the night, Sienna's sobs gradually quieted into a silent stream of tears, but the ache in her chest only grew. The rest of the journey to her mother's house passed in a haze of grief and disbelief, each mile taking her further away from the life she had known and closer to a future she wasn't ready to face.

As soon as the car had parked, the door swung open and her mother stood there, beckoning Sienna toward her.

Sienna sank into her mother's embrace. Her mother ushered her into the house, where Taissa was sitting with her husband, her daughters, and Eddy, all of their faces shocked and soaked with tears.

CHAPTER 24

Justine tried to keep a respectful distance from Sienna's grieving family. She'd met Taissa and recognized the other's faces from pictures at Sienna's apartment and it was easy enough to see who was who. She took a deep breath and overlooked the emotional wreckage of what had happened. From what she'd learned, Bobby Bright had been out riding his motorcycle and had fatally crashed. That's all she knew—that's all anyone seemed to know at this point.

"Hi." The older man walked up to Justine. "I'm Eddy, Maxine's husband. Sorry we have to meet under these circumstances. Can I get you anything? Water or something stronger?"

Justine shook Eddy's hand. "Justine." She didn't really know how to introduce herself. Who was she to this family? Sienna had told her that her mother and sister knew about them, but how much did Eddy know? "Sienna's in this, um, movie about my life." How stupid did that sound? Especially in the light of what had just happened. Sienna and Taissa had lost their father. "We were all having dinner at the director's place when Sienna got the call."

"Thanks for bringing her here," Eddy said. "How about a drop of scotch?"

Justine nodded. At least, if she had a drink, she could stay a while longer, and keep an eye on Sienna. Justine would never know what it felt like to have her father pass away so suddenly, but she knew very well what it felt like to lose a parent, just like that. To become an orphan, even if your parents were still alive. She would try to be there for Sienna as much as she could—as much as Sienna would let her.

"Hi, Justine." Maxine Brewster walked up to her, her arms wide open. "God, what a mess." She shook her head, before pulling Justine into a loose hug.

What a way to meet your girlfriend's mother, Justine thought, as she stood stiffly in Maxine's arms. Until now, Justine's love life had never included any meet-the-parents moments, and this was not how she'd pictured it when it had to finally happen. Yet, that's how life was. Full of cruel and shocking turns.

"Here you go." Eddy had returned with a glass of scotch. "I'll get some for the girls as well. I think they need it." He put his arm around his wife's shoulder and gave it a squeeze. Maxine leaned into his touch for a split second, then straightened her spine.

"I'll be honest, I don't know what to make of you and Sienna," Maxine said when Eddy was out of earshot. "But I'm so glad she has you right now."

"I know a thing or two about dealing with the hard stuff life throws at you," Justine said. "Sienna can count on me."

"Thank you." Maxine fixed her gaze on Justine. "We're all just so shocked right now."

"I bet." Justine sipped from the scotch. She didn't have the palate to know whether it was cheap or expensive—from the mansion she was standing in, she gathered the latter—but it did its job of calming her nerves somewhat.

———

"Thanks for staying so long." Sienna's eyes were red and her cheeks blotched. What Justine wouldn't give to take this pain away from her, or to shoulder some of it, but she didn't have that power—nor could she turn back time and prevent Bobby Bright from getting on his motorcycle. All she could do was physically be here.

"Of course." Justine took Sienna's hands in her. "Whatever you need."

"I'll stay here tonight, with my mom."

"That makes sense."

"Taissa and her family are staying as well." Every word Sienna spoke sounded as though she had to force it through her choked up throat.

"You should be together." Justine wanted to draw Sienna near, but she didn't want to take that initiative with her family sitting so close by. "Do you want me to stay a little longer?"

"You've been here for hours already. You should go home. Get some rest."

"Okay. If you're sure." Justine discreetly caressed Sienna's palm with her thumb. "Call me anytime. I mean it. Anytime."

Sienna gazed into her eyes and her body seemed to deflate completely. She threw herself into Justine's arms. Within seconds, Justine's neck was slippery and wet with Sienna's tears. Justine did all she could do, which was hold Sienna tight. No one in the family seemed to bat an eyelid at this—under the circumstances, they couldn't care less.

Taissa and her husband got up to put their daughters to bed, while Eddy topped up his and Maxine's glass.

"I feel so fucking empty," Sienna managed to whisper in Justine's ear. "It's impossible to believe he's gone."

"I know." Justine stroked Sienna's hair and held her close. "Why don't I stay? You can sleep in my arms." That's what they're for, she thought, because she felt for Sienna so much—because she cared for her. Because Justine was madly in love with this grief-stricken, broken person barely hanging on in her arms.

Sienna's chin nodded against Justine's shoulder.

————

Sienna had lain awake in Justine's arms, quietly sniffling, for hours. She didn't talk, as though she had lost the power of speech altogether. She just lay there, absorbing the shock, processing what had happened—that her father had lost his life in a stupid accident.

Before they'd gone to bed, a police officer had called with more information. Apparently, Bobby had lost control of his bike and had collided with an overpass on the freeway. He had died instantly. He hadn't been under the influence of alcohol or drugs and, thankfully, no other vehicles had been involved in the accident. So much for small mercies. Because Sienna and Taissa had still lost their dad.

Justine was glad that Sienna had finally fallen asleep, but she was wide awake. In the end, they hadn't eaten—Mimi hadn't had the opportunity to serve whatever feast she had prepared—and Eddy's scotch sloshed in Justine's empty stomach.

Although not very experienced with sleepovers, Justine had spent the night at Sienna's penthouse plenty of times, but staying at her mother and stepdad's house was entirely different. The scotch hadn't helped with that either—nothing could help these wretched circumstances.

She maneuvered gently so Sienna slid off her. The bottle of water on the nightstand next to her was empty. Justine stayed perfectly still for a few moments, making sure Sienna was still asleep, then slipped out of bed, in search of some water and, if at all possible, something to eat.

She tiptoed to the kitchen, where she found Maxine in the low light of a dimmed lamp, crying over a bowl of soup.

"I'm so sorry to intrude," Justine said when Maxine spotted her.

"You're not. Please, sit with me." She wiped the tears from her cheeks. "I don't even know why I'm crying. I divorced Bobby eons ago, and for very good reasons."

"He's the father of your daughters," Justine said, as she slid onto one of the stools surrounding the giant kitchen island.

"He was not a bad man." Maxine got up and, without asking, served Justine a bowl of soup. "But he was a really shit husband and not the best of fathers either." She placed the soup in front of Justine. "In case you're hungry. It's tomato."

"Thank you." Justine shot Maxine a warm smile. It could probably be anyone sitting across from her now. She just wanted to vent, release some of the things that weighed heavy on her mind.

"We tried to stay friends, but Bobby was a hard man to stay friendly with," Maxine murmured. "I know I shouldn't speak ill of the dead, but his worst fault was that he was so unreliable and hurt the girls over and over by being like that. I hated him for that—for hurting them. For not being there. For not being the dad I wanted him to be." She huffed out some air. "But he *was* their dad and they wouldn't be who they are—these two amazing, talented, smart, and beautiful women, without his… contribution. And now he's gone, and I can't believe it." She shook her head.

"Life can be a real bitch," Justine said.

Maxine surprisingly chuckled in response. "Ain't that the truth." She went quiet again, then said. "Sienna's very sensitive and she was much closer to her dad than Taissa. I guess she saw him as her acting mentor. They bonded over that, at least. She might take this very hard." Her eyes glistened with tears again.

"I understand," Justine said. "She can count on me."

"Is it… serious between the two of you now?" Maxine asked.

Good question. "Getting there," Justine said, quickly realizing how inadequate that was as an answer—no matter how truthful. "I mean, um, my intentions are good. I think the world of Sienna and I have strong feelings for her." *Jeez.* Justine had just gone in search of some food—and she hadn't even touched her soup yet—but now she was sitting in Maxine Brewster's swanky kitchen, answering questions about her relationship with Sienna. But she and Sienna were in a relationship, that much they had established. And they liked each other a lot and loved sleeping with each other, although Justine wasn't going to tell Maxine that.

"I'll be honest." Maxine fixed her gaze on Justine. "After Sienna first told me about you, I had my assistant do some in-depth research on you."

"Excuse me?" Justine's eyes grew wide.

"I'm sorry, but it's the kind of mother I am and my hackles went all the way up when the girls were talking about this 'middle-aged white lady' Sienna was seeing." She shot Justine an apologetic smile. "Of course, I'd heard about you. Even before Sienna told me about this movie. You've made quite the name for yourself in this city. And my assistant didn't dig up anything negative about you. Nothing. Nada. Like you're some saint or something. Los Angeles' very own patron saint for homeless queer kids."

Justine scoffed. "I can assure you I'm no saint, but I do take my work very seriously."

"Because you've been there?" Maxine asked.

Justine just nodded.

"If Sienna's going to be with an older woman, then I'm happy it's with someone as conscientious and serious as you." Maxine's smile grew a little warmer. "It's also obvious that you care about my daughter a great deal and I get the distinct impression she's pretty crazy about you too, so…"

And she's thirty-six years old, Justine thought, but it was not the time or place to say something sharp like that. Justine was sitting in Sienna's mother's kitchen purely by circumstance and, for that reason alone, it was futile to wonder whether this conversation, and everything Maxine had just said, was a good thing or not. Justine was here and Maxine was sort of—that's how Justine read it, anyway—giving them her motherly blessing.

"Granny!" A child's voice came from the living room. "Granny, where are you?"

"I'm here, baby." Maxine stood up and, as she headed out of the kitchen, briefly touched her hand against Justine's arm.

CHAPTER 25

Taissa stared at the piece of paper in her hand again, then looked at Sienna.

"I guess we're loaded," Taissa said, as though they hadn't been rich before they'd inherited their father's many millions.

Sienna would give back every single penny for one last hour with her dad. For a chance to say goodbye. For a frank and honest conversation about his shortcomings as a dad and her own as a daughter. Because more often than not, she hadn't painted him in a very positive light. But no one was perfect, and Bobby Bright certainly hadn't been—although the dozens of obituaries written about her famous, larger-than-life movie star dad would have you believe otherwise.

Bobby's net worth had been much higher than Sienna could ever have imagined—she had never given it much thought— and everything he owned was to be split evenly between her and her sister. Bobby had never remarried and hadn't fathered any other children—possibly because he knew he wasn't really cut out for parenting, although Sienna would never have the chance to ask him. She'd never be able to ask him anything ever again. All she could do from now on was speculate about Bobby's motives.

That cold hard fist that had wrapped itself around her heart when she'd heard of her father's death was still there, albeit a little less tight. She'd had a week to process that first, horrible blow. Now, what remained was this aching void inside her that she, sometimes, found hard to explain, because she hadn't even been that close to Bobby. If it felt like this—utterly devastating and grim—when her father died, Sienna couldn't possibly imagine what it would be like to lose her mother. The thought was too horrific to consider for even a single second because Sienna predicted she'd never want to get out of bed again if the world was without Maxine Brewster.

Now, the world was without Bobby Bright. Her dad being who he was, Sienna's phone had been blowing up non-stop with messages and condolence calls. Bobby's death was still in the news every day. Every angle of the accident was being examined and re-examined. So many people that Sienna had never heard of had something to say about her father.

The family had discussed at length what his funeral should look like: a small, intimate gathering or a large celebrity circus. No matter how much they might have wanted the former for themselves, they owed Bobby the latter. Because Bobby Bright was a Hollywood icon. One of the last real movie stars. A ridiculously charismatic man of undisputed talent who had died well before his time. People living on the other side of the world who had never met him, who knew him only from the movies he'd starred in, mourned his death as if he'd been a friend. Most of all, everyone who'd actually been close to Bobby, knew in their soul that he would have wanted the biggest, most lavish funeral possible. They could no longer do anything else for him, but they could honor his spirit—his very essence. No matter how much they might have been annoyed by it when he was still alive.

His never-ending hankering for attention. His constant pursuit of fame and adoration. His need to be the focus whenever he entered a room with his extravagant, extroverted charm.

To see his name on a billboard so it could draw millions of people to movie theaters around the globe. That's what Bobby had lived for. On many occasions, it had been far more important than spending time with his kids—than being a father. But none of that still mattered, because Bobby was dead. Sienna's father was dead.

She'd never be able to tell him how much he had inspired her to become an actor. How much he had taught her, just by doing what he did and being who he was. How much the advice he had given her had meant to his youngest daughter. She could only hope that he knew, because she'd certainly never told him. That was not the kind of relationship they had.

The day before, Sienna and Taissa had been summoned to their father's lawyer's office. He had given them each a sheet of paper with the amount of money they'd inherit written on it. It was an amount that had to be scribbled on a folded piece of paper so that it didn't have to be said out loud—like in those gangster movies from the eighties her father was still so adored for. He'd probably stipulated in his will that they be notified this way—that was also the kind of guy he was. Sienna concluded that giving her and Taissa the full amount of what he owned was his way—the only way he still had left when it came to it—of showing them the extent of his love for them.

"Shall we do this, sis?" Taissa put the piece of paper in her bag and rose. "Shall we say goodbye to dad?"

Bobby's big send-off, that was open to anyone who wished to attend, was about to begin.

"Let's do it," Sienna said on a sigh. She wished it was over already—and that she didn't have to share her grief with all these people.

But at least Justine would be there to hold her hand. Sienna was so extremely grateful to have Justine in her life today.

———

Taissa leaned against her husband's shoulder. Even Maxine, who hadn't been married to her dad for such a long time, seemed overcome by emotions, and perhaps also the grandiose circumstances, and held on to Eddy for support. Sienna was the only one who didn't have a significant other to lean on. Because Justine was not there.

They were supposed to meet at Sienna's mom's house before going to the church—Bobby considered himself a lapsed Catholic and wanted a religious funeral—but Justine hadn't shown up by the time they'd had to leave. She hadn't responded to Sienna's texts. Sienna had tried calling her before switching off her phone—she needed it off for the service, because it was still blowing up with messages about her dad—but it had gone to voicemail.

Justine had a front row seat next to Sienna in the church but that seat had remained empty. Just before the service had started, Sienna had looked into the vast crowd behind her, hoping to spot Justine somewhere in the back. She had seen Rochelle and Rita and Nora and Mimi and Alexis and almost everyone else from the *Gimme Shelter* set, but no Justine Blackburn. Where the hell was she?

Sienna was worried—especially after Bobby's accident—and perhaps also a little angry because the very least Justine could have done was send a message.

But Sienna couldn't spend too much energy worrying and being angry at Justine because she was saying goodbye to the man responsible for half her DNA, the man she had loved simply because of his role in her life, but had also thought the worst of more often than she should have.

Her and Bobby's relationship had been complex and it certainly hadn't been a straightforward father-daughter relationship, but he had always been her dad and he had always loved her, even though he couldn't always show it—but who could?

His death had ripped something open inside Sienna, like an

extra reservoir of love she had for her father that she hadn't had access to when he'd still been alive. As if he'd had to die for Sienna to find it. A newfound appreciation for how he was and what he meant to millions of people.

Bobby Bright had not been an ordinary man with an ordinary life. Sienna had never known him before he'd shot to fame. He'd always been a famous movie star to her and she'd never been very impressed by it—she'd been annoyed by it most of the time—but as she sat there, as Peter Kaminski, one of Bobby's best friends, was giving something between a eulogy and a roast—something Bobby would have undoubtedly loved —Sienna considered that she'd seen her dad through a too-narrow lens. That she'd focused on his faults more often than his qualities. That she would miss the hell out of him and the deeply flawed but wonderful person he'd been.

Tears trickled down her cheeks and she wished so fervently that she could lean into the warm embrace of someone she loved—a special person to get through this tough time with. She wanted nothing more than to find comfort in the arms of someone who understood, someone who'd been there for her all week. And Justine had been there. The death of a parent was not something that scared off Justine Blackburn—on the contrary. So where was she now? Why had she decided to leave Sienna to deal with all this without her, today of all days? At this excruciatingly emotional event. At the time when Sienna needed her most of all.

Sienna glanced at the empty seat next to her, which had literally become a waste of space. If she'd known Justine wasn't going to show up, she'd have asked a friend to sit with her. She would have made sure she'd had a shoulder to cry on.

She caught her mother's eye and, in response, her mother scooted over and put her arm around Sienna. She took a deep breath as she found so much more than comfort in her mom's embrace. The tears that dripped from her eyes multiplied. Because what Bobby's death had also done was trigger an irrational fear of Sienna's mother dying—just like that, the way Bobby had done. And who would hold her then?

As the service continued, and that front row seat remained conspicuously empty, Sienna's sadness over her father's death morphed into mad fury over Justine's glaring absence.

CHAPTER 26

Justine knew she had screwed up, but she also knew in her bones that she didn't have a choice. Try as she might, in all of her fifty-four years, she still hadn't found a way to be in two places at once. And today of all days, she'd had no choice but to put Ashleigh first, no matter how unfair it was to Sienna.

By the time she'd had the chance—and the presence of mind —to call Sienna, the funeral service had begun and Sienna had been unreachable. When the doctor had assured her that Ashleigh was stable, Bobby's funeral had almost finished. After Justine had—finally—been able to briefly talk to Ashleigh, to assure her that she wasn't alone in this, that Justine was there for her no matter what, the reception at Maxine's house was well on the way.

Justine sat in her car outside. Her old Subaru stuck out like a sore thumb between all the gleaming black town cars with drivers at the wheel. She'd been getting dressed for the funeral service when she'd received the call about Ashleigh, and at least she was wearing a black suit, but it was wrinkled and her white blouse had a coffee stain on it. As soon as she went inside that house, she would stand out like a sore thumb as well—and not just because of her disheveled looks.

Justine had texted Sienna when she'd left the hospital, but she hadn't received a reply. She wondered if she should try calling Sienna and ask her to come outside so they could talk in private so Justine could explain what happened. But Sienna had just buried her father and Justine felt like it was too much to ask —especially after she had failed to show up. Being there for Sienna was truly the only thing she'd had to do and she had utterly failed at this simple task—just like she had done so many times for others in the past.

Justine huffed out a breath, gathered her courage, and made her way inside—she'd faced much worse in her life, after all.

The house was packed with people, some of them surely celebrities, but Justine didn't recognize any of them. She spotted Sienna talking to someone by the big table in the dining area but before she could reach her, Maxine intercepted Justine.

"I'm not sure you should be here." Maxine's stare was cold and hard on Justine. "You're a little late."

"I know and I'm sorry."

"What excuse could you possibly have for not being there for Sienna at her father's funeral?" Maxine hissed.

"An emergency at the shelter," Justine said. Maxine was not the one she wanted to have this conversation with and she wasn't going to give her any details about what had transpired with Ashleigh. "I'd like to speak to Sienna, please."

As if she'd heard her name being spoken through the hubbub of the crowd, Sienna looked in Justine's direction. Their gazes met, but it was impossible to read Sienna's face—that lovely, warm, usually so expressive face.

"What you did was not okay," Maxine said. "You sure picked a day to show your true colors." With that, she turned around and walked off.

Justine tried to advance, to get closer to Sienna, who seemed to pretend Justine wasn't even there, but it was as though everyone in the room knew what she had done and was trying to prevent her, just by standing in a certain way and blocking the path.

When Justine finally reached Sienna's side, she was exhausted. It had been a day and a half already.

"Can we talk, please," she said to Sienna's back.

When Sienna turned around, her eyes were moist and her face a mask of raw pain.

"I needed you today," Sienna whispered. "Fuck, how I needed you."

"I know." Saying sorry seemed so insignificant, but an apology was all Justine had. "I'm so sorry, babe. I would have been there if I could. Please, can we talk?" Justine urged again.

"I just can't right now, Justine." Sienna looked in such agony. Actually saying goodbye to her dad and the ritual of the funeral must have wrecked her. Justine completely understood. "I needed you today and you weren't there." Tears pearled in her eyes.

"I'm sorry." The words sounded as inadequate as they felt to Justine as she uttered them. "I'm here now," she said, hoping—in vain—that it was enough.

"As what?" Some of the pain on Sienna's face had turned into hardness. "My girlfriend? My friend, even?" She gave a terse shake of the head. "Everyone else was there. Rochelle and Rita were there. Drew and Shanti from makeup? They were there. A whole bunch of people I don't even know, they were there." She pointed a finger at Justine. "And you? Where the fuck were you? I can't do this right now. I'm sure you had what seemed like a huge emergency, although I only figured that out after I saw your text and I could finally be sure that you hadn't been in an accident, the week after my father died in a motor-cycle crash. So no, I don't want to talk to you today. Not tomor-row, either. I never want to fucking see you again."

"Hey, sis." Taissa had made her way through the crowd, most of whom were staring at Sienna and Justine. "Why don't you come with me? We'll get something to drink in the kitchen." Taissa put her arm around Sienna and, without even acknowledging Justine, ushered her sister away.

Justine had clearly incurred the wrath of all the Brewster-Brights—perhaps rightly so.

Sienna was also right about today not being the day for Justine to explain why she hadn't been at Bobby's funeral. Sienna was too wrung out by all the emotions of the day, and the past week.

There was no point in staying at this reception in Bobby Bright's memory. Justine had hurt his daughter, possibly beyond repair, and she was damn sorry for it.

———

"This is what you always do," Rochelle said. "You're not there when it really matters."

"Ashleigh tried to kill herself, Roche." Justine had stopped by the hospital on her way to see Rochelle and Rita and, all things considered, Ashleigh was doing okay. "I'm not losing another kid. I can't lose another one." She shook her head.

"I feel for Ashleigh, you know that, but Sienna—the woman you are dating and are supposedly madly in love with—lost her dad." Rochelle shook her head with even more force than Justine, as though they were in a contest. "The shelter has so many volunteers. You could have asked Darrel to go to the hospital to be with Ashleigh. They would have done it in a heartbeat, you know that."

"I had to be there for Ashleigh myself. We have a connection."

"If I have to convince you that you made the wrong choice today, there's really no point," Rochelle said. "In that case, Sienna being so angry with you might as well be the end of it. Then you shouldn't even try to salvage whatever's left of what you had."

Justine closed her eyes and pinched the bridge of her nose. "I know that I made the wrong choice, but—"

"As long as there's a 'but', you shouldn't even apologize to Sienna." Rochelle wasn't pulling any punches today. She never had, but it had also never had the power to change Justine's behavior.

"I think," Justine said, "in this particular situation, there's simply no such thing as a wrong choice. It wasn't even a choice, not a conscious one, anyway. I got the call and I drove to the hospital." It's who I am, Justine thought but, perhaps, only she would ever understand that.

"For a minute there"—Rochelle's gaze softened—"I truly believed it would be different with Sienna. You were different with her. You sat in that same chair and told me how easy it was to be with her, to show up for her. And I know you showed up, that you were there for her every single day after her father died. I was so impressed by that. I really was. Ask Rita. I told her in those exact words. Rita and I even talked about how you and Sienna might actually work out somehow—we couldn't put our finger on what was so different this time around. Maybe, first of all, that you let yourself really fall in love for once but also, more importantly, that you let Sienna do the same with you. That you let whatever chemistry you had organically grow into something potentially beautiful and—who knows?— lasting. But today showed us that you still think the shelter is more important than anything or anyone else."

"Because it is," Justine confirmed.

"More important than Sienna on the day of her father's funeral?"

"No," Justine contradicted herself, because that's what this whole situation was. One big contradiction. Both Sienna and Ashleigh mattered a great deal, but in very different ways.

"I hate to say this to you, Justine, but just like Bobby Bright, you're not going to be around forever." Rochelle really was too much sometimes, but it was also why she'd been Justine's best friend forever. "The Rainbow Shelter will be there long after you've gone. It's unlikely, but you might even consider retirement one day, or at least scaling back." Rochelle held up her hand, indicating that she wasn't done talking and that she had a further point to make. "What I'm trying to say is that there are other, equally capable people who work at the shelter and can fill in for you when needed—when you have to be at a funeral you can't miss. If you'd called me this morning, I would have gone to the hospital to be with Ashleigh. You know that. And Darrel will graduate their management course soon."

"I wasn't thinking. I just did what I always do when I get a call. Hop in my car and go so I can deal with the situation. It's what I've been doing for thirty years." *It's what they're making that fucking movie about.* "I hate that I hurt Sienna. It's the last thing I wanted to do." Justine couldn't shake that first heart-wrenching glimpse she'd caught of Sienna's face at the reception earlier. The profound pain and deflation in her glance. "I really care about her. A lot." Justine looked into Rochelle's eyes. "I may need some advice on how to fix this."

"Do you want to fix it?" Rochelle brought her hand to her chest. "Do you feel that in here? Like it can't possibly be any other way?"

Justine nodded. That was precisely how she felt.

"Let me put it differently, then." Rochelle narrowed her eyes. "If you could do today all over again and you got the call about Ashleigh while getting ready for Bobby's funeral, what would you do?"

Justine scoffed. She knew what Rochelle needed *and* wanted to hear. Whether that was what she would actually do, given another chance, was impossible to honestly say.

"I would call you," Justine said regardless. "I would ask you to be with Ashleigh so I could be with Sienna."

"Sure." Rochelle didn't sound as though she fully believed Justine—and why would she? "Your best bet is to convince Sienna that's the truth."

"What a fucking mess." Justine closed her eyes for a moment. This was usually the moment she knew she had to retreat from the relationship, for her own sake, but also for the other person's sake. Yet, even though she had behaved the way she had, and made a spur-of-the-moment decision that put her relationship in grave jeopardy, Justine felt no desire to pull back from Sienna—on the contrary.

CHAPTER 27

The production staff had rearranged the shooting schedule so that Sienna could have the maximum number of days off after her father's death. She only had to go back on set next week. She was still staying at her mom's house because not only was she grieving the loss of her father, but her burgeoning relationship with Justine had also come to an abrupt end. After Justine had left the house during the reception, in a fit of rage, Sienna had blocked her number. She hadn't found it in her to unblock it yet. The rage hadn't subsided sufficiently, even though Sienna was self-aware enough to realize that her anger wasn't just aimed at Justine.

She was angry at Bobby for owning a motorcycle in the first place—for being the quintessential guy in his sixties who believed he was indestructible.

She was angry at herself for being so annoyed at her dad when he'd visited the *Gimme Shelter* set—the last time she had seen him. For believing that she saw right through him and his motives while, in hindsight, maybe all he truly wanted was to spend some time with her and see his daughter in her element.

She was angry at Taissa, who seemed to have picked her life

back up as though not much had happened—as though their father hadn't unexpectedly died.

She was angry at all the gossip sites that kept rehashing Bobby's accident as if talking about it non-stop could possibly undo it.

Mostly, she was furious because she couldn't think of or do anything that would bring her father back. Bobby was gone and it was all just so terribly infuriating.

Sienna was also angry at herself for being so angry at Justine for simply being who she was. For being every inch the kind of person—which was really just an incredibly caring, kind human being with a few personal boundary issues—she'd always said she'd been. The kind of person Rochelle had warned her about. Because, of course, Justine would have rushed to Ashleigh's bedside as soon as she'd got the call about her suicide attempt. Every cell in Justine's body would have been utterly and completely convinced that she was doing the right thing, despite it preventing her from going to Sienna's father's funeral. And where did that leave Sienna? It told her a harsh truth: nothing and nobody came before the shelter in Justine Blackburn's life. Not if you wanted to put yourself before someone like Ashleigh, who had been so depressed and desperate she'd actually tried to take her own life.

Rochelle had stopped by the house a few days ago to explain to Sienna where Justine had been last Saturday and Sienna understood—of course, she understood—but that didn't mean she had to accept it. In the state she was in, still so full of pain and rage, she couldn't possibly accept it, even if that made her the most selfish person on the planet. For that reason as well, she was very angry at herself. At the whole fucking world. Because it was all so goddamn unfair.

————

"I had Dion work his reservation magic," Sienna's mom said as she walked into the living room. "He got us a table at that Korean place you can't shut up about for tomorrow evening."

Sienna had been flicking through the channels. She switched off the TV and put the remote away. "Min-ji's?" she asked.

"Yep." Her mother all but batted her lashes.

"I'm impressed."

"This is LA, where name-dropping still works like a charm, no matter what anyone says." Her mother's assistant, Dion, was a legend at talking his boss into a table at the most coveted restaurants in town on short notice.

"It'll just be the three of us girls. It will do us good." Her mother sat next to Sienna.

"Thanks, Mom." In need of human contact, Sienna instinctively sank against her mom's side. Her mom put an arm around her. What Sienna had missed most of all, were Justine's hugs. Especially now, when she was in such need of a pair of loving arms around her.

They were startled by the sound of the bell.

"Are you expecting anyone?" Sienna's mom asked.

Sienna shook her head.

"I'll go see who it is." Unhurried, her mother pressed a kiss on the crown of Sienna's head before walking off. "It's Justine," she shouted from the room next to the kitchen where the security video was fed into a screen.

Sienna huffed out a deep breath. "I'm not here," she yelled back. Tell her to fuck off, she thought. Sienna might miss Justine's arms around her, but Justine had lost the right to do that when she'd failed to show up at Bobby's funeral. As soon as Sienna heard her mom say Justine's name, that fist of steel clenched harder around her heart. As if Justine had come to stand for all the pain that coursed through Sienna so mercilessly after her dad dying.

Sienna sank back into the couch and waited for her mother to return. When she didn't, Sienna switched the television back on. An image of her father looked back at her from the big screen.

————

There was no other way for Justine to show how sorry she was than to turn up at Maxine Brewster's house. She knew from Rochelle that Sienna was staying at her mother's. Maxine had spoken to her through the intercom when Justine had rung the bell, and asked her to wait outside because she wanted to have a word.

Maxine Brewster was by all means a formidable woman—a true force of nature who had single-handedly changed the status of Black women in Hollywood, according to Rochelle— and she was another hurdle for Justine to negotiate while trying to regain access to Sienna. While trying to get some face time with her. To just catch a glimpse of her face, to erase the memory of Sienna's wounded expression when Justine had seen her last.

Maxine appeared and closed the security gates behind her.

"You have a lot of nerve," Maxine started as soon as she was close enough to Justine to be heard. "To come here." She pointed at the massive mansion behind her. "After you sat across from me, in my own kitchen, and promised me that you'd be there for my daughter."

"I get that you're upset, Maxine." Justine knew how to keep calm in situations like this, even though Maxine's accusation wasn't entirely justified. Not in Justine's book anyway, although she might be the only person who felt that way about it. "But if I could just talk to Sienna. Just for a few minutes."

"She doesn't want to see you and I don't blame her." Maxine crossed her arms in front of her chest.

"Does she—" Justine tried to say, but Maxine cut her off.

"I think it would be best if you left Sienna alone." Justine had dealt with far more menacing people than Maxine Brewster, yet she was intimidated by her. She was like a mama bear protecting her cub—like the mother Justine never had, and she could only respect that. "She doesn't need another person in her life who she can't rely on. Like the one who just died."

It was a bit rich to compare Justine to Sienna's absent father, but she guessed Maxine was hurting as well—if only by seeing her children grieve—and lashing out at Justine was easy enough. Apparently, it was the best way for all the Brewsters and the Brights to blow off steam, although Justine could only wish that Sienna would at least hurl some accusations at her face-to-face instead of shutting her out completely.

It was obvious this mama bear wasn't going to let Justine anywhere near her child. To have a mother like that, someone who came out swinging and fought your battles for you, who was willing to take that first, biting sting of pain for you. Poor Ashleigh, in her hospital bed, now battling even more guilt and shame, could only dream of a parent like that.

"Okay." Justine held up her hands in supplication. "I'll go." She looked Maxine straight in the eye. "Please, tell her…" Justine didn't finish her sentence, just shook her head. It wasn't as though she didn't understand all this hardness, all this posturing and putting up a shield. She was an expert at it. All she could hope was that, unlike with some of the scars on her own heart, a touch of softening would occur before it was too late. Before the scar tissue became permanent.

She turned around and trudged back to her car. More patience and time would be required.

CHAPTER 28

Sienna wasn't shooting, and Justine needed some punishment. She couldn't think of a better place to get what she deserved than the *Gimme Shelter* movie set. Whatever plan she could possibly hatch would have to wait until Sienna was at least willing to talk to her again—to answer the phone when Justine called. Maybe it was a good thing, because Justine had not been able to come up with a plausible plan just yet—especially after Maxine's reprimand.

She showed up at the set without giving it much thought and, perhaps, also because Rochelle had assured her that, even though it would surely hurt, it would still be healing.

There was a different kind of energy in the air than last time Justine had visited and she soon found out why. Nora Levine was shooting her scenes as Justine's mother today.

Just as she was thinking of leaving—Justine didn't need *that* much punishment—she spotted a familiar figure. Someone she hadn't seen in years but whose tall stature was so distinctive, Justine would recognize it anywhere. No-Mercy Marcy.

When Marcy noticed Justine walking over, she did a visible double take.

"I know this movie is about you," she said in her deep voice. "But never in a million years did I expect you to be here."

"Why not?" Even though things hadn't ended well between her and Marcy, Justine opened her arms to her ex. "Although, to be honest, I didn't know they were shooting Nora's scenes today. The schedule's been overhauled so much, I can't keep up."

Marcy gave her a tight bear hug which, for Marcy, was just a normal hug.

"Given your presence," Justine said, "I take it you're still torturing Nora on a daily basis?" Marcy had been Nora Levine's personal trainer for a very long time—Nora didn't like change and Marcy got excellent results.

"Correct, although I also have another reason for being here." Marcy stood there beaming, looking strong and healthy and, come to think of it, ridiculously happy. "The director is kind of my mother-in-law."

Justine tilted her head while running the names of Mimi's kids through her head. Her son was engaged to a member of Nora's posse, and she couldn't remember Mimi's other children.

"I'm with Jennifer, Mimi's daughter," Marcy explained. "We've been together almost a year." She pointed at a woman of about Sienna's age who was chatting to Mimi next to the soundstage.

"I'm so happy for you, Marcy. I really am."

"What about you?" Marcy shuffled her weight around—she was all impressive muscle and shapely long limbs. "I've heard the rumors. It's hard not to in the St James family."

Mercifully, the call for silence on set came.

"We should grab a drink after this," Marcy whispered. "For old times' sake."

"We should?" Justine looked Marcy in the eye.

"Definitely." Marcy was not the kind of person you said no

to—although Justine had said no plenty of times when they'd been going out.

"Okay."

Another call for silence came. Maybe because of Nora's professional presence the vibe was more tense than the previous times Justine had visited. Or maybe it was the scene that was being shot.

Before she knew it, and very much against her will, Justine was drawn into it.

Justine had no idea how the makeup department accomplished this, but Alexis had been made to look a lot younger than in the other scenes, when she was meant to be twenty-five. But seeing Nora was the biggest shock to Justine's system. Yes, that was Nora's face, one of the most recognizable faces in the world, yet she conjured up Justine's mother effortlessly. Many had considered Monica Blackburn a beautiful woman. Maybe, on the outside, she was. But to Justine, she would always be the woman who had kicked her out of her house instead of the mother who was meant to care for her. There was nothing beautiful about that.

She watched the scene and the distress of seeing Nora as her mother quickly subsided as Justine's heart turned into stone again. She needn't have worried about this scene—about being here while it was shot. It could no longer touch her. Justine had made herself so strong, had armored her heart with fortified steel of the highest order, Monica Blackburn, or anyone else for that matter, could never hurt her again.

———

"Jen wanted to get in shape and was looking for a personal trainer," Marcy said. "Nora recommended me." She waggled her eyebrows. "And here we are, a year down the line."

Marcy looked utterly content. She popped a piece of fried

chicken in her mouth—not something Justine could remember her ever doing when they'd been dating.

"She has softened my hardest edges just a fraction." Marcy grinned at her. "Yum. Why is this chicken so damn delicious?"

"Because Min-ji is a wizard in the kitchen," Justine said.

Jennifer had been called away for an emergency at work—something with a mobile app Justine didn't fully understand—and the drink she and Marcy had decided to grab had turned into an impromptu dinner at Min-ji's.

"But she's not even in the kitchen," Marcy said. "She's front of house. She conjured up this table out of nowhere for us."

"You know better than to ask me why a piece of food is so good." Justine shrugged. "I wouldn't know the first thing about it.

"Correct." Marcy fixed her deep-brown gaze on Justine. "Some things never change."

"I'm glad you're so happy. That you found someone who, um, really gets you." Justine knew better than most how difficult that was.

"It wasn't easy." Despite what she was saying, Marcy's face lit up. "Jen was"—she curled her fingers into air quotes—"'self-partnered' at the time. She was truly convinced in her heart that she, herself, was the best partner she could ever find."

"Hm." Justine had never thought about things like that. "That's very interesting." Maybe she should consider it. Who understood her better than she did herself? Even the people who made the effort to get what Justine was all about, like Rochelle, didn't last, because—Justine knew this about herself as well—she simply wasn't prime relationship material. Maybe a self-partnered relationship with herself was all she could hope for.

"Try to compete with that." A wide grin broke on Marcy's face. "But Jen kept booking more and more sessions with me until, well, they weren't really personal training sessions anymore." She threw in a chuckle. "We had our hands all over each other for all sorts of exercises that really didn't require such a hands-on approach."

Marcy was so obviously in love—of course, it made Justine think of Sienna. She missed her and she wished she could be there for her—that was, at the very least, something Justine knew she was good at. She could help Sienna through this hard time. She was certain of that. If only she'd let her.

"What happened with you and this hotshot actor playing your ex-girlfriend?" Marcy's gaze softened.

"I fucked up." Once, Justine thought. One single time. "A girl at the shelter had to go to hospital on the day of Sienna's dad's funeral."

"And you had to go with her?" Marcy's tone was not judgmental, which was refreshing.

"I did." Justine could regret making the wrong choice, but she would never regret what she actually did. She couldn't regret being there for Ashleigh when she needed her most.

"I take it Sienna Bright doesn't see it that way."

"No, and I get that. I completely understand. She's lost her dad. She's in pain. She needed me." This was also true. But two things could be true at the same time. "I wasn't there. Story of my life, right?" Justine gave a half-smile.

"Of your love life, sure," Marcy confirmed. "I never felt so neglected than when I was dating you. The hours I spent waiting for you." She puffed out some air. "It annoyed the hell out of me because it so clearly said what you could never say to me in words. That I could never mean as much to you as your job. As the shelter. Jen's busy too, but it's completely different. It's a lot more… respectful and communicative. You were always so totally absorbed by what you do and the kids you were looking after. I gather that hasn't changed either?" Marcy's gaze on Justine was kind and understanding, despite what she'd just said. Justine didn't take it as an insult. Being there for the shelter residents was never an insult. It was who she was. It was Justine Blackburn to her very core.

"Still, it was different with Sienna," Justine admitted. "In my heart, I feel as though I have been there for her." It probably wasn't a good idea to tell Marcy, her ex, how effortless it had been to find time for Sienna—something she had failed at big time with Marcy. "Although I do know that I fucked up. She doesn't want anything to do with me at the moment. She's still in so much pain. I guess I can only bide my time." Sienna was still in the movie. They'd have to see each other at some point in the near future.

Marcy narrowed her eyes and looked across Justine's shoulder. "What the—" she said, her voice trailing off. "Either my mind is fabricating images of Sienna Bright because we're talking about her or she just walked into this restaurant."

"What?" Every single last one of Justine's muscles tensed up. Sienna was here? She turned around and saw Maxine and Taissa take a seat at a table on the other side of the room. And then, sure enough, she caught a glimpse of Sienna's gorgeous face before she sat with her back to Justine.

CHAPTER 29

"Who told you about this place again?" Taissa asked, looking over the restaurant.

"Justine," Sienna said on a sigh. Perhaps coming here hadn't been the best idea, but she knew her mother had secured the reservation to make Sienna feel better—and because she had, indeed, not been able to shut up about Min-ji's heavenly food.

"That makes sense." Taissa put her hand on Sienna's arm. "Because she's here."

"No way," their mother said. "Oh, come on."

Sienna didn't have a choice. She had to have a peek. She looked over her shoulder, straight into Justine's face. She quickly glanced away, wondering who the tall, Black woman with the shaved head was opposite Justine.

"We can leave," Sienna's mother said. "We'll get take-out and eat at home."

Sienna shook her head. "No. It's fine. We're going to be in the same room sooner rather than later. I'd best get used to it." Who the hell was that woman? And why did seeing Justine sitting across from her make Sienna feel more uneasy than looking into Justine's face? It was hardly rocket science. Sienna was jealous. How beyond ludicrous.

"If you're sure." Her mother looked Sienna in the eye. "I want you to feel better. That's the only purpose of this restaurant visit. If *her* being here prevents that, there's no point in staying."

"The food will be delicious. I want you and Tai to taste it."

Min-ji appeared at their table. Sienna introduced her mother and sister and then asked Min-ji to bring them whatever she thought was best—just as she'd done on Justine and Sienna's first date, that hadn't been a date at all, until one thing had led to another.

Sienna was sure Justine would never admit to it, but this was the place she brought people to that she wanted to secretly impress. Was she on a date with that improbably broad-shouldered woman?

Sienna couldn't stop herself. She glanced over her shoulder again. Justine and the woman appeared in deep conversation.

"Keep your attention on us," Taissa said. "Fuck Justine."

"I'm just wondering who she's here with," Sienna whispered, as though Justine might overhear.

"Oh, I know who that is." Taissa's eyebrows arched all the way up. "That's Marcy Baptiste, Nora Levine's notoriously tough personal trainer. I read about her in a fitness magazine."

Marcy? Justine's ex-girlfriend? Was she rekindling an old flame now that Sienna had broken things off? That was a bit quick—as well as impossible for Sienna to stomach.

"Does it look as though they're, um, together?" Sienna asked her sister, who had a better view of Justine's table.

"Baby, come on," her mother said. "Forget about Justine. What is this? The middle school lunch table?" Her mother fixed her gaze on Sienna. "We're all adults here. Let's not regress to teenage girls gossiping about their exes."

Min-ji brought over the first plate of food—the same kind of scallion pancakes Sienna'd had when she'd come with Justine. Sienna soon realized that they should have taken the food to go.

She couldn't eat with Justine only a few feet away from her. With Justine on a possible date with her ex, Marcy.

"I don't know what Justine's like," Taissa said, completely ignoring their mother's admonishment. "But surely she's not already dating again. She only turned up at the house asking for you the day before yesterday."

Sienna nodded, but so much could happen in a few days— her father had died in the blink of an eye. Maybe Justine needed a shoulder to cry on and she had, in a moment of weakness, called her ex. Hadn't it ended on bad terms between her and Marcy? Sienna could speculate all she wanted, she'd never know. She was going a little nuts at the mere sight of Justine. They hadn't had proper closure—that much was true.

Taissa cleared her throat, pulling Sienna from her foolish train of thought.

"Looks like she's coming over," Taissa said. "Don't worry. We've got your back."

Then Justine was standing right next to Sienna. She ignored Maxine and Taissa and focused on Sienna's side of the table.

"Can we talk, please?" Her voice was soft and low. "Just for a few minutes? We can go outside."

"Sienna doesn't—" her mother started, but Sienna held up her hand to cut her off.

"It's okay, Mom. I can speak for myself." Her mother had been doing a bit too much talking for Sienna lately. She glanced up at Justine. "Yes, we can talk." She pushed her chair back and told her mother and sister she'd be right back.

Justine, who clearly knew her way around the place, led them to a door at the back. This gave Sienna a chance to get a good look at Marcy. This was the kind of woman Justine dated? She looked like an Amazonian warrior, with muscles so pronounced you could easily see them through her T-shirt.

A few moments later they stood in the restaurant's small backyard.

"Thanks for, um, agreeing to—"

"Is that your ex?" Sienna asked.

"Oh, Marcy? Yeah. I ran into her on set." She pursed her lips. "She's dating Mimi's daughter now. Small world, right?"

For the first time since seeing Justine with Marcy, Sienna could properly breathe again. She had been irrationally jealous. But so what? She was also still angry at Justine.

"Hey, um," Justine said when Sienna didn't reply. "I haven't had the chance to properly tell you how sorry I am for not being at your dad's funeral. I am really sorry, Sienna. I need you to know that."

"It made me feel I can't trust you," Sienna said.

"I get that, but—" Justine took a step closer.

In response, Sienna stepped back. She didn't want to stand closer to Justine. She wasn't sure what it might do to her. Justine was looking all Justine again with her practical clothes and chaotically pushed back hair, impossibly regal and righteous all at the same time, despite being in the middle of an apology to Sienna.

"It made me feel like you don't have my back because I'm not important enough to you," Sienna said. "That's not how I want to feel when I'm dating someone." Not at this stage, anyway. Sienna was all for trying to win over someone seemingly impenetrable—someone exactly like Justine—at the beginning of a relationship, but when push came to shove, they had to show up for her. That was the ultimate pay-off. And Justine had failed the biggest test life had thrown at her—at them.

"There's not much I can say to make this better. I did what I did and I can't rewind the clock and do things differently. But sometimes our actions don't reflect how we feel, because I hate that I made you feel like you're not important to me. Because you are. You're so important to me. You must know that."

Justine was right about one thing. Nothing she said could change what she had done. On top of that, what she was saying now was totally inadequate and didn't make a blind bit of difference to Sienna.

"I'm not just angry at you for leaving me in the lurch like that." When Sienna lay awake, counting slow minutes through another sleepless night, the image of that empty chair at the church often came back to her—the very symbol of Justine's glaring absence. "I'm also angry because my anger makes me feel like a selfish brat after what happened to Ashleigh. It's not that I don't get that you wanted to be there for her. That's who you are. I know that. It's one of the reasons I'm so attracted to you. But you've still made this impossible for me."

"It was kind of an impossible situation," Justine said, her voice nothing more than a broken whisper.

"Yeah." Sienna swallowed something out of her throat. "It's sad because I really like you. But I don't want to be with you anymore. I can't. That would be a big mistake and really stupid of me. I know that much." A tear dangled from Sienna's eyelash and crashed onto her cheek. "I'm not going to give you my heart to have you trample all over it again next time the situation is impossible. I can't count on life being easy that way. And I can't count on you either." Sienna tried to steady herself by taking a deep breath. If she stayed here any longer, the waterworks would start churning uncontrollably. "I'm going back to my family." She walked past Justine to the door.

"Sienna, please." Justine tried to grab Sienna's hand, but Sienna avoided her grasp. She had to get out of there pronto. She had to get away from Justine—she had to protect herself.

CHAPTER 30

"It's okay," Mimi said. "We'll do another take after you've had a longer break."

Sienna closed her eyes. She was so tired, she could fall asleep right there, dressed as Rochelle in her mid-thirties, on the *Gimme Shelter* set. That's what if felt like in that moment, but the truth was that Sienna couldn't sleep to save her life. Not here, not anywhere, and certainly not in bed at night.

The last time's she'd gotten more than a few hours of uninterrupted sleep was the last night Justine had stayed with her, when she'd slept in her arms.

Sienna glanced over at Rochelle for some moral support. She was fucking up the scene and she knew it. Everyone was very understanding about it because it was Sienna's first day back on set, but if her father had taught her anything, it was to always turn up as a pro. Ironically, it was his fault that Sienna was failing spectacularly at being a professional today.

"Come here." Rochelle beckoned her over.

Sienna walked over and Rochelle put her arm around Sienna's shoulders.

"It's going to be okay. You just need some more time. This is completely normal," Rochelle said, but she wasn't in charge of the shooting schedule, which had already been stretched to its limits in order to give Sienna some much needed time off.

They walked to Sienna's trailer. "If only I could get some fucking proper sleep." It wasn't just a lack of sleep that made Sienna a horrible actor today. It was being back here, working on this movie about Justine's life, and having to act opposite Alexis-as-Justine that was messing with her head as well as her ability.

"Can I ask you something?" Sienna looked at Rochelle. The more time they spent together, the more she'd grown to appreciate her.

"Of course." Rochelle smiled at Sienna. "Anything."

"Do you think I'm being too hard on Justine?"

Rochelle shook her head. "That's not a question I can answer. I know what she's like, but she's my best friend."

"I should have listened to you when you warned me about her."

Rochelle shook her head again. "Since when have mere words ever stopped anyone from falling in love? Words don't have that kind of power."

"I *was* in love with her." *Still am.* "I still think Justine is an amazing human being. I love her passion, but… I can't forgive her. What she did is just not something I can live with. I can't separate it from my dad's death. It's all so intertwined in here." She brought her fingers to her temples.

"You need to take your time to grieve and to heal, Sienna. These things always take a lot more time than you think. It's only logical you can't separate the two."

"Ashleigh's doing better?" Sienna asked.

"Yeah." Rochelle just nodded. It was unethical for her to share more information about the poor kid's health. "You don't have to worry about Ashleigh. It's not your battle."

Not anymore, Sienna thought.

"Listen to me." Rochelle narrowed her eyes. "It's okay to put yourself first. It's not something Justine has ever learned to do.

The shelter is her life because it's how she has dealt with her own trauma. Just as you said things are intertwined in your head, Justine's life and trauma are inextricably linked with the shelter. The two can no longer be separated and it's become second nature for her to put the shelter, and kids like Ashleigh, first. And I really mean first—before anyone else. In Justine's head, rushing to Ashleigh's bedside, no matter what else is going on, will always be the only right thing to do." Rochelle paused to take a breath. "As someone who loves her, it can be very frustrating, but I've learned to live with it. I've accepted that about her, because well, firstly, it's hard to hold it against her and, secondly, she's so much more than her flaws. I couldn't be her partner. I tried but it was impossible for me, but it's an honor to call her my best friend. So I get it. I completely get it, Sienna. You want her, but she's near impossible to be with because she'll never be able to put you first, which is where you belong in a romantic relationship."

Rochelle really could hit the nail right on the head. "She's damn lucky to have you as her best friend as well," Sienna said. "I hope you know that." Maybe out of the two of them, Rochelle was the real saint—for always being there for Justine and letting her be who she was. Although Sienna knew that Rochelle gave her best friend plenty of flak for her obsessive behavior sometimes.

"Maybe we're just lucky to have each other." Rochelle's face conveyed only pure tenderness.

Sienna expelled a deep sigh. Her eyes were prickly from lack of sleep.

"I'm so sorry I don't seem to have it in me today to do a good enough job of playing you. I want to do you justice, Rochelle." Sienna rolled her head back onto her shoulders.

"It'll come back to you." Rochelle really was sweetness personified.

"During a shoot, time literally is money. There's no time for me to be this mediocre," Sienna said.

"There's always time. Take it and don't feel bad about it. They may not act like it, but producers are people too. They know shit happens. Cruel, unexpected shit. It's what they make movies about, after all. So, it's okay. You're dealing with a lot."

"If only I could sleep. I'm so tired."

"I wish I could help you with that, but you're a smart woman. I'm sure you've tried everything I could suggest."

"At night, in my bed, when everything is quiet and dark outside, I just feel so intensely alone," Sienna admitted. "I get so scared that something will happen to my mom as well. Or to Taissa or Eddy and I just… I end up not being able to breathe and I have to get up to calm myself down."

"Are you talking to someone about this? A professional?" Rochelle asked. "I can recommend someone. You don't have to go through this alone."

"A therapist?" Sienna blew out some air. She'd had plenty of therapy in her early twenties, mostly to deal with her daddy issues.

Rochelle nodded. "A couple of sessions can work wonders in a situation like this."

"Yeah. I have someone. I'll think about it."

A knock came on the door of Sienna's trailer.

"Hey." Mimi appeared in the doorframe. "How are you, Sienna? I hope you know that we all understand if you need more time."

Sienna shook her head. She didn't need more time, nor did she need to talk to someone. She just needed to get some shut-eye. And then she needed to get on with things.

"Let's try again." Sienna shot up, mustering as much energy as she could. She'd have to try and channel some of Bobby Bright's legendary professionalism.

———

The first couple of nights after her dad had died, Sienna had slept in Justine's comforting arms. After Justine hadn't shown at the funeral, Sienna had to sleep alone. She'd turned to sleeping pills, but she didn't want to go down that route for too long. Besides, the pills made her even groggier in the morning than if she hadn't caught any winks at all.

She tried meditation, hot baths, cold showers, chamomile tea, wine, and too many shots of whiskey, but nothing could sufficiently quiet the panic lurking in her brain.

She lay tossing and turning, staring at the ceiling in her bedroom at her mother's house. Maybe she should move back into her own apartment. She couldn't stay here forever, and it wasn't as though it helped her sleep.

Sienna reached for her phone and considered emailing her former therapist to arrange an appointment, as Rochelle had suggested. It was worth a try. Sienna was ready to try anything she hadn't already tried, because nothing was more maddening, more demoralizing, and more destabilizing to her acting skills than not being able to sleep.

She was half-delirious with fatigue as she toyed with her phone. It was one thirty-four in the morning. She had to be on set early the next day. She had a lot of scenes to catch up on.

Her thumb must have made a false maneuver because Justine's old messages appeared on her phone screen. Justine wasn't much of a texter—she didn't have time for that particular type of finger fiddling. Justine Blackburn was the kind of person who preferred the efficiency of a good old-fashioned phone call, even to someone she was in the early stages of dating.

Fucking Justine. And this fucking movie. Both Sienna and Justine now had plenty of reasons to have a love hate relation ship with *Gimme Shelter*.

Sienna scrolled through the few text messages she had received from Justine—before she'd blocked her number. What would happen if she unblocked it? Would she get the messages that Justine had tried to send her? There was only one way to find out.

Sienna unblocked Justine's number but nothing happened. Her phone didn't blow up with unread messages. Of course, it didn't.

Sienna stared at her phone as memories of Justine scrolled through her mind, as if conjured by seeing her name. Of Justine's arms around her. Of the incomparable soothing effect her warm body had on Sienna's rattled nervous system. Something flared inside her. It could be exactly what she needed to regain the ability to simply doze off. To get some sleep. To restore some peace to her exhausted mind and wrecked body.

She dropped her phone on the bed. Sienna knew she wasn't thinking straight. Her brain was operating on the bare minimum of sleep, on endless tossing and turning and mulling everything over in her head. But didn't Justine owe her one decent night of sleep? At the very least, Sienna thought. Didn't she owe Sienna the consoling warmth of her body? Just for one night?

Oh yes, she fucking did.

Sienna arranged a car to pick her up in ten minutes. Because she was going to get what she was owed. What she had been denied by Justine being, so infuriatingly, Justine.

CHAPTER 31

When you slept in the street for long enough, you forever lost the ability to sink into a deep slumber that allowed you to snooze through anything. Subsequently running the shelter hadn't helped because the emergencies were frequent, and often happened after dark.

So Justine woke with a start, but was barely rattled by the banging on her door. She didn't share her home address, but kids were savvy these days, and it wasn't very hard to find out where Justine lived. She jumped out of bed and pulled her worn old robe around her, thinking it might be Ashleigh as she hurried down the stairs. She'd been admitted to a psychiatric unit but maybe she'd escaped. Anything was possible.

"All right. All right," Justine shouted at the door. "Hold your horses." She unlocked the door and threw it open, only to come face-to-face with Sienna.

Sienna didn't wait for an invitation to come in. She barged past Justine into the cramped hallway of her small house. She looked a little unhinged. Her eyes red-rimmed with blue-black half-moons underneath them. Her blouse was done up all wrong, with gaping holes between the buttons and she was wearing slippers that weren't meant for the outdoors.

"This isn't forgiveness," Sienna said. "It's nothing of the sort."

"Okay." Justine examined her face to ascertain Sienna wasn't sleepwalking—that she was actually fully awake. "Hey." She tried to lock her gaze on Sienna's, but Sienna wouldn't—or couldn't—look her in the eye. "Are you all right? Physically, I mean?" Justine gathered Sienna must be in quite some mental distress to turn up at her house in the middle of the night looking totally unkempt.

"Am I all right?" Sienna's eyes grew wide for a moment. "Of course, I'm not all right. I can't sleep. For the life of me, Justine, I cannot go to sleep." She narrowed her eyes to slits. "And you owe me a night of sleep. I just—" Her shoulders slumped. "I need someone to hold me so I can go the fuck to sleep." Tears started streaming down her cheeks as though a rain cloud had burst over her head.

Justine bridged the distance between them. "Is it okay if I touch you?"

Sienna nodded.

"Come here." Justine folded her arms around Sienna as gently as she could. "I'm here. It's okay," she said. "I'll hold you."

Instantly, as soon as they touched, Sienna's body went limp against Justine's. In a matter of minutes, Justine's robe was soaked with tears.

"It's okay. Let it all out." She held Sienna a little tighter, more of their bodies touching.

They stood entangled like that, Sienna sobbing and heaving, for what felt like hours, until Sienna calmed down. But she didn't let go of Justine's body. If anything, she squeezed her arms around Justine's waist with a tighter grip.

"Can I sleep here tonight?" Sienna whispered. "I'm just so tired."

"Of course, you can." Justine cupped the back of Sienna's head in her palm.

"In bed with you. I need you to hold me. I need to sleep."

"Yes." Justine didn't have to think about this for even a split second. Sienna needed her, and this time, she was going to be there all the way, no matter what it took. "Shall we go upstairs? Or do you want to talk more? Have some water first?"

Sienna's chin moved from left to right against Justine's chest.

"Come on." Justine untangled their limbs. She took Sienna's hand and led her up the stairs.

In her bedroom, she sat Sienna on the edge of the bed and crouched before her so she could slide off Sienna's inadequate footwear. Then she took a respectful step back, because it didn't feel appropriate to help Sienna undress. This wasn't forgiveness, after all.

Sienna tugged her wrongly buttoned blouse over her head and tossed it to the floor. She wriggled out of her jeans and then, without saying anything else, unhooked her bra. In just a pair of briefs, she slipped under the covers of Justine's bed.

Justine let the robe slide off her shoulders and hurried into bed with Sienna.

"Do you want me to spoon you?" Justine asked.

"Yes," Sienna whispered. "And take off your top, please. I need to feel your skin."

She hadn't come to mess around either, but Justine did as Sienna asked of her. It was the least she could do.

Justine pressed her naked body against Sienna's back and curled an arm around her waist.

"Is that okay?" she asked.

"Yes," was all Sienna said.

Justine didn't say anything else either. It was pretty obvious that Sienna hadn't come here, in the dead of night, to talk. She looked as haggard and drained as anyone would in the midst of such unexpected grief. It was no wonder Sienna couldn't sleep. If what she needed was Justine's arms around her, it was Justine's privilege to provide just that.

———

Five minutes in Justine's arms was all it took. Like fucking magic. Like swallowing the most amazing sleeping pill alongside something that stopped the endless churning in her brain. Sienna's eyelids grew heavy because, somehow, she felt safe. She was being held. Despite what she had done—or had failed to do—Sienna knew, all the way in her bones, that Justine cared deeply about her. It didn't matter that they could no longer be together. As Sienna had made clear as soon as she'd crossed the threshold, this wasn't absolution. There was no hidden motive behind any of this. She just wanted this. She just wanted to sleep. And sleep she did.

———

Sienna blinked her eyes open. She felt like she had returned from a trip to outer space, that's how deeply she had slept. She blinked again. Oh, fuck. Justine looked back at her, her blue eyes all kindness and understanding. Last night came back to Sienna. Leaving her mother's house in a state of utter madness. Turning up at Justine's in the middle of the night and demanding—there was no other word for it—she let Sienna sleep in her arms.

Oh damn. What time was it? Sienna shot up and threw the covers off her.

"Relax." Justine gently put her hand on Sienna's shoulder. "You have time. I made sure of that."

"What do you mean?" Sienna checked her watch. It was well past nine o'clock and her call time was in about fifteen minutes. Her mother was probably also going mad with worry, wondering where she was.

"I texted Maxine that you're safe and I called Mimi to tell her you're going to be late," Justine said matter-of-factly. As though her taking care of these things for Sienna was the most normal thing in the world.

"You did?" Relief washed over Sienna. Then she realized her upper body was naked. She folded her arms in front of her chest, as if that made any difference now.

Justine nodded.

"Thank you." Sienna fell back onto the mattress. It wasn't just relief washing over her; a tension she'd been carrying around since the news about her dad seeped from her muscles. She closed her eyes.

Six hours of unbroken sleep was like a dream, but the effect that weeks of insomnia had on her body couldn't be undone by just one night.

"I'm so embarrassed," Sienna whispered while opening her eyes to slits. "I'm sorry for turning up out of the blue like that." Embarrassing though it was, it had helped. Sienna had actually slept—and Justine had been the missing ingredient to make it happen.

"My arms are always here if you need them again," Justine simply said. "I'm serious."

Sienna turned on her side to face Justine. She was wearing a T-shirt but she didn't look as though she had showered or gotten ready yet for what was probably another busy day in her life.

"Really?" Sienna drew up her eyebrows.

"My arms are yours." Justine stretched out her arms for effect. "You might as well write on them: property of Sienna Bright, until further notice."

Sienna chuckled. She'd been so angry at Justine, she'd almost forgotten how kind she was—how giving.

"You have no idea how much I appreciate that." Tears pricked behind Sienna's eyes again, but she didn't care. "Not being able to sleep is such a bitch."

"I know." Justine smiled at her. "It makes you feel like you're losing your mind."

A part of Sienna wanted to crawl toward Justine and nestle in her arms a while longer, not to sleep, but just to lie there, feeling safely ensconced in her embrace before heading out into the world again.

"I should get ready. I need to go home before I go to the studio."

"You can come back tonight if you want to. I'll be here," Justine said. "It's up to you, but I'm here if you need to sleep."

She looked so gorgeous in the morning light, her tangled blonde locks shimmering softly and her gaze tender but sparkling. But Justine could, in Sienna's eyes, be the most beautiful woman in the world, and have the best, safest, warmest arms to doze off in, she would always be who—and how—she was. Rochelle had confirmed that much in their conversation the other day.

"I might have to take you up on that," Sienna said, despite the warning signs flashing in her brain. "For the purpose of the movie, of course. I can't keep fucking up this movie about your life now, can I?"

"The purpose doesn't matter to me," Justine said. "Just come over if and when you feel like it. I'll be here. I promise."

Sienna wanted to do much more than bridge the distance and disappear into Justine's arms. She wanted to kiss her and rip that T-shirt off. But she didn't.

"You're too kind," Sienna whispered instead of giving in to her baser urges. "Thank you. Really." Words couldn't express Sienna's gratitude for Justine helping her, but she had other ways of thanking Justine—a bank account full of them. "Maybe I'll see you tonight, then."

"I would like that." Justine moved her hand towards Sienna's face, but then retracted it, as if thinking better of what her instinct was telling her to do.

Sienna didn't want her to get the wrong idea—although she didn't really know what that was at that point—and slipped out of the bed she had slept so deliciously in.

CHAPTER 32

Sienna came back every night that week, always late, and always ready to go straight to bed. As soon as Justine closed her arms around her, Sienna's naked body relaxed against hers, and mere minutes later, Sienna's breathing slowed before settling into the most adorable purr. She was exhausted in every single way, that much was obvious.

Despite her father's sudden death, Sienna was a professional making a movie, and she wanted to do more than just a decent job. Those two things—grieving and playing Rochelle in *Gimme Shelter*—were clearly all she had energy for right now.

If Justine's only contribution was to let Sienna fall asleep in her arms each night, she would gladly oblige. She had patience. She had time. They could talk later.

But of course it moved her, in more ways than one, to hold a near-naked Sienna in her arms every single night. To push her breasts against Sienna's soft skin and feel the heat of her body radiate onto hers for hour after hour.

Justine was still madly—and maddeningly—in love with Sienna but, apart from turning up to sleep in her bed, and arms, every night, Sienna hadn't given any signs of wanting anything more from Justine.

It was Friday and if Sienna showed up tonight, she wouldn't have to rush off to the studio in the morning. They might find some time to talk tomorrow—they might even have breakfast together. Although sometimes Justine considered that it was to her advantage that Sienna didn't stick around for anything else than sleep, because it helped to curb the increasing urge to kiss her. Or to reach for her in the night, when their bodies had separated during sleep, and do so much more than just hold her.

Justine might have patience and time, she also has a wildly pulsing clit each night and surely Sienna must feel how hard her nipples grew when Justine pressed her breasts against her back?

Time ticked away and it was well past midnight when Justine stopped puttering about. She'd been keeping herself busy, waiting for Sienna, who still hadn't turned up. The evenings before, she had always texted to politely inquire if it was okay to come over, but Justine hadn't received a text yet tonight. Maybe Sienna had other plans tonight. Maybe she was out. Maybe she was with her family. Maybe she was fully rested. Or maybe—who knew?—she was on a date. Either way, her plans didn't include Justine which made perfect sense because Sienna had told her that she couldn't be with Justine. That it was too difficult. That she couldn't trust her.

Still, you didn't turn up at someone's house each night to sleep in their arms, as though it was the only place in the whole wide world where you could find some peace, and not have some sort of feelings for them. Signals were mixed and things were complicated. That was pretty much the story of Justine's life.

Because of Sienna's presence in her bed, Justine hadn't gotten enough sleep herself, and she was exhausted. She got ready for bed but kept her phone on, as always, and put it on the nightstand.

But Justine couldn't sleep. Not without Sienna in her bed. Not so much because she needed her there, but because she was worried. Sienna was fragile. Only a few days ago she had turned up at Justine's door in the middle of the night looking completely unhinged. Even though there was an explanation for that—severe sleep deprivation—there were a million other reasons why Sienna could go off the rails. There were the obvious ones that Justine knew about such as her father's death. And the woman she was seeing not turning up to the funeral. But it was the reasons Justine didn't know about that worried her the most. Because Justine knew what feelings that lurked under the surface could do—what they could make you do. She knew how vulnerability could make humans react in ways that weren't in their best interest because she witnessed the result of that every single day.

But she didn't want to call Sienna. She didn't want to put that kind of pressure on her. Nor did she have any claims to make. Sienna hadn't made her any promises—on the contrary— and Justine had offered her help freely and unconditionally. Worries after midnight were the price she had to pay.

Justine must have nodded off, despite her worries, because she was woken up by the doorbell. She hurried downstairs and, sure enough, Sienna stood in the doorway.

"Once again," Sienna said. "This isn't forgiveness." She all but pushed her way into Justine's house again, but instead of walking past Justine, she grabbed her by the shoulders, and pressed her against the nearest wall.

Sienna gazed at Justine through red-rimmed eyes—Sienna's pain had obviously gotten the better of her again.

"I didn't want to come, but now I can't stay the fuck away," Sienna whispered, before leaning in and touching her lips against Justine's.

Oh, fuck. Justine wanted to kiss her back so badly. And she did, but only for a short moment. Sienna was in no state to do this. She was obviously not herself. She was hurting and stressed because of the movie and all the scenes she still had to shoot. She was blowing off steam and it took all of Justine's willpower to say no, because all week long, she had craved this very thing. But this was not how she wanted to resolve the tension between her legs. Nor did she want it to be something that Sienna might regret tomorrow—that would be the hardest to bear.

Justine pulled back as much as she could while standing with her back against the wall.

"Let's talk," she said. But Sienna came for her again, pressed her lips against Justine's again.

"It's too late to talk," Sienna groaned in between kisses. "I don't want to talk."

"Okay." Justine put her hands between their bodies. "Time out. Stop."

Instantly, Sienna took a step back. The look of hurt dejection on her face was almost too much for Justine to bear.

"Let's take a breath," Justine said softly.

"I don't want to talk," Sienna repeated. She took a step back and crashed against the opposite wall. The hallway of Justine's house was so narrow that they were still standing close to each other. "I just don't want to feel like this anymore."

Justine closed the remaining distance between them. She took Sienna's hands in hers. "I know it's hard. I know that it hurts."

"I wasn't even that close to him. I don't get why it feels like I've been torn in half. Like a part of me is missing." Tears trickled down Sienna's cheeks.

"He was your father," Justine said. "He was a part of you and he always will be."

"I don't know what to do to feel better." Sienna's voice broke all the way.

"Can I hug you?" Justine asked.

"Please." Sienna's voice was barely audible, but Justine heard.

Justine folded her arms around Sienna and held her close.

Sienna put her head on Justine's shoulder and cried and cried.

Justine couldn't take away Sienna's pain, but she could offer her arms and all the tenderness she had inside her. Although tenderness may not be the perfect antidote for pain, it was the best place to start healing.

———

Sienna woke up with her head sore from all the crying she had done the night before. All those tears she was shedding for a man who had barely made time for her still didn't make much sense. But now that the shock of Bobby's death had subsided, it had left her surprisingly unsettled. Like a permanent dent had been inflicted on her previously carefree life—a hole in her soul that not even time could mend.

It was early and Justine was still sleeping. Sienna examined her still shape, her peaceful face, and it made her feel a little bit better. It made her feel as though, when all was said and done, she could learn to live with that dent. Being with Justine made her feel as though her soul, even with a big Bobby-shaped hole in it, might find unexpected ways to be all right. Because Justine was all kindness and patience, even after last night and how Sienna had turned up at her house—once again filled to the brim with hurt and demands.

When Sienna had started composing her usual text message to Justine to ask if she could sleep over, something had come over her. An unshakable urge to feel something other than all the nothingness inside her. Something, she knew, only Justine could provide. Something much more intimate than just sleeping in her arms.

Sienna realized she had gone about it the wrong way. Maybe she'd even deliberately sabotaged herself because she knew Justine would not respond to how strongly she was coming onto her—although you never knew with Justine. She presented as the epitome of being dependable only to not show up at your father's funeral.

Perhaps it could have gone either way, but Justine had put a stop to it immediately. In hindsight, it was a good thing, because Sienna hadn't been thinking clearly. She seemed to have lost that ability ever since she got that dreadful call about her dad. Because how could you possibly think clearly, or expect to have a logical, sane thought ever again, when a person's life could be over in the blink of an eye? When her dad could be alive one second and be gone the very next. When nothing made sense any longer.

Justine turned on her side toward Sienna, and Sienna was engulfed with a wave of something. She didn't know if she was still in love with Justine. Probably. Why else was she here? Why else had she tried to kiss her last night? But Sienna didn't trust her own thoughts, let alone her feelings. Nothing about her could be trusted right now.

With her eyes still closed, Justine reached for Sienna. She put a warm hand on Sienna's belly, then slid it over her side, onto Sienna's back.

Sienna might be grieving, might be experiencing a brand-new kind of pain in her life, but she also knew that Justine was the one who made it more bearable. Justine not only helped her sleep—she did so much more than that. Maybe that's why Sienna had tried to get it on with her last night. Her body, once recovered from the shock, had not stopped wanting Justine. If anything, it wanted more of her. And soon, only Justine's arms around her would no longer suffice. Justine might have stopped their kiss—and rightly so—but something else hung in the air.

Sienna scooted closer to Justine, until their bare breasts touched. A flutter stirred in her belly. Maybe, last night, Sienna had just followed her gut. And yes, she had been too aggressive, but Justine had just stopped her—she hadn't turned Sienna away. She hadn't asked her to leave.

Justine's eyes were still closed so she was presumably still sleeping, yet her hand tightened around Sienna's waist. Maybe she was dreaming. Maybe even of this.

Sienna couldn't possibly know that, so she quickly dismissed the thought of making Justine's potential dream come true. All she could do was wait for Justine to wake. But Justine had slipped her hand around Sienna's waist, so Sienna could do the same to her. She did. Their bodies pressed closer together and it was a natural movement for Sienna to position her head just above Justine's breast. It was a hell of a lot more than the naked-but-chaste spooning they'd been doing all week, yet it felt, to Sienna, exactly as things should be.

"Hmm," Justine groaned low in her throat, making Sienna wonder whether she was really still asleep.

"Are you awake?" Sienna whispered.

"Hmm," Justine replied, then shifted so her lips were dangerously close to Sienna's.

Next thing Sienna knew, Justine's lips were on hers. Justine was kissing her. Half asleep or not, Sienna kissed her back. Sleepwalking might be real, but Sienna had never heard of sleep-kissing before.

Justine's hand slid from Sienna's back to her belly, then, deliciously, up to her breast. Oh, Justine was very much awake. Maybe she didn't want to acknowledge it. Maybe she needed this to happen in that fuzzy dreamlike state between being asleep and awake. Justine cupped Sienna's breast and slipped her tongue inside Sienna's mouth.

It was all Sienna wanted. It was what she needed. She craved Justine's soft skin. Her deft, unique touch. Sienna had missed it so much, she instantly wondered why she had denied herself this. Why she had denied herself Justine. Because if anyone could make her feel the tiniest bit better, it was Justine Blackburn—and her alone.

Justine skated her thumb along Sienna's rock-hard nipple, then let her hand travel down. Instinctively, Sienna rolled onto her back and spread her legs. God, how she wanted Justine.

How she wanted to feel her fingers inside her. How she wanted to feel something else than all this grief and pain she'd so suddenly been saddled with. Not just for her dad, but for Justine letting her down when she needed her the most. But none of that mattered right now, because Justine's fingers were traveling down still, slowly but securely, to exactly where Sienna wanted them.

"Fuck me, please," Sienna whispered. "Oh fuck, Justine, I need you."

Justine's fingers slid between Sienna's legs. If she could, Sienna would spread farther, but she was already spreading as wide as she could. For Justine. But also for herself. Just as the warm embrace of Justine's arms around her had helped her sleep, maybe this could help her heal. Or at least help her some-how, if only by being connected to another human being, by feeling alive instead of numb for a few moments, by experi-encing the closeness of intimacy and the power of a climax delivered by someone who—unmistakably—cared for her.

Justine gently stroked Sienna between her legs, her finger-tips featherlight and oh-so controlled, making Sienna aware of how fully awake she must be. This was not the handiwork of someone half asleep. Justine kissed her way from Sienna's lips to her neck, then to her ear.

"I'm here for whatever you need," she whispered, then pushed herself up and looked Sienna straight in the eye as she, gently and slowly—as was her way—slipped her fingers inside Sienna. As she did—again—what Sienna had asked of her. As she fucked her.

Sienna's breath stalled and, with it, all the agony that had been eating her from within came to a stop as well. It disap-peared to a place from where it could no longer hurt her. Because Sienna was captured in Justine's tender gaze, by the smooth strokes of her fingers, and the nimble positioning of her thumb over her clit. There was no room for anything else, espe-cially not for pain and grief. Effortlessly, Justine took her back to the time when Sienna's father had still been alive. When she and Bobby, although estranged, still had all the time in the world to get to know each other. To forge a better father-daughter bond. To, quite simply, be better at being a parent and a child. Everything was still possible because Justine was doing the one thing that was impossible. She stopped time. When she looked into Sienna's eyes, with all that love so brazenly, so easily, on display in her face, she made the minutes stop. Justine had that power. And Sienna loved her for it.

It didn't take long—not nearly long enough—for Sienna's body to surrender to Justine's touch, but most of all to her attention, to her care and focus and understanding. To all that she had given Sienna from the instant she had come knocking on her door.

Justine's fingers were no match for Sienna's exhausted body, her defenses crumbling as though made out of water instead of something stronger.

Sienna came hard and loud and with her muscles shuddering at Justine's hands. Of course she did. Such was Justine's power over her.

CHAPTER 33

Sienna lay with her head in the crook of Justine's arm. When Sienna had reached for Justine earlier, when she wasn't fully awake yet, Justine hadn't been able to resist. Sienna's intention might have been the same as last night, but the gesture had been so different. Neither one of them seemed to regret what had just happened—Justine certainly didn't.

"When I saw you at Min-ji's with Marcy," Sienna said, "I was so jealous."

Justine chuckled softly, making Sienna's head bounce up and down a little, but she didn't say anything else. She wanted to let Sienna talk. To let her say whatever she wanted to say in this delicate post-orgasmic moment.

"I was jealous of this improbable giantess with the most impressive shoulders I've ever seen," Sienna mused. "The possibility that you might be on a date with her drove me mad."

"A date? Really?" Justine could no longer keep quiet when she heard something preposterous like that.

"You never know," Sienna whispered, her voice growing small again.

"Maybe not," Justine said, "but I hope you know now."

Sienna's chin bumped against Justine's chest as she nodded.

A silence fell. Despite everything that had happened, it was glorious to have Sienna lie in her arms like that. It felt right. Like the only possible way to spend a Saturday morning although, as usual, Justine had a million things to do. But for Sienna, she would make time. She would take the hours she was unable to give her on the day of her dad's funeral and multiply them by a thousand, and give all of them to Sienna from now on.

In the end, Justine didn't need to hatch a plan to get Sienna to come back to her. She had come back of her own accord. First, to sleep. Then, last night, for more.

"I'm sorry for coming on so strong. That was not okay," Sienna said softly while her hand drifted up and down Justine's belly—driving Justine insane with lust.

"Nothing I can't handle." Justine tried to make her voice sound normal.

"You can handle anything and understand everything," Sienna said.

"Not true." Justine's voice had shot all the way up. "Because right now I'm having big trouble handling your fingers on my skin like that."

"Oh, really?" Sienna dipped her fingers lower, stroking Justine's belly.

Justine could only reply with a sharp intake of breath. All week, the tension in her body had been building. A week of Sienna sleeping in her arms, her skin warm and inviting against hers. Justine had plenty of understanding, but she really couldn't handle much more of this. Especially not after making —and watching—Sienna come earlier.

"Are you sure you have time for this?" Sienna's fingers skated lower, to an inch above Justine's clit. "I know you are a very busy woman. You must have better things to do than this." Sienna removed her hand from Justine's belly and brought it to her lips. She sucked the tip of her index finger into her mouth, making a smacking sound, then lowered her hand again. Ever

234

so softly, she placed her moist fingertip right next to Justine's clit.

"I couldn't be more sure," Justine said.

"I had no idea you were into muscle chicks like Marcy." Sienna drew a slow circle around Justine's clit. "What are you doing with the likes of me?"

"Oh, fuck." Justine wasn't really listening anymore to what Sienna was saying. Maybe she really had been jealous. Maybe it had played its part in Sienna turning up at her door like that. Either way, Justine would much prefer it if Sienna stopped talking now—especially about Marcy. She knew the perfect way to make that happen. "I need your mouth," she groaned. "I want your tongue."

Sienna turned on her side and found Justine's ear with her lips. "I'll give you much more than that," she breathed into Justine's ear.

Her finger was still circling and Justine was highly combustible, but she could wait for that utterly divine moment when Sienna's tongue touched against her clit. She had dreamed of it a couple of times too many when Sienna lay sleeping in her arms, but she was only human. She had feelings and urges too. And Sienna was gorgeous. Her body wasn't all muscle tone and hard abs like Marcy's, that much was true, but it was luscious and sexy and deliciously soft in all the right places—and Justine couldn't get enough of it.

Sienna kissed a path down Justine's neck. She paused at Justine's breasts to plant kisses on her nipples, and leave a trail of moistness on Justine's skin, leaving it ultra-sensitive.

Justine let her knees fall apart for Sienna, so she could take position. Sienna maneuvered between her legs, her braids fanning out over her belly and thighs. Somehow, between the curtain of her hair, she managed to find Justine's gaze. It made Justine's clit pulse extra hard with desire.

Sienna looked away again and kissed Justine's inner thighs. Teasingly slow, as though she had a mile of distance to cover instead of the tiniest stretch of skin, Sienna's lips made their way to Justine's clit. When she finally reached the spot, Sienna didn't touch down immediately. Justine could feel her hot breath on her. She could feel how Sienna waited, how she drove Justine totally crazy.

But then the moment had finally come—the moment Justine had not dared to believe would ever arrive again. Sienna's tongue skated against her wildly pulsing clit, and Justine could finally surrender. She could finally let go. She could let her own tears stream down her cheeks—just this once.

For all the confusion in her brain about what this was. For all that she had lost and all the love she had been denied, but had also denied herself and others.

Was this love? It sure felt like it. But if it was, why did Justine allow herself to give in to it now? Why wasn't she protecting herself? And even if it was love, this didn't mean that she and Sienna were dating again or would ever get back together.

Justine might have bottomless reserves of understanding because she knew how devastating life could be, but she got confused too. Her feelings for Sienna perplexed her. She usually didn't let things get this far—Marcy had been a stark reminder of that. She had fucked up with Sienna as well, yet the tip of Sienna's tongue was driving her to greater heights as the seconds ticked away. Maybe they were just two people who needed each other at this specific time in their lives. Justine didn't know. She had no clue. All she knew was that, with just a few more divine strokes of her tongue, Sienna was about to make her come.

"Oh, baby," Justine groaned, digging her fingertips into the flesh of Sienna's shoulders. "Oh, fuck." It was so easy—too easy —to surrender to Sienna's touch. To everything about Sienna. And maybe Justine did know, even though it scared her more than anything.

This *was* love.

She may come to regret it, but she loved Sienna. She loved who she was and what she stood for. She loved the depths of her dark gaze and that flicker of light in it, earlier, when she came. She loved how she was so unafraid to get what she wanted. She loved how she played Rochelle. She loved the sound of her gentle snoring when she slept in Justine's arms. She loved all those things about Sienna in such a way that she had a hard time imagining her life without it.

More than anything, right now, she loved the pure pleasure Sienna was giving her. Because she was very good at that. Just as that bubble of tension dissolved in Justine's belly, as it transformed into a joyous sparkle spreading throughout her entire body, Sienna gave her the 'much more' she had promised earlier. She slipped her fingers inside Justine, intensifying her climax, stretching it out, wave after delicious wave, until Justine's body sank into the mattress, drained but utterly satisfied.

Sienna wiped off her mouth with the back of her hand and the sight was so sexy, so lustful and brazen, it made Justine want her all over again, despite being totally spent.

"Come here," Justine said, not caring that her cheeks were still wet with tears. "I need to tell you something."

Sienna crawled into her arms and looked at her.

"I'm more in love with you than ever before," Justine said.

She watched how Sienna swallowed hard. She didn't say anything back, not that Justine expected her to. Sienna looked her in the eye, though. She wasn't one to avert her gaze when it mattered—another something Justine loved about her. Seconds ticked away in a silence that grew more and more strained.

"We should probably talk now," Sienna said, instantly sucking all the romance out of the air—and dashing most of Justine's hope.

"I didn't say that to pressure you into anything," Justine was quick to say. "It was probably just that climax talking." Ah, there was good old Justine again. Where had she been hiding the past few days? The past few weeks and months since she'd met Sienna and let herself get carried away like that?

"I need a shower." As though suddenly in a hurry, Sienna jumped out of bed and rushed into the bathroom.

Maybe it's for the best, Justine thought. Because despite meaning every word of what she'd just said to Sienna—and the love she felt for her—Justine also knew herself. She knew all too well she wasn't cut out for this and, obviously, Sienna had caught on to that as well.

CHAPTER 34

"The thing is," Sienna said, trying to reproduce the speech she had put together in her head while in the shower, "that I can't be trusted either right now. I'm grieving and I'm all over the place." She took a slow sip of coffee. "Clearly, I'm drawn to you."

Like a moth to a fucking flame. Sienna couldn't stay away. She couldn't even sleep in a bed that Justine wasn't in. "And I have feelings for you. Of course I do. But..." *It's all just such a mess right now.* "I don't expect you to change for me. I don't expect that of anyone. I've learned from having the father that I had that is a completely unrealistic expectation." Sienna looked away from Justine. From her kind blue gaze and her hair that always looked so sexy when she just got out of the shower, all wet and slicked back, accentuating her high cheekbones. "But I also don't expect myself to change. I don't want to go into too much psychobabble about this but, probably because of my absent daddy issues, I need to come first. I certainly don't want to feel like I'm in a contest for your attention with underprivileged kids. Because that makes me a terrible person. Maybe I am a terrible person. The point is that I don't want to be ques-

239

tioning that about myself every other day just because I am with you."

"You are not a terrible person," Justine said. "Trust me, I've come across plenty of those and you are absolutely not one of them."

"I know I'm not, but that didn't stop me from feeling like I was after the funeral." She rolled her eyes, mostly at herself. "I'm so over that. It's fine. I get it. You had to be there for Ashleigh. But I can't ignore how it made me feel when you weren't there." She shook her head. "And I do forgive you. Of course, I forgive you, even though I said last night that this wasn't forgiveness. I have forgiven you, because this is who you are and that's not something you need to be forgiven for. Both you and Rochelle warned me about this and I ignored it because I was attracted to you and then I was falling in love with you and you were always there. I had no reason to believe it was even true. Until I did."

Sienna took a breath. Was she making this too complicated because she couldn't think straight? She was here, for crying out loud. What was she even doing at Justine's house if she didn't want to be with her? Being with Justine, being in her physical presence, in her arms and in her bed, was exactly what she wanted. It was what came after that scared her to death. It was the possible future hurt she couldn't deal with right now. Not when she was still reeling from her dad's death. The prospect of it was simply too much.

Justine rose and walked over to Sienna. She went to stand behind her as she sat at the counter and put her fingertips against the sides of Sienna's head. "It's been a lot, and you might be getting a bit lost in here." Justine gently swept her fingertips along Sienna's temples. "I think what we have is not very rational," Justine whispered, but her voice was clear —commanding even. "Last week, when you couldn't sleep, your body brought you here. Your deepest self made you come here. Listen to your body instead of all of those thoughts in your head. Most of the time, our body knows best."

Even after what Sienna had just said, confessing to her doubts about being with Justine after she'd welcomed her into her home and her bed every single day, Justine's empathy knew no bounds. She let the back of her head fall against Justine's chest.

"How about…" Justine massaged Sienna's head. "We just take it day by day? What else can we do, anyway?" She slanted forward so she could meet Sienna's gaze. "Walk away from this?"

Fuck no, Sienna thought. She wasn't walking away from this. She was keeping Justine firmly in the center of her life. Sienna shook her head. "I get the feeling you wouldn't let me walk away," she joked, just to lighten the mood, then tilted her head back so she could see Justine's expression.

"That's not true. Do whatever you feel is right for you, but I meant what I said earlier." There was not a hint of a smile on Justine's face.

I'm more in love with you than ever before. The words might as well be etched into Sienna's brain. For some reason, they had scared the living daylights out of her. Sienna tilted her head forward, away from Justine's gaze, and took a breath. She was in love with Justine as well, but both of them having strong feelings for each other wasn't as simple, as straightforward, as two plus two equaling four. There was so much else at play here. And Sienna's head was still a mess.

"Okay." Sienna nodded and pushed herself out of the chair. She turned to fully face Justine, to look her in the eye when she said, "One day at a time. Let's do that."

Then Justine's phone rang—of course, it did.

Justine checked the screen. "It's Darrel. Is it okay if I take this?" she asked, as though Sienna would say no to that or, even if she did, Justine would listen.

Sienna just nodded and watched Justine take the call. She

listened to how she spoke to Darrel, her voice this peculiar blend of worry and efficiency. And Sienna realized that she hadn't just fallen in love with the parts of Justine that were endlessly understanding, always kind, and oh-so hard to resist. She had fallen in love with the whole person, and that included her full commitment to the shelter and to the kids who stayed there. Come to think of it, it was a huge part of what drew her to Justine because it made up most of her personality. Of who she was. Sienna didn't get to pick and choose which bits of Justine she loved. As with everyone else—with her dad, but also her mother and her sister and her friends—it was all or nothing. Besides, she had plenty of flaws herself—such as, also not unlike her dad, the unshakable need to come first in someone else's life.

"Do you happen to feel like making someone's day?" Justine had hung up and smiled broadly at Sienna.

"If you put it like that, it's hard to say no." That was the other thing about Justine. Even though the Rainbow Shelter housed kids in precarious circumstances, the place made her light up like nothing else. It gave her strength and purpose. It made her stand taller than she already was.

"A surprise visit from Sienna Bright would most certainly make Ashleigh's day," Justine said.

———

Before meeting Justine, even after having signed up to play Rochelle in *Gimme Shelter*, Sienna would never have considered visiting a homeless kid in hospital. The thought had simply never occurred to her. Now, on their way back from seeing Ashleigh, Sienna's smile was just as big and persistent as Ashleigh's had been when Sienna had walked into her room. All Sienna had to do was show her face for Ashleigh to light all the way up. And that for a kid who'd been through hell and was a psychiatric inpatient. Ashleigh didn't have too much to smile about, yet she hadn't been able to stop smiling at Sienna.

"Thanks for coming." Justine put a hand on Sienna's knee. "Ashleigh was over the moon."

"Honestly, it was my pleasure." Sienna pointed at her lips. "Have you seen the smile on my face?"

"You enjoy making other people happy." Justine gave Sienna's knee a quick squeeze. "I told you that you were the opposite of a terrible person."

Sienna did, indeed, feel the opposite of terrible. She felt as though, just for a few hours, the blow that life had recently dealt her might be manageable. Especially if she could find more opportunities to get her head out of her own ass. Making a vulnerable teenager grin from ear to ear was a hell of an antidote against wallowing in her grief. It also made her understand Justine's irrepressible can-do attitude about everything. It was right there in the *Gimme Shelter* script and now Sienna witnessed it in real-life action. Justine had saved herself by saving others. Helping others, helped Justine. And Sienna had made the mistake to hold that very thing against her.

Sienna put her hand over Justine's. "I'm sorry for giving you such a hard time about you not being at my dad's funeral."

"You really don't need to apologize." Justine gave her a quick look. "Your father died and, well, for lack of a better word, I was your… girlfriend. My place was there, with you."

"My *girlfriend*?"

"I did say for lack of a better word." Justine stopped at a red light. She looked sideways at Sienna and shot her one of her crooked grins.

"And that for someone who usually has no lack of words." Sienna grinned right back.

"What does that mean?" The light turned green and Justine accelerated. "I always thought of myself as a woman of action more than words."

"Even though you were my *girlfriend*." Sienna brought her

hand to the back of Justine's neck. "I get why you couldn't be there." She caressed the soft skin of Justine's neck. "I get why you do what you do. Why you put all this energy into it. It's everything to you."

"You're pretty important to me too." Justine leaned the back of her head against Sienna's hand. "You are my ex-girlfriend, after all."

"I don't feel like your ex at all. Especially not after this morning."

"That's because you're not." Justine focused on the road, but the vibe in the car intensified. "You're so much more than my ex-girlfriend. You're very special to me."

For now, Sienna thought, it was more than enough. The only thing she could do was wait and see where taking it day-by-day would lead them. She didn't even know where Justine was driving them right now, let alone where they would end up together in the next few weeks. And there was no talk of being *girlfriends* again just yet.

CHAPTER 35

To be at the wrap party of a movie about her life was already absurd enough for Justine, but to be there with Sienna Bright, who was playing her ex, was beyond surreal.

Whether they were actually each other's girlfriend—whether Justine could ever really be someone's girlfriend—was up in the air, but what was more than obvious was that they enjoyed each other's company. They spent most of their spare time together—and every single night in each other's arms.

They didn't waste a lot of that precious time talking, but Justine felt it in every cell of her body. When Sienna so much as rang her doorbell, her stomach flip-flopped. When she kissed her, Justine knew no one else's kiss would ever do again. All the while, they did as they had agreed. They let the days pass, lived their lives, and grew closer.

Sometimes, Justine had to cancel a date. Other times, instead of rushing to the shelter the way she'd always done, she asked Darrel to handle an emergency that previously she would have believed only she could deal with. Darrel would finish their management course next week and as their graduation present, Justine was giving them a larger chunk of responsibility as well as a pay rise—thanks to Bobby Bright's donation. The shelter was still everything to her, but Sienna was quickly becoming equally important.

A hush went through the crowd at the party. They were being silenced.

"Time for the director's speech," Rochelle said to Justine.

Mimi St James stepped onto the stage, microphone in hand. She'd never looked the way Justine had imagined a director would, and she certainly didn't tonight. She was dressed in a stark white pants suit, a fuchsia blouse underneath, all no doubt costing more than a month's worth of Justine's salary.

Mimi thanked the cast and crew profusely for all their hard work the past few months, then paused to smile before continuing.

"Directing a movie was my childhood dream. I've wanted to become a director since I was a teenage movie nerd. I became a lot of other things in my life. A mother. A TV show producer. Nora Levine's lesbian lover." Everyone laughed at that, Justine included. "And it was Nora who planted the seed in my mind that, just because I'm in my sixties, it's not too late for my teenage dream to come true. It was also Nora who came up with the idea for this movie." Even Justine felt a twinge of emotion as she witnessed how Mimi gazed so lovingly at Nora. The things love could do—the very thing Justine had run away from for such a long time. Until it came knocking on her door so brazenly, so irrevocably, that she could no longer ignore it.

"But, of course, this movie wouldn't exist without its amazing subject." Mimi fixed her gaze on Justine now. "I know you're not fond of the spotlight, Justine, so I'll be brief. But make no mistake, me being brief does not mean my appreciation for you, for what you do, and everything you stand for— the message you send every single day by tirelessly doing what you do—is any less. On the contrary. I am merely the director of *Gimme Shelter*, but you are its undisputed star. Let's give it up for Justine Blackburn, everyone!"

"Whoop," Rochelle shouted next to Justine.

On her other side, Sienna grabbed her hand.

Justine felt more than a twinge of emotion now. Nothing about this movie had gone as she had expected. Instead of mostly ignoring that there was a movie, and instead of getting on with her life, Justine had spent a lot of time on set. She'd cried bitter tears while watching some of the scenes. She'd felt her heart open a fraction and perhaps it was no coincidence that, as her defenses had stretched and then softened, Justine had fallen in love with Sienna Bright—helplessly and recklessly so. Against all expectations, she was secretly looking forward to watching the finished product.

Justine did what she wasn't very good at. She accepted the applause. Not because of her so-called accomplishments, but because of who she was now as opposed to on that day when Alexis Dalton and Sienna Bright had first come to Rochelle's house. Because of how this movie had changed some significant aspects of her life. Because, girlfriends or not, she and Sienna were in a relationship.

Because Justine was in love.

————

They were at Sienna's apartment and, as she always did now, Sienna took a moment in front of a picture of her dad on the sideboard.

"How are you feeling?" Justine asked.

"I'm sad that he's not going to see our movie." Sienna had referred to *Gimme Shelter* a couple of times as 'our movie' now, and Justine had stopped correcting her. It didn't even bother her that much anymore. "And that he'll never get to know you."

Justine had only met Bobby briefly and talked to him on the phone once, but she'd forever be grateful to him for two huge accomplishments in his too-short life: donating all that money to the Rainbow Shelter and fathering Sienna Bright.

"Yeah. It's sad and unfair." Justine beckoned Sienna over to her.

Sienna crashed next to her on the couch and lay down with her legs dangling over the side and her head in Justine's lap.

"How are *you* feeling after that wrap party?" Sienna gazed up at Justine.

"It was okay." A strange sensation that she couldn't really place had started creeping up on Justine from time to time. "I quite enjoyed it, actually." She suspected that, in that dark, shadowy place where she preferred to bury a lot of her feelings, she might actually feel something akin to pride. Because that movie had reminded her how far she'd come. Justine had literally seen her own past come to life before her very eyes.

"Remember when I said we'd walk that red carpet together?" Sienna smiled up at her.

"I don't know much about the movie industry, but I do know a hell of a lot of time passes between wrapping a movie and the premiere."

"This one is low on the special effects, but yeah," Sienna mused. "I'm fully expecting some reshoots. I wasn't always at the top of my game."

"How long do you reckon? Ballpark?" Justine didn't have a clue about the actual time frame.

"Six months minimum, but it could be longer." Sienna waggled her eyebrows. "Either way, no matter what happens to us, we'll both be there."

Justine nodded. "Let's hope we'll still be on speaking terms."

"On much more than speaking terms." Sienna looked deep into Justine's eyes, and Justine knew what that look meant. Their hunger for each other had only grown. Justine couldn't possibly imagine no longer speaking to Sienna, for whatever reason. But life was wholly unpredictable, that much she also knew.

Justine bowed and kissed Sienna's forehead. "If I remember

correctly, you said it would be an honor to walk the red carpet with me." She broke into a grin. "That honor would be very mutual."

Sienna's gaze softened, and the hunger in her eyes changed into something else. "Can I tell you what would be an even bigger honor for me?"

"Of course." Justine couldn't wipe that grin off her face even if she wanted to.

Sienna took her sweet time saying whatever she was going to say. She gazed into Justine's eyes. If she was trying to convey with that look that she was crazy in love with Justine, it was working. If she was trying to say something else, Justine was missing it completely—her brain was too saturated with the hormones unleashed at this stage of infatuation.

"If you told me something about your parents," Sienna said.

Way to kill the mood. Someone might as well have just placed a glass dome over them, robbing the room of all oxygen in one fell swoop.

But instead of reacting, Justine took a breath. She had experience with this question and *Gimme Shelter* had only increased that experience the past two years. Being a part of this movie was always going to raise questions.

"I wish I'd been there when Nora was shooting her scenes," Sienna said. "I know you were there, babe. How did it make you feel?"

Justine understood that Sienna had questions. She was in the movie, she was dating Justine, and she'd just lost a parent.

"It didn't make me feel anything," Justine said, truthfully. "It was strange to see Nora Levine play my mother. A hell of a lot weirder than seeing Alexis play me, and that's already been such a trip. But I don't have any residual feelings for my parents and I honestly don't know if they're still alive." Justine could only assume that someone, although she didn't know who, would let her know when her parents died. She couldn't predict how it would make her feel, but she suspected not a whole lot.

"I also don't care. They might as well not be my parents because I clearly stopped being their child." While your child should be the most precious thing in your life. "It was their choice, not mine. I came to terms with that a long time ago."

"What were they like… before?" Sienna was a bit too curious to Justine's liking, but it was easy enough to cut her some slack.

"I guess these days you would call it bougie." Justine was used to joking about them. When she'd had to describe her parents to Charlie for the screenplay, she'd gone about it the same way—perhaps the only way. "But the worst kind, you know? Everything had to look a certain way for the outside world." Justine shook her head. "The right kind of clothes and the right kind of car. Until my twelfth birthday, my mother made me wear a dress every single day, even though I made sure she knew how much I hated wearing them. That kind of stupid, pretentious bullshit." Justine ran her fingers through Sienna's braids. It soothed her, and perhaps allowed her to continue more easily. "They were always so formal with each other, like they were business associates more than a married couple. With me as well. There wasn't a huge amount of love on display, only a lot of expectations and, well, disappointment, I guess." None of this still agitated Justine. "I came out to them in a fit of blind rage. God, I was so angry back then. I was a typical teenager. All out-of-control fury and feeling misunderstood. Although I have no idea who I got my rebellious streak from. I have no idea where I get any of my personality traits from. I always felt like such a stranger in my own family. Like I couldn't believe these two uptight hypocrites made me." Justine looked into Sienna's beautiful face. "I wanted to leave home as soon as I could, but I wasn't ready when they kicked me out. I was hoping college would be my big escape, but I didn't even graduate high school. They didn't give me the chance."

"I'm so sorry." Sienna reached up her hand and found Justine's. "Thank you for telling me."

Justine shrugged. "It's all going to be in *that fucking movie.*"

"*Our* movie." Sienna squeezed her hand.

"I think Mimi might disagree with you calling it that." Justine was more than ready for a change of subject.

"Maybe." Sienna narrowed her eyes. "Did you really only agree to it for the money?"

"Of course, what other reason could I have had?" Justine intertwined her fingers with Sienna's. "When I said yes, I didn't yet know that Sienna Bright was going to play Rochelle, otherwise that would have definitely swayed me much earlier."

Sienna chuckled. "I know for a fact that you'd never heard of me before I was cast. You certainly hadn't seen any of my movies."

"I've seen them all now." Some even more than once.

"You didn't agree to the movie because, deep down, you were hoping for some sort of closure?"

"Closure of what?" Justine shook her head. "I made my peace with what happened a long time ago. I don't need a movie for that. I did it for the money because funding a homeless shelter for queer kids is very expensive."

"You do realize that I'm hella rich now, right? Half of Bobby's money puts me in the 1%."

"Good for you."

"Once all the paperwork is done, I will definitely donate more to the shelter."

"Really?" Justine's insides fluttered like a field of butterflies in the wind. "I do vividly remember that's how you seduced me last time, but you've already got me now."

Sienna burst out laughing. "There's so much to unpack from what you just said, but I choose to only focus on that I've got you."

"You have." She bowed down again, to kiss Sienna fully on the lips this time. "You've totally got me," she whispered, before letting her tongue slip into Sienna's mouth.

CHAPTER 36

"Come with me if you don't believe me," Sienna said to her sister. "We sure can use the extra pair of hands."

"*We?*" Taissa gave her a look.

"All of us at the Rainbow Shelter." They were sitting in their parents' back yard. Sienna was telling her sister all about the virtues of volunteering. But Taissa wasn't sleeping with the shelter's founder, nor did she seem to need something extra—something different and good for the soul—to help her get over their father's death.

"What do you even do there?" Taissa asked. "You're hardly the type to be cleaning toilets."

"There's nothing wrong with cleaning toilets," Sienna said, despite never having cleaned one in her life. "But the shelter's not a hotel. There's a strict chore rotation system. The residents do most of their own cleaning."

Taissa gave her the kind of look Sienna had to respond to—all skeptical and full of judgment.

"What?"

"That's exactly what I should be asking you." The skepticism in Taissa's eyes softened.

"Why?"

"Is it official now? You've gone back to her? After what she did?"

I need her, Sienna thought, but she wasn't going to admit that to her sister. "Justine... she helps me. Being with her makes me feel better. She helps me cope with dad's death better. Being with her makes me feel as though Bobby dying doesn't have to tear me to pieces every day."

Taissa shook her head. "She wasn't there for you on the only day she had to be there. I will never understand that. Maybe you have forgiven her, but I can't just do that." Taissa pursed her lips. "Please don't tell me what she did to you that you forgave her so easily for letting you down like that. It must have been spectacular but, as your sister, I don't want to know."

"I'm still in love with her." Sienna had no trouble admitting that.

Taissa expelled a long sigh. "I know there's no such thing as reasoning with a woman in love, but are you sure she's right for you? She's a lot older, for starters and, well, clearly not very dependable."

"Of course, I'm not sure and of course Justine's not perfect." Although, Sienna thought, maybe Justine's exactly the person she needs to be. "Neither am I. Neither are you, for that matter. No one is." Sienna's heart grew a size in her chest. "But I do know that she's kind and patient and wise." As well as stubborn and messy and often late, Sienna didn't add out loud. "She's so special, Tai. Yeah, she's in her fifties and absolutely nothing's more important to her than the shelter, but I know in here"—Sienna dramatically tapped her chest—"that I *can* depend on her." Night after night of sleeping in Justine's soft embrace had taught Sienna that. "I have to believe that and I do." Justine was also endlessly fascinating and there were parts of her that Sienna might never get to know, might not even scratch the surface of, even though, at times, Justine had started to open up more about her past.

"God, you really are a smitten kitten."

"Meow." An inadvertent grin tugged at Sienna's lips. "I think that once you see this movie, you will understand Justine more."

"I don't want to have to see a movie to know that my sister is dating someone good for her. That's not how this works." Taissa sent her a soft smile. "I know you're in pain and Justine is probably there for you in ways that your family can't be, but if she hurts you again, I swear, she will have to answer to me. And to Mom!"

"Aren't you in pain?" Sienna'd had enough of defending her renewed connection with Justine to her sister. She didn't know where it was going; she only knew what she felt on any given day. And every morning, Sienna wanted to spend more time with Justine. That was the only thing she was certain of.

Taissa huffed out some air. "Bobby's death affects me, no doubt, but, honestly, I often thought of him more as my sperm donor than my dad. We weren't close like you and him, if you could even call that close. We didn't have a big thing in common like acting. How can I miss someone I barely saw? Someone who hardly made time for me, or his grandkids for that matter? He was a shit dad, no matter how you twist or turn it. He was never there. And when he was, he always made me feel like he had something much better to do than spend time with me." Taissa shrugged. "All of that may be terribly disrespectful, but that's the honest truth of how I feel."

Sienna could hardly argue with Taissa's statement that Bobby had been a shit dad, but his death had ripped something apart deep inside her nevertheless. Justine understood this, without Sienna having to explain. Justine understood everything and, in her arms only, Sienna could feel something resembling whole again.

"He did leave you a humongous wad of cash," Sienna said. "What are you going to do with all that money?"

Taissa shook her head. "I don't know. Set up a trust for the kids, I guess."

"Did you know that dad gave a quarter mil to the Rainbow Shelter before he died?"

"No, but it doesn't surprise me." Taissa all but rolled her eyes. "He was buying your love. It's all so transparent. He'd rather give us a million bucks than spend a holiday with us. It's so quintessentially Bobby."

"He visited the *Gimme Shelter* set a few days before he died," Sienna said, remembering how much Bobby-being-Bobby had annoyed her at the time. "He called me out of the blue and turned up fifteen minutes later. Just like that."

"He was putting on his I'm-such-a-regular-and-caring-dad act. He was a really good actor, you have to give him that."

"He did care for us, Tai." Tears pricked behind Sienna's eyes again.

"That may be so, but if he did, how was I to know? He certainly never told me and the only way he ever showed me was by paying for everything."

"You never refused the money he gave you." Just like a penthouse for Sienna, Bobby had bought Taissa a huge mansion in Brentwood.

"Why would I refuse the only thing he could give me? I tried with him so many times. And he broke my heart over and over again. Some people are not meant to parent and Bobby was one of them. I'm fine with that. I had Mom and Eddy and you. But I'm not going to spend my time grieving a man who never made time for me. And I will spend the money he left me with a big smile on my face."

"A big 'Bright' smile," Sienna said, repeating one of their dad's favorite things to say.

"A big fucking Bobby Bright smile." A shadow crossed Taissa's face.

She probably loved Bobby more than she would ever admit, and she'd inherited some of his emotional avoidance behavior —although Taissa never bailed on you or flaked at the last minute. And she was a hell of a mother.

"What are you going to do with all your dough?" Taissa asked.

"I have some ideas." Sienna had been mulling things over in her head and she needed to speak to her financial advisor before she could set things up but, if it was up to her—and thanks to Bobby—the Rainbow Shelter wouldn't have to worry about funding for a very long time to come. "Mostly charity. I'll let you know."

"You're not going to give all of Bobby's money to Justine, are you?" Taissa was as straightforward as they came—she got that from their mom.

"Justine is not the shelter," Sienna replied.

"Could have fooled me with how she left you alone at the church, when you were burying your father, for an emergency at *her* shelter."

"I get your reaction. I'm also sensitive to someone not showing up when you need them most. It's trademark Bobby stuff. But Justine is nothing like Bobby, I can assure you that, Tai."

"I'll have to take your word for it." Taissa's gaze had gone soft like melted butter. "I'm also not blind. I can see that she makes you feel better." Taissa reached for her glass of wine and lifted it toward Sienna. "To Bobby," she said.

"To dad, may he rest in peace." Sienna clinked her glass against her sister's. And to Justine, she thought, who's the only person who can give me a modicum of peace right now.

CHAPTER 37

Because Sienna was independently wealthy, she always scheduled a few months off after wrapping a movie. She wasn't like her dad, who had still believed, after decades at the top, that his career would be over if he didn't book back-to-back projects. Bobby Bright had been a textbook workaholic and it had brought him the fame he'd so craved, a fortune he'd been unable to spend in his short lifetime, and two more or less estranged daughters. Her father's life was a lesson Sienna wouldn't easily forget.

The free time Sienna had on her hands, she spent either in private with Justine, or at the shelter. At first, all she'd had to do was show up and hang out with the kids, but the novelty of having Sienna Bright around soon wore off. Any new residents were still easily impressed, but the kids who'd been at the shelter a while soon realized—and rightly so—that there was nothing inherently special about Sienna just because she was an actor and appeared in a few movies. Even Ashleigh, who'd been released from the hospital, no longer had to suppress a grin every time she saw Sienna.

Justine's days consisted of a lot of arranging, meetings with social workers and child welfare people, and a barrage of questions from everyone around her. Meanwhile, she was trying to secure a home placement for Ashleigh at Francis Delgado's. She was on the phone to some authority figure right now, making her case, which was never an issue for Justine. Operating within child welfare regulations was complicated, but when it came to things like this, to going the extra mile, to making that frustrating phone call, and filling in yet another form, Justine was tireless. She also had a vast network of contacts within the various city departments responsible for runaway kids and unhoused teenagers.

It only took a few days at the shelter for Sienna's admiration for Justine to skyrocket. What Justine accomplished in a day was remarkable, what she achieved in a week was, to Sienna, superhuman, and what she'd pulled off over her lifetime so far was nothing short of miraculous.

At first, when contemplating what to do with the millions her father had left her, Sienna believed that buying Justine free time was the way to go. Funding an extra full-time position at the shelter seemed like a good idea, but witnessing how Justine was when she was working—all focus, intention, and limitless amounts of compassion—soon taught Sienna that buying time off for Justine would be a punishment to her. It was obvious why Justine worked the hours she did, why she hardly took a day off, and never even discussed taking a vacation. Taissa had been right. Justine was the shelter.

She'd gradually been giving Darrel more responsibility but it didn't have any effect on her own workload, because working less was the last thing Justine wanted. Helping kids energized her, even if that meant being on the phone with a city official for an hour. It was what Justine did—it defined her personality completely. This all became crystal clear to Sienna within days. And she only loved Justine more for it. Because never in her life had Sienna seen this kind of utter selflessness on display.

Sienna found herself increasingly captivated by Justine as she watched her manage the shelter with such grace and beauty. As the days turned into weeks, the importance of Justine missing Bobby's funeral diminished into a mere footnote in their shared history. Sienna could now see firsthand what she hadn't been able to understand back when she'd waited fruitlessly at the church—that loving someone like Justine could be both maddening and the best thing she'd ever do.

———

"Come here," Justine said from the couch in Sienna's apartment. Sienna glanced up from her phone. Her agent had emailed, saying he'd be couriering over a promising script tomorrow. It made her think of her father, because when it came to deciding whether to audition for a part or not, she always asked for his opinion. Even when abroad, Bobby would jump on a quick call and ask Sienna to give him the broad strokes. Who would she ask for advice now?

"Where?" Sienna asked, even though she knew exactly what Justine meant—and she recognized that look in her gorgeous pale-blue eyes. She sat there looking very Justine again. Her jeans were worn at the knees and her T-shirt had an actual hole at the seam, but Justine couldn't care less. The fact that she didn't, made her all the more irresistible to Sienna. Because it meant that she cared only about things that really mattered and those things were also becoming the things that Sienna cared more and more about.

"Come here and I'll make you feel better." Instead of beckoning her over, Justine sucked two fingers into her mouth and let them fall from her lips with an intoxicating smack.

"Feel better about what?" Sienna didn't know why she was putting up this fight. Seeing Justine's fingers disappear into her mouth was more than enough to quicken her pulse.

"I can read your face like an open book, baby." Justine threw in a sultry, crooked grin. "Let me make you feel good and…"

She narrowed her eyes to sky-blue slits. "Lose those jeans on your way over here."

Sienna was brought up in the glitzy part of Los Angeles, where women—and most men—plastered their face with layers of makeup and put on the kind of clothes designed with the sole purpose of making them look their best. Justine had redefined Sienna's take on what looking good—and sexy—meant. Not a single person had ever looked sexier to Sienna than Justine Blackburn did right now. She didn't need designer garments or weekly hairdresser appointments. It was all there in the fierceness of her gaze, in the timbre of voice, in how she held up two fingers to Sienna and the promise they entailed.

So Sienna did exactly as was asked of her, because she knew how Justine would make her feel—not just better, but ecstatic. She took off her jeans as well as her panties before straddling Justine.

"I have to tell you something." Justine gazed at her while trailing her fingertips along Sienna's naked behind.

Sienna's skin reacted instantly to Justine's touch and she only managed a throaty "Hm" in response.

Justine kissed Sienna lightly on the cheek, then nibbled a path to Sienna's ear, ready to whisper a sweet nothing into it—one of her favorite things to do.

"You are beautiful," Justine breathed into her ear. "You're sensational and you take my breath away and…" Justine paused. "I love you."

That was a new one. Sienna pulled back a little so she could see Justine's face. "You do?" That was no longer pure lust coursing through Sienna—it was so much more than that.

"Fuck yeah," Justine said. "You've proven utterly impossible not to love." Her face was as serious as Sienna had ever seen it. Justine wasn't playing around.

Sienna didn't have to think about it—because she already felt it. She'd been feeling it, and letting that sensation grow inside of her, since she'd rocked up at Justine's house in the middle of the night, claiming that she couldn't forgive her. But to turn to Justine in her biggest moment of need, when the pain had been so obliterating, could only ever reveal one thing.

"I love you too," Sienna said.

Justine's smile shone through in her eyes. She caressed Sienna's cheek with her hand and pulled her near. Before she kissed her, Justine said, "I want to be inside you. I need to feel you."

The entire expanse of Sienna's skin broke into goose bumps. With her lips glued to Justine, she wrestled her blouse and bra off her, until she sat naked across Justine's lap.

Justine skated her fingers softly along Sienna's entrance, making her clit pulse hard between her legs. Sienna needed to feel Justine as well—she craved her intimate touch inside her. Because of course she loved her.

She'd let the days go by, sleeping in Justine's arms night after night, and there had only been one way for that to go. Love had taken over and filled up some of the negative space her father's passing had left. Some of the pieces her heart had shattered into would forever be unglued—and Sienna would never be the same again—but she had not only lost. She had gained a person that she loved with all her heart.

At first, she had directed most of her anger at Bobby dying so callously, so unexpectedly in that tragic accident, at Justine. It was the easiest thing to do at the time and Justine was an easy enough scapegoat. But Sienna's body had known well before she'd let her brain catch up, that doing so was foolish. That losing two people she loved was infinitely worse than one—and her dad was never coming back, no matter how much she wanted him to.

Like most humans, Justine was infuriating and beautiful. Mostly beautiful, though. She was older, but she was also wiser. She had limitless reserves of empathy and was much better than Sienna at regulating her emotions. Justine had seen the worst of humanity and she'd risen above it. She had remade herself into the most beautiful person Sienna had ever met. To be able to call

Justine her partner—her *girlfriend*—was the privilege of a lifetime.

Justine's fingers slid inside her. Their kiss stalled because Sienna had to catch her breath. She had to look Justine in the eye. It was as though now that they'd said it out loud to each other, Sienna could finally allow her body to absorb all the love they felt for each other into every last cell.

Justine gently stroked inside of her and Sienna would never have guessed it when she'd met her that first time—when she'd been all straightforward bluntness—but Justine's inherent tenderness was not only surprising, it was what floored her most of all.

Justine could coax Sienna to a climax with the minutest of gestures, with an almost stillness that seemed to multiply inside Sienna, with a tenderness that, because of its serenity and depth, touched her to her very core. It was no different this time, such was the hold Justine had over her. Because she wasn't just a hot older woman, she was the best person Sienna had ever had the honor to know—and to love with everything she had.

CHAPTER 38

Sienna wasn't one of those typical LA barely there girls, neither in body, nor in attitude. She was the kind of person who filled a room, who drew the eye and—in Justine's case—infinitely more than just the eye.

Sienna's tongue slid along Justine's most intimate parts, like a paintbrush that, with just a few expert strokes, can produce a perfect image that didn't exist before. Sienna was licking Justine straight into seventh heaven again, yet it felt like a brand-new sensation. Because Justine had just told Sienna that she loved her—and Sienna had said the same to her.

Granted, saying those three words moments before her fingers were about to slide inside Sienna's soft wetness was perhaps a touch dramatic, but it was all the more reason for Justine to say them then. Because this was how it had all begun. Some innocent flirting at Min-ji's. Sienna's unexpected reciprocation. The drive to Justine's house. The hot sex with a movie star that, in hindsight, had perhaps overwhelmed Justine much more than she could ever admit to anyone, herself included. Justine Blackburn was not the sort to be impressed by movie stars, not even the one chosen to play her best friend and ex-partner Rochelle—who had once changed her life forever, and infinitely for the better.

Now Sienna was having the same effect on Justine's life all over again. As though playing Rochelle had paved the way for that. As though making 'that fucking movie' as Justine had referred to *Gimme Shelter* a bit too often, had made that possible. Every tiny thing that had happened had played its part and was responsible for Justine lying between Sienna's million thread count sheets in her bed that was big enough for three.

Justine might have claimed, in her hardened way, that closure was bullshit and agreeing to a movie being made about her life was not about that, yet it had brought her something so much more life-changing than closure. It had planted Sienna Bright right in the middle of her existence—and that after she'd already sold her life rights.

From the very beginning, Sienna had made it feel easy—as if it was nothing—for Justine to let herself be loved. Something, according to Rochelle at least, Justine had never been capable of before. Look at her now. Legs wide, Sienna's gorgeous body bent toward her, her hair fanning out over her belly. Justine's body on the way to climax—without hesitation or even a hint that it might not happen, unlike that first time they'd slept together.

It may forever remain a mystery how she did it, and why, but Sienna had succeeded in dismantling the walls around her heart at exactly the right time—when Justine was ready for it. When *Gimme Shelter* was being shot. Maybe, for that reason, it could only ever have been her. Maybe that's why Justine had flirted with her so brazenly that first evening when they'd met. Maybe she and Sienna were just two people who were meant to meet at exactly the time they met, although Justine would never be able to fully believe that. What she could believe—what she had no choice but to believe—was that life was unpredictably magnificent one moment and viciously cruel the next. That the ebbs and flows of it were inevitable and that, finally, on the cusp of fifty-five, she was ready to face those ups and downs with someone else by her side.

She allowed Sienna into her life—into her arms and her bed —day after day. She made time for her, although she didn't have to try that hard because Sienna was at the shelter with her almost every day.

Sometimes, Justine even talked about her parents, about the years of her life before she left home, and about the girl she was back then. Sienna was unafraid to ask a hard question and, with Sienna, Justine found, more often than not, the power to reply. Although talking about those times would never be easy. Making 'their movie' might have changed Justine's life—and Sienna's, for that matter—but her history could never be altered. It didn't have to be. All Justine's dreams had come true nonetheless.

How could Justine not feel like the luckiest person alive with Sienna Bright's tongue twirling between her legs? Sienna, who was so audacious and, when it came to certain things, so deliciously without qualms. Justine would never forget those very simple, direct words she had spoken when they'd only just met. "I like you and I like sex." A few hours before Sienna had spoken those irresistible words, Justine had never even met her. She'd never seen a movie she was in. Sienna Bright was still more a concept to her than an actual person. Hours later, that very same person had been in her bed and she had kept coming back. Most surprising of all: Justine had let her.

She had opened her arms wide in the middle of that dark night when Sienna came knocking on her door, and they had remained open since. Sienna needed her then, but Justine had needed her too. And being part of *Gimme Shelter* had, for the first time in Justine's life, given her enough strength to be vulnerable—vulnerable enough to let another human pierce the concrete around her heart. And what a human Sienna was.

Tonight, in Sienna's bed, Justine was plenty vulnerable enough to let a climax roar through her. A warm, pulsing glow spread through her. The world narrowed to the riot coursing inside her. The sensation was as overwhelming as Sienna saying she loved her, as though Sienna's words had instantly increased Justine's body's capacity for joy. Ever since she had come into her life, Sienna had increased that capacity in every aspect of it.

The kids' smiles whenever Sienna visited the shelter had a direct line to Justine's heart. To just sit with her on the couch after a long day, to feel Sienna's presence next to her, was such a simple but profound pleasure. To catch secret glimpses of the look on Sienna's face when they watched one of her movies together—that special blend of pride and expectation and doubt —was positively addictive. But to know that Sienna loved her, despite everything they'd both gone through, was the biggest joy of all.

Sienna also had an extremely deft tongue and Justine's muscles tensed, then gloriously released, leaving her breathless. Her heart hammered against her chest, each beat echoing the deep, satisfying love that unfurled within her. All Justine's nerves were buzzing, until slowly, the waves receded, leaving a tender calm in their wake.

Sienna crawled up to her, that devilish smile on her lips, her chin glistening with Justine's wetness, and Justine opened her arms again. She closed them around this gorgeous, sensational woman that she loved so much, not intending to ever let her go again.

————

Justine stood in front of the mirror, adjusting the cuffs of her glittery suit that Sienna loved so much. The reflection staring back at her was confident, poised, and ready for Maxine's birthday celebration. Sienna emerged from the bathroom, a vision in her elegant dress, and they shared a moment of silent admiration.

"You look stunning," Justine said.

Sienna smiled her irresistible confident smile. "You don't look half bad yourself."

They moved toward each other, but just as their lips were about to meet, Justine's phone buzzed on the dresser. She glanced at the screen and saw Darrel's name flashing. Her heart skipped a beat.

"Hey, Darrel, what's up?" she answered.

Darrel's voice was strained. "We've got a situation with Lila. She's barricaded herself in the toilets. She's breaking things, crying, and won't let anyone near her."

Justine felt the familiar pull, the instinct to rush to the shelter and take control. It was a feeling she knew all too well, a drive that had shaped her life for as long as she could remember.

She looked over at Sienna, who was putting on her earrings, her face showing a flicker of concern. Justine knew Sienna accepted her commitment to the shelter, but she would not be happy if their plans were derailed by another crisis Justine believed only she could solve.

Taking a deep breath, Justine made a decision. "Darrel, I need you to handle this. Call Taylor; she's experienced with these kinds of situations. She's built a rapport with Lila over the past few weeks. I trust you both to manage things until I can check in later."

There was a pause at the other end—a moment of surprised silence. "Are you sure?" Darrel asked. "You always handle these situations yourself."

"Yes, I'm sure. Keep me updated, but I'm not coming in tonight. I have plans with Sienna, and I need to be there for her."

She ended the call and turned to see Sienna watching her, a mixture of surprise and relief in her eyes. Justine walked over and took Sienna's hands in hers, feeling the warmth of her skin, the gentle strength in her fingers.

"You're staying?" Sienna asked softly.

Justine nodded, her throat tight with emotion. "Tonight, I'm choosing us. Darrel and Taylor can handle it. I want—*I need*—to be with you and your family."

Sienna's eyes shimmered as she leaned in and kissed Justine. It wasn't a kiss of passion, but one of gratitude and love, a recognition of the significance of this moment. Warmth spread through Justine—a sense of rightness and balance that had eluded her for so long.

As they left for Maxine's party, peace settled over Justine. She knew she wouldn't change overnight, that there would still be struggles and moments of tension. But this was a step, a conscious choice to prioritize the woman she loved, to find a way to be true to both her life's work and her heart.

She could be there for Sienna and still be committed to the shelter. It wasn't all or nothing; it was about finding the moments that mattered and choosing love when it counted. As she walked hand in hand with Sienna into the celebration, Justine knew that this was one of those moments.

Tonight, she was exactly where she needed to be.

CHAPTER 39
THREE WEEKS LATER

Sienna was sitting on the balcony of her apartment, holding a large envelope in her hands. Los Angeles seemed somehow quieter with Bobby gone. As if someone had turned down the volume on life itself—such had been her father's loud presence, despite Sienna not having had nearly enough time with him.

The sunset painted the LA skyline in strokes of orange and pink. Justine came to sit beside her.

"I didn't have enough of these with my dad." Sienna nodded at the setting sun. Her father had not been the kind of guy to quietly enjoy the end of a day.

Justine reached out her hand and covered Sienna's with hers; it was warm and reassuring.

Sienna leaned into Justine's shoulder. Something about her made it easier to breathe, to accept the heaviness of grief without letting it pull her under. Justine had this quiet strength that made Sienna feel safe and protected.

Being with Justine was like discovering a secret pathway through the wilderness of her emotions. Justine's maturity was a light in the dark, guiding Sienna through this unexpected grief with a gentleness she hadn't known she needed. It wasn't only Justine's age, but everything she'd gone through. It made her empathy as deep as the roots of an old, sturdy tree.

"I have something for you." Sienna toyed with the envelope. "For the shelter, actually." She gave Justine the envelope. "It's not really from me. It's from my dad."

"Oh, babe." Justine's eyes moistened. She was, no doubt, clever enough to guess what was in that simple, brown envelope. "Thank you." Justine's voice was soft and solemn, as though she wanted to honor the moment with her tone.

Justine pulled out a stack of papers. The first page said, in big black letters:

The Rainbow Shelter Endowment Fund

Sienna had worked with her lawyer and financial advisor to set up a special investment fund that would generate a steady yearly income for the shelter. The profits of the fund could only ever go to the Rainbow Shelter, no matter what happened.

Justine leafed through the pages. Her eyes went wide as saucers when she saw some of the projected numbers.

"Oh my god, babe." She glanced at Sienna. "Is this for real?"

"It's very real."

"Fuck me," Justine muttered under her breath.

"Maybe later," Sienna joked.

"Seriously." Justine swallowed the lump in her throat. "Five million a year?" She huffed out an incredulous breath. "I can't believe this." She turned her head and fixed her damp gaze on Sienna. "I don't know how to ever thank you for this."

"It's for the shelter and it's Bobby's money." Sienna had put nearly all the money she had inherited from her father into the fund. She already had all the money she needed. She had this place—that her father had bought for her. The kids at the shelter had nothing. "You don't have to thank me. If anything, I should thank you."

Sienna hadn't scheduled any future auditions yet. Helping out at the Rainbow Shelter, dressed down in one of Justine's old shirts and with zero makeup on her face, turned her into a version of herself that she'd, perhaps, never been. Because Sienna had always been Bobby Bright's daughter and she'd started her acting career as early as she'd been able to.

These days, at the shelter, she could work a shift at reception without being recognized—the kids coming in had other things on their minds—and it gave her such an unexpected thrill. To simply be a volunteer working at the shelter, with Justine milling about as she did, helped her cope with her father's death most of all. To use the money she had inherited from him for the shelter made all the more sense because of that, no matter how much her mother and sister had disagreed at first. But they'd changed their minds after Sienna had invited them to come and see, with their own eyes, what the shelter was about. It also helped them to accept the fact that Justine was firmly back in her life. That Sienna and Justine were back on and had every intention of building a future together.

"I'm thanking you anyway." Justine threw her arms around Sienna and showered her in kisses. "Thank you. Thank you. Thank you," she said in between every kiss. "Who knew this movie about my life would be the best thing that ever happened to me?" Justine said. "Because it brought me you."

"To think that my dad warned me against playing a real person," Sienna managed to say.

"I'm so glad you didn't listen to him." Justine pointed at the papers that were spread on the floor between them. "Although Bobby has my eternal gratitude as well."

"Rest in peace, Bobby Bright," Sienna whispered, while she nestled into Justine's arms.

"You know what's really funny," Justine said. "When Rochelle and I founded the shelter thirty years ago, we were only able to do so because of the money she raised through her Hollywood connections. For a long time, she managed all the funding. Now, you've played her in a movie, and you're also funding the shelter."

As a response, Sienna huddled deeper into Justine's embrace. The last of the sun dipped behind the distant skyscrapers and Sienna felt a calm settle over her. The endowment fund for the shelter was more than a donation; it was an investment in a future she believed in deeply—and it would always connect her to her father as well as to Justine.

CHAPTER 40

EIGHT MONTHS LATER

The movie hadn't even started but Justine's eyes were already watery. This whole affair had grown totally out of proportion and defied any expectations. It was one thing to put her signature underneath a contract giving access to her life rights, but it was a whole other ball game to sit in this movie theater, the lights dimming around her, Sienna on one side of her, Rochelle on the other, the hum of anticipation fizzing audibly in the air, and have it unfold in front of her.

For a split second, Justine considered that she couldn't do this. That she couldn't sit through this screening of *Gimme Shelter*. That it would be too painful, too confrontational, too everything she tried to avoid. But that was old Justine. That was Justine-before-Sienna.

Because just as Justine had strutted onto the red carpet earlier, holding onto Sienna's hand for dear life, and had let herself enjoy it—let herself bask in that gloriously outrageous moment—she could actually enjoy this.

She and Sienna had been officially together for almost a year —certainly a record in Justine's recent history when it came to amorous relationships. Most Sundays, when Justine had the time, she was welcomed into Maxine Brewster's lavish mansion. Maxine, Eddy, and Taissa and her husband were sitting in the row behind them. Some days, Justine had to pinch herself, because it kind of felt like she had a family.

Justine let the tears flow freely as she watched Alexis Dalton play that long-ago version of her. That lost, angry, lonely young woman who, according to this movie, had found the strength to set up a shelter for homeless queer youth because of love. Because she met Rochelle and together they were stronger than the sum of their parts. Even though it was dark and Justine couldn't see her face, Rochelle sat beaming with pride beside her. Justine didn't have to see her best friend's face to know that with absolute certainty. Their romance in the movie might have been dramatized for effect, as Charlie and Mimi had called it, and not entirely true to how it had actually transpired, but Rochelle had still changed everything. Just as Sienna had done thirty years later.

Justine squeezed Sienna's hand. She hadn't let go of it all night—she found that she couldn't. Sienna looked dazzling in an emerald gown, courtesy of Francis Delgado, that matched Justine's tuxedo perfectly. And yes, Sienna was gorgeous and beyond generous and one of the undisputed stars of this movie, yet Justine hadn't considered herself unworthy of walking the red carpet by her side. Because Sienna had done the one thing that Justine had always thought unimaginable: she had made it possible for Justine to love her, with all her heart and all her soul. With every fiber of her being.

As the movie progressed, and Justine witnessed her own grand transformation on the big screen, she remembered being on set when some of the scenes were being shot. The sucker punch to the gut that seeing the movie version of the Rainbow Shelter for the first time had been. That scene with Nora Levine playing her mother, when Justine's heart had still been so locked-up, she hadn't felt a thing—unlike now.

All the emotions she had gone through that had led her to this moment when, ever so slowly, she was going through another huge transformation. As Justine sat in the theater, the broken parts of herself that she'd always wanted to hide at any cost, became a little less broken.

On the screen in front of her, Justine's partnership with Rochelle was able to move mountains; now, her partnership with Sienna had allowed a sea change inside her very self.

Justine still lived for the shelter. It was still her everything. But it wasn't the only thing and her reasons for doing what she did had changed along with her. Most of all, the accusations Rochelle loved to hurl at her about her emotional unavailability were no longer correct. Justine had left the door to her heart ajar, and Sienna, with her irresistible, straightforward way of loving, had succeeded in throwing it wide open. Because of that, Justine could, in the end, truly enjoy this movie. This moment that she'd so dreaded, she didn't even want to think about it when she first met Mimi—Justine's preferred way of dealing with unwanted emotions. But Justine could experience a difficult emotion about herself now and resist the urge to run away, to bury herself in work, to find something more important to do than tend to her own feelings. Because Sienna didn't let her get away with that any longer and Justine was ready—more than ready—to accept that. She was ready for love. And this fucking movie had made it possible.

———

As soon as the credits rolled, everyone jumped out of their seats for a standing ovation. While Justine still found it rather silly to clap for a movie about herself, she joined in. Because the work Mimi, the crew, and the actors had accomplished was astounding. To witness this movie being made had not only been a privilege, but also an unexpectedly powerful source of healing some of Justine's oldest, deepest wounds. That did deserve a little round of applause.

The lights came on and Justine looked around, at everyone

who was attending the premiere of *Gimme Shelter*. There was Mimi with Nora by her side. There were Mimi's kids, one of whom had Marcy's strong arm around her shoulder. And a few rows ahead, there was Min-ji and her partner with, next to them, Raffo Shah, also with her girlfriend. More than four rows in this massive theater were filled with ex-residents of the Rainbow Shelter, and that made Justine's heart swell most of all.

After this, a big party was planned, and Justine couldn't wait to catch up with the likes of Raffo, to check in and see how life was treating them. She didn't have to check in with Min-ji. If it were up to Sienna, and it often was, she and Justine would go to her restaurant at least once a week.

Justine spotted Francis and his husband a few rows down. In between them stood Ashleigh and the sight of her, with a big fat smile on her face, made Justine's heart ready to burst.

"I'm so incredibly proud of you, babe," Sienna whispered in her ear.

"Me?" Justine pointed a finger at herself in jest. She shook her head, but then thought better of it. Justine hadn't made this movie, but she had allowed it to be made. And just like allowing herself to be loved, it had only gone and changed her life.

GET THREE E-BOOKS
FOR FREE

Building a relationship with my readers is the very best thing about writing. I occasionally send newsletters with details on new releases, special offers and giveaways.

And if you sign up to my mailing list I'll send you all this free stuff:

1. An e-book of *Few Hearts Survive*, a Pink Bean Series novella that is ONLY available to my mailing list subscribers.
2. A free e-book of *Hired Help*, my very first (and therefore very special to me) lesbian erotic romance story.
3. A free e-book of my first 'longer' work, my highly romantic novella *Summer's End*, set on an exotic beach in Thailand.

You can get *Few Hearts Survive* (a Pink Bean Series novella), *Hired Help* (a spicy F/F novelette) and *Summer's End* (a deeply romantic lesfic novella) **for free** by signing up at www.harperb liss.com/freebook/ or scanning the QR code below

GET THREE E-BOOKS FOR FREE

ABOUT THE AUTHOR

Harper Bliss is a best-selling lesbian romance author. Among her most-loved books are the highly dramatic French Kissing and the often thought-provoking Pink Bean series.

Harper lived in Hong Kong for seven years, travelled the world for a bit, and has now settled in the Belgian countryside with her wife, Caroline, and her photogenic cat, Dolly Purrton.

Harper loves hearing from readers and you can reach her at the email address below.

www.harperbliss.com
harper@harperbliss.com